TREMBLE

TERRAWAY
BOOK TWO

MARY E. TWOMEY

MARY E. TWOMEY, LLC

TREMBLE

BOOK TWO IN THE TERRAWAY SERIES

By

Mary E. Twomey

COPYRIGHT

DEDICATION

For Tiffini.

Thank goodness they don't charge for phone calls by the minute anymore.
We'd be in some serious trouble.

I love you, girl, plain and simple.
Though you are anything but plain or simple.

1

TAKE AWAY DESSERT

Mariang cried the whole way to the mansion. Her cooing sniffles were the only sounds as we walked inside and awaited my doom. I didn't want to think about the fact that I'd just murdered the Goblin King, Titus. Each time I closed my eyes longer than a blink, I saw his wrinkled Christmas Elf body turning to stone and crushing into pebbles when I'd lost my mind after he'd threatened Mason.

My head hung as I waited outside the conference room at Ezra's mansion. I guess Ezra was going to be my stepdad when he married Bev, but in this capacity, he was my boss. I'd just screwed up royally my first week on the job. Instead of reaping enough souls to feed the nations of Terraway, I'd managed to wipe out one-seventh of their nations in a single blow. Titus had tied himself to his people, connecting his life with all the Goblins in Terraway. It had been a solid plan to survive a famine – if he ate, none of the Goblins starved.

I don't think Titus counted on a fight when he crossed me.

Ezra opened the door to the conference room with a closed expression, ushering me inside. I gasped at the remnants of Titus' body that had been shoved in the corner next to the fichus. The statue that had mere hours ago been a living, breathing being was still intact from the neck down – solid stone though it was. One leg was raised higher than the other, and his arm was outstretched, frozen as it reached out to snatch at the stone, or at me. I backed away, my heels skidding on the short carpet. My anxiety brimmed at the evidence of madness that could only belong to me.

Mason's hand on my back was supposed to be reassuring, but I'm not sure anything could've calmed me enough to make me forget I'd just slaughtered an entire people in one go. I kept my head down, accepting whatever sentence the council of Terraway had for me.

My hands were shaking as I scratched at the skin on the backs of them. I didn't bother sitting at the long oval-shaped polished wood table. My insides felt hollow and painted in a thin layer of white coldness that had nothing to do with the chill I got from reaping.

Mason sat in his chair, representing either Hayop or Sombi, I wasn't sure. He patted the seat next to him that had been selected for me. I stood, knowing I didn't deserve a spot at the cool kids' table after what I'd done. Danny wasn't permitted a seat, since he was a Reaper only. He stood in the corner, observing with a quiet intensity that made me itch. Kabayo, Captain Finn, Sylvia and Langgam all stared at me with a new kind of curious fascination that was mingled with a wary watch-out-for-that-one;-she's-nuts looks.

I was sorely missing Von, who still hadn't shown up for work. They would lock me up for sure, and I wouldn't even be able to say goodbye to him.

The worst was that I wouldn't be able to explain things to Ollie. I'd just disappear in some Terraway jail, separated from my big brother, who would never be the same. He'd think I'd abandoned him, like our sister Allie had done to us.

Ezra and I were the only ones standing. I lowered my chin when he took the floor to start my private hearing. "We've been discussing at length how to handle this situation, and have come to the conclusion that your involvement in this should be kept secret, Lady October."

My head whipped up to gaze at Ezra, but I didn't say a word.

"It's in the best interest of Terraway to let Titus' arrogance of tying himself to his people, as if he were immortal, stand as a lesson not to dabble in such things. He was foolish, and now he and his people are dead. Who did it doesn't matter at this point. What matters is that no other kings feel tempted to bind themselves to their people in the same way."

My mouth fell open in shock. It wasn't until Ezra's verdict that I glanced up and took in the casual demeanor of everyone on the council. Kabayo was leaning back, his black horse head mildly interested as he tapped his fingertips on the arm of his chair. Captain Finn had his hands folded across his stomach, his left combat boot crossed over his right knee. He had a calm look about him, like he was watching the whole thing on television on a Sunday afternoon. Even Sylvia, the woman with a crescent-shaped face and bat-like enhancements only wore an expression of mild concern.

Like I was there for a traffic violation. Like I hadn't just murdered a whole race of people.

Ezra waved his hand in my direction. "You can carry on about your day, then. That's all. Just keep this to yourselves the next time you're in Terraway."

My head whipped from one end of the table to the other, my somber expression mutating into indignation. "No! Are you kidding me with this? I just murdered probably thousands of people!"

Kabayo raised his finger to correct me. "Hundreds of thousands. And Goblins aren't people; they're a plague. Good riddance to the whole of them."

Prince Langgam wasn't even interested in the conversation, but played with one of the cockroaches as it skittered up his muddy arm. "Is the meeting over yet?"

I glowered at Lang. "I'm smack in the middle of talking, you jag."

Finn quirked a dark blond eyebrow at my outburst. "Do you want us to hang you? Then where would we be? Even with the Goblins taken off the list of creatures the souls you reap have to fuel, Terraway will still starve without a healthy Omen. Lady Mariang can't keep up with the demand anymore." Finn inclined his head apologetically to Ezra out of respect for speaking disparagingly about his daughter.

Kabayo stood, as if the whole meeting was adjourned. "Frankly, you only did what everyone in this room wishes they could get away with. Goblins have been stealing food from the neighboring lands when they don't actually need it, since they were tied to Titus. Every time one of our horses takes ill, it's from some Goblin's curse."

I tried to picture the reverse centaur standing before me actually riding on a horse, but it was too weird a visual. I cleared my throat to address the room as an equal. "You all should be ashamed of yourselves. I killed baby Goblins who didn't even have a chance to change their people for the better. I killed the good people as well as the bad. You can't let me off the hook for this. It's not right."

Sylvia eyed Titus' stone body warily. "There's no such thing as a good Goblin. None that I've seen, anyway. They all grow up the same – greedy and sneaky."

Mason's hand on my arm was gently trying to tell me to shut up and be grateful, but I ignored him. I leaned my knuckles down on the table, resolute in my conviction. "No. I won't help a world that has no checks and balances. No one's above the law, not even the people in this room. I mean it. I'm not leaving until I'm punished in some way."

Ezra softened, pinching the bridge of his nose. "What would you have me do? If I throw you in jail, it only punishes the people of Terraway who continue to starve."

My eyes met Ezra's with no hint of optimism or peace. "I just committed genocide. I hope you understand that. I don't care if the Goblins were a people worth saving. On your payroll is a mass murderer. Don't you dare tell me you can go to sleep with that on your conscience." I shook my head at Ezra. "I'm a correctional nurse. I believe in the justice system. Know me a little bit, Ezra."

Captain Finn's smile told me that no matter how insistent I was, they weren't going to take this as seriously as they should. "Kabayo, why don't you take the new Omen down to your prison? Let her look around at how many cells were opened up when the Goblins turned to stone."

"More than half. The statues are being moved to the palace garden right now, actually."

"No one's above the law," I argued, furious. "That's the whole point of having a law! I mean, honestly!"

Prince Langgam stood, and several dozen cockroaches skittered across his shoulders and trailed down his mud-streaked arms. "Are we done here? I've got to get back."

"No, we're not done! You can't let me do this with no repercussions."

Captain Finn scratched the gills on his neck and stood. His short caramel-blond hair was ruffled on the left, and I wondered if he ever worried about things like bedhead. He was wearing that same cocky smile that had a hint of cruelty to it as he stared across the table at me. "Expect a shipment of gold from King Banak in the morning, expressing his gratitude. You've done Terraway a great favor, Lady October."

I jabbed my finger in his direction, livid that this was all a joke to them. "Don't you smile at me. Don't you dare smile about this."

Kabayo bowed slightly to Ezra, and then to me, chuckling at my indignation. "She wants to be punished? Take away her dessert, Ezra. No cake for a whole day." He extended his hand to shake mine, but I refused, sniffing at the offensive offer. Kabayo shook Mason's hand instead, and then vanished before my eyes. I jumped, and then remembered the kings and important blowhards all had enhancements that allowed them to transport their bodies between worlds on a dime.

Sylvia inclined her head to me. "We've been trying to ward off the Goblins for years, but they keep encroaching on our territory. Thank you for helping us." She placed her hand on the table and met my eyes with sincerity I couldn't shrug off. "Truly."

"But I didn't..." I tried to protest, but no one was listening.

Sylvia and Captain Finn vanished, and then Lang

followed suit after he walked behind my chair and squeezed my shoulder.

Mason exhaled when it was just Danny, Ezra and me with him in the conference room. "We got lucky there." Then he craned his neck up at me with a scolding expression from where he sat at the table. "Are you trying to get yourself killed? Take the pardon and run next time."

"Are you kidding me with this? This is wrong, Mason. You should know that a country's leaders should have to follow the same rules as its citizens."

Danny's arms were crossed over his chest. "I can't believe you're upset about getting off without punishment. You're just trying to be difficult."

"Hello, I work at a prison! I see every day that checks and balances matter. I know in my heart that I belong in jail on death row. I killed a man in cold blood just because he..." My eyes fell on Mason before they closed to shut out the world for a few seconds.

Mason stood, his hand rubbing circles into the middle of my back. "You thought Titus was going to kill me. I can't tell if you were right, but I know you did what you had to do. It was Titus' fault for tying himself to his people with the *tahi* charm. We all warned him of the danger."

"Don't," I warned quietly. "Don't you let me off the hook, too." Mason's body was warm and inviting. I don't know why I felt the tug of a magnet in my gut, but it drew me to him so I could wrap myself in his comfort.

For three whole seconds I breathed, inhaling the relief

of his calming presence that smelled like patchouli, pine and grown man.

I stiffened when his hand trailed to the small of my back. It was such an intimate space on my body, but the alarms weren't because his hand felt wrong there – my hackles rose because his touch felt all too right. I didn't deserve comfort, and I was soaking it in like a glutton. I pushed Mason back and stomped out of the room, running down to the basement where the cell I knew I deserved was waiting for me.

2

PRISON BREAK

The steel bars taunted me with their sturdy nature. The construction was no joke, and went from the concrete floor to the ceiling. The cell was meant for Von – my half-vampire Reaper who was still MIA. When Von couldn't suppress his blood cravings anymore, he locked himself in this cell to keep the world safe. He also did it to keep himself from drinking the blood of a whole human and transitioning to a full-vampire.

I locked myself in the cell with the key to keep the world safe from me. I was dangerous, and the worst kind of person. I was up there with ruthless dictators who slaughtered instead of thought things through. The council wouldn't keep the monster I was under control, so I knew I had to do it.

I sat in the far corner of the cell of the basement that was lit only by the stairway light. I hugged my knees to my chest and contemplated the horrible person I'd become, and the steps that had led me there.

It was twenty minutes before Mason came bounding down into the basement. I clutched the key in my hand to make sure he couldn't get me out of my self-imposed prison.

When his eyes found me in the dimly lit concrete corner, a soft smile played on his lips, his shoulders relaxing. "What are you doing down here?"

"Hosting a tea party. You can tell Ezra that I'm not coming out, either."

Mason glanced to the empty hook on the wall and frowned. "Where's the key?"

I displayed it in my hand, and then went back to clutching my knees, resting my head on them in my utter despondence.

"Give me the key, October." Mason moved to the side of the cage, chuckling when I leaned away from his reach. "You really have no idea how strong I am, do you."

"All I know is I'm where I deserve to be."

"Seems like talking you out of this isn't going to work." Mason tsked me, as if I was a petulant child instead of a mass-murderer. Then he clutched the door to the cell on either side and yanked it clean off its iron hinges with barely more than a grunt.

I yelped and plastered my body to the wall. "I can't believe you just did that!"

"I can't believe you thought you could do *this*. You're an

Omen now. That means you don't get to take a day off, not even to go to jail." He examined the door with a grimace as he rested it to the wall. "I'll have to fix that later, in case Von needs this place."

I remained on the floor, not needing a door to hold me inside. "Leave me alone, Mason."

Mason cocked his head to the side, sizing me up. "No. We're in this together. That means you don't get to go rogue and ask the council to lock you up or hang you. It means that if you're locked up, then I go with you." He sat down next to me, pulling his knees to his chest, as I was doing. "This is actually kind of nice. I didn't get much sitting down time before meeting you."

"This isn't nice. This is a prison. Nice is upstairs. In here is for criminals."

"And you've gone from hero to villain in a single morning? That's impressive."

His teasing tone threatened to soften me, so I hugged my knees tighter to brace myself against it. "Go away. I'm serious."

"Oh, I know you are. I've never seen anyone question the council like that, especially not over a favorable ruling." His arm draped around my back, bringing me in to his side.

That magnet feeling tugged in my gut again, and the warmth spread through me like hot chocolate. I wanted to resist, but the desire to stay in his shelter kept me in place. "I killed children, Mason. Little Goblin babies who didn't do a thing to me." My eyes started to water, and I knew I wouldn't last long with my pride intact if I kept going. My confession came out in an agonized whisper. "I killed thousands of children."

Mason buried his nose in my cheek as he held me, relishing the connection that was still new, but somehow also felt like the most natural thing in the world. "I could feel that you were down here. Ezra was looking upstairs in the guest rooms, but I knew you were here. I barely know you, but I can feel you." He tapped his heart. "So strange."

"Don't say sexy things to me. I don't deserve it."

Mason stiffened, but then relaxed again. "You think that's sexy? I guess that's good. I didn't know what to make of it." He thumbed my other cheek, melting me in his arms afresh. "We should get going. Danny's worried about continuing the workday this late. Thinks we won't meet the quota."

"I can't go on with life like what I did is no big deal."

"Then pay your penance to Terraway by making sure they have enough to eat. Help Mariang build up the souls so we can get out of this hole of constant starvation."

I mulled over his suggestion, and finally ruled that Mason's way was the best route; I would be able to punish myself and still be helpful. "Okay." Mason made me blush when he kissed my cheek, pulling me up with him as he stood.

"You saved my life," he said as his hand clasped mine. I jerked my hand out twice before letting it rest back in his grip. He was patient with the untamed side of me. I weighed the damage of how many germs Mason might have, and if he was a safe person who wouldn't contaminate me. We both calmed a little at the contact that was foreign to me, but felt like the most natural thing in the world with Mason. I don't know how he did that, but I suspected a fair amount of pulling was involved.

"Mason? Don't let me kill anyone else, okay?"

He squeezed my fingers as we walked toward the stairs. "I'll do my best, *hani*."

3

HIS LIPS, MY LEGS

I took Mason's advice to heart and set my sights on making myself useful to Terraway. I reaped my way through nine people on the first floor, five on the second, and then four more on the third floor. Mariang reaped five people before she collapsed in Danny's arms. He carried her to the car, but I still had some fight left in me after I'd turned my self-loathing into fuel. I knew that if I went back home, someone would make me talk about the Titus incident. I didn't want that, and was ready to avoid the confrontation at all costs.

Mason's hand on my shoulder was soothing. "October, you can be done for the day. Eight people is all you need between you and Mariang combined." He gulped. "Well, seven, I guess, now that the entire nation of Goblins is dead." He closed his eyes to scold himself when my posture slumped in shame. "Sorry. I meant that to be more of a positive thing."

"Well, I'm at eighteen souls, so that should stock up some extra days for us. The trek through Terraway to deliver the sagrado stone might take more than a day, you know. The sooner..." I stared down the long hallway that seemed a mirage with its unending tunnel-like haze. "The sooner, the sooner," I ruled, not caring if I made perfect sense. I gripped the wall and leaned on it, trying not to double over. I knew the second I did, the work day would be over.

"This isn't healthy. You need to rest. The souls are poison, you know. You're inhaling *poison* all day long, and more than you need to. When was the last time you ate anything?"

"One more," I ruled, not answering his question. I felt too yicky to eat anything. Reaping makes you sick to your stomach, sure, but I'd just killed a man, and an entire nation. I didn't deserve a meal, unless it was my last meal before I was taken off the planet for being a horrible person. I deserved to be behind bars with the inmates who grabbed my butt when I wasn't looking.

"Okay. One more and you're done. I mean it." Mason offered his arm to me, and I took it, leaning heavily like a drunken sorority girl on him. I pointed vaguely to a room that the tug in my gut was guiding me toward. Mason reached over the nurse's station and did a slight pull on the two sifting through endless paperwork behind the desk. That little consideration allowed us to move into rooms without anyone calling security on us.

When we reached the hospital room, my arm was so weighted that I could only manage two light bangs from my fist. Mason let us in, and I found a middle-aged balding man sitting next to his wife, who was sleeping in the hospital bed.

The man stood, but I had no preamble for conversation. I'd used up all my finesse long ago. The tug led me not to the woman, but to her husband. I trembled as I placed my hand on his shoulder, sucking his freezing soul out of him. "I'm so sorry. This isn't room 306?"

"No. It's 317. You're almost there." He gave me a good-natured smile, not knowing that while he was worried about his wife being in the hospital, the person he should really be worrying about was himself. He would die within twenty-four hours, and there was nothing to be done about it.

Even though Mason was holding onto me so the soul could have a straight shot into him, he didn't reap it fast enough. The shock of the cold let the last of the air out of my tires. I collapsed in Mason's arms, not caring where I landed, so long as I could sleep.

~

MY SUDDEN PLUNGE INTO UNCONSCIOUSNESS BROUGHT ME TO a dream that was set on a Caribbean beach. It looked exactly like the postcards and pictures I'd seen. The water was clear and so deeply blue, it looked like it had a bucket of dye dumped in, or like, a dozen blended up cookie monsters or something. The sand was pure white, and I dug my bare toe in, smiling at the sensation my mind worked overtime to make more powerful.

I wore a skimpy gold bikini to match Princess Leia's. I would never have the nerve to wear something so revealing in reality, so I vanished the scar on my arm and the one on my thigh to make the picture complete. In real life, I was covered enough to conceal my more obvious curves. In my dreams, I could be a woman without the fear of an inmate grabbing at me, or that my guy friends would get stupid ideas in their heads.

I lay back in the sand, basking in the sunshine that chased away the cold so much reaping had immersed me in.

I frowned when a shadow crossed over my body, squinting up to find the same guy with white-blond hair and a killer body I'd enjoyed at the Eiffel Tower in my other dream. He was smiling down at me in nothing but red and white striped swim trunks that looked like they were from a style done about a hundred years ago. "Is this spot available?" he asked, making me chuckle at his "Is this seat taken?" line he flirted with.

"Pull up some sand and enjoy the view."

"Oh, I intend to. The view from here is spectacular." His eyes raked over my form, and because my imperfections had been erased, I felt no shyness or shame. My smile bloomed as he sat next to me, looking around at the scenery as if he'd never seen it before either. "This is pretty. Where are we?"

"I think it's Cancun. I've never been. Needed a good escape."

"Long day?"

"I'll say. This reaping thing is no joke. I'm trying to be what they need, but I overdid it today."

"Yeah? How many did you reap?"

I loved that I didn't have to explain what reaping was to him. He was a figment of my imagination, the cutie. "Too many. Terraway will eat well, hopefully."

"You're a good person, giving yourself up for them. You sure it's worth it?"

"I'm sure I can't live with myself if a whole world goes starving and I could've done something about it."

"This is going to be harder than I thought," he murmured under his breath. He looked me over with obvious lust poking through his gentlemanly demeanor. "I've never seen a woman clothed in so little."

"You've never seen a woman in a bathing suit before?"

"Not one like that, no. You're stunning."

"You're not so bad yourself. You got a name to go with

that smile?" I felt a little slutty that I'd made out with him in my dream before without bothering to give him a name. "If you're going to be making reoccurring appearances in my dreams, you might as well have a name. Fair warning, you've got some steep competition. It's usually Ian Somerhalder in my nighttime boy fantasies."

The man pursed his lips that were just the right amount of plump. "I could tell you what my friends call me, but if you keep dressing like that, I don't think we'll be friends much longer."

"Philip," I breathed, dubbing him the name of the prince in one of the fairytales that Allie used to read to me when I was little. The illustrated prince in the book had a chin dimple, just like my dream guy did. "Let's call you Philip. And I'll be Gracie. I always liked that nickname best."

"Very pretty. It suits you. Too gracious for your own good." We laid back on the sand, and I grinned when he touched his toes to mine. I loved my dreams because my OCD didn't inhibit me here. I was free. Philip's feet were large, his toes long in comparison with my smaller feet. "I like it here. What made you pick this place?"

I shrugged and adjusted my bikini strap, which made his gaze drift to my chest.

That's right. I've got moves. I only use them in my dreams, but still.

"It's far away from where I am in real life."

"And where are you in real life?"

"Someplace I don't want to be." I watched the gentle waves come in and wondered if I would someday learn how to swim. My smile died on my lips as I pondered all the choices that had led me to work for Ezra and permit complete strangers into my space. In the span of a couple days, our little group had grown closer – close enough to lean on. Most of my friends I'd known a decade now weren't close enough for me to want to lean on. I wasn't sure what it was about this group that made them the exception.

Philip leaned his shoulder to mine. "But where? Where's your home?"

"Here," I said, pointing to the ocean. "I live here now. I was thinking of putting a sofa over by the shore so I can watch the ocean like it's a TV."

Philip smiled at me through his note of irritation that I didn't want to talk about reality. "You're a stubborn one. It plays in your favor that you're a pretty little thing."

I'd never loved the idea of being called a thing, but I went with it, since he looked at me like I was beautiful when he said it. "Then why'd you come back?" I realized I'd probably brought him here, wanting another taste of his lips.

"I wanted to see you again. Get to know you."

I shook my head. "Not much to know. Gracie Reese. 5'5", nurse, and imagination surf champ." I shook my head. "I came here to forget reality for a while."

Philip moved his body to cover mine and leaned over

me, his taut muscles looking almost photo-shopped. "I think I can help with that."

When his lips touched mine, all talk about home stopped. There was nothing but his lips, my legs, his hands and the beach.

4

BYGONES AND BULLY

I was warm and comfortable when I slowly came back to myself. Passing out from too much reaping was an ordeal I was unfamiliar with, so I was grateful I slept through the bulk of it with such a pleasant dream. The whole nightmare of Titus and his head crumbling beneath my hands felt like a distant Dali-esque hallucination tinged with surrealism that was all too real. The world was wreathed in a fuzzy white hue as I tried to grasp onto the reality I was certain had a fair amount of "oh crap" to it.

The crap sandwich grew more unavoidable when I finally opened my eyes and saw Von in a chair next to the bed.

Not my bed.

Not my house.

I sat up, my body moving slower than I would've liked.

The sheets weren't mine. I couldn't be sure they were clean. I tried to extract myself from the stranger germs that were no doubt crawling all over me by now, but only managed to twist myself in the bedding more, until I was swimming in a sea of pea green fabric and no doubt dangerous amoebas.

"Whoa, calm down. I've got you." Von ripped the comforter off me, and instantly I could breathe easier.

"Where am I?" I swung my feet over the side of the bed, but they were clumsy and flopped against the bedframe like rubber. "Stupid useless feet. Come on. Get it together, guys."

"Take it easy, love. You're in no condition to run a marathon just yet."

"I'm fine." In the back of my mind, I knew it was a dumb idea to stand up, but I was too stubborn to listen to Von or my brain. Determination. That was the only language I spoke. My attempt at standing on my own was short-lived. My knees buckled, and I collapsed on the floor, banging my elbow hard on the ground. "Ow! Oh, that stings."

Von stood back, hands on his hips as he surveyed the mess that I was, sprawled out on the light beige carpeted floor. "Well, I told you to calm down. You were flopping around like a manatee out of water." He reached down and lifted me gently, ushering me back to the bed. I loved how Von said "water". Such a simple word, but his British accent did wonders with it.

I sat up with my feet over the side, a mix of frustrated and embarrassed. "Thanks. I guess I'm not firing on all cylinders."

Von whipped out his phone and said into it, "She's awake, but you were right. Her body's not cooperating just yet." He paused, studying my face as if looking for something to report back. "Yeah. Come on up." He hung up and shot me a reassuring half-smile. "Better now that you're not on the floor?"

"Much. Where am I?"

"Ezra's house."

"Seriously? Again?" I looked sideways up at him. "You alright?" I asked of his absence that morning.

"I am. I spent the day getting myself taken off your case, apparently." He sighed, and that haunted look of too much weight on his shoulders dimmed the jokes his eyes and lips usually danced with. "It was fun while it lasted, yeah? The whole upstanding 9-5, or in your case 7-7, wasn't for me. Not a huge surprise when Danny's right, but he never tires of the confirmation."

I nodded slowly, my brain taking longer than usual to digest the information. "I guess that makes sense. Fun night with Katrina?"

"Very fun night, though you were right about her trying to steal my knickers. Fun little fetish, but I and my underwear escaped."

"Thanks for the report. So now what? Can I stop being a Death Omen?"

Von watched my face, taking a beat before answering. "No. You can't get fired quite as easily. Mason can replace me on his own well enough."

My shoulders slumped. I'd expected as much, but the verification sucked. "You need a letter of recommendation or something?"

Von let out a humorless chuckle. "No. I'll go back to what I was doing before, though I don't imagine Ezra will rehire me now. There's plenty of work for Duwende outcasts who didn't graduate the Academy, though not a lot for half-vampires." He cleared his throat, not meeting my gaze. "I had an errand to run this morning, and it took longer than expected. That's why I didn't show up to the house at seven."

I nodded, not wanting to get into a fight. I was still pretty pissed that I'd been attacked by Titus, and I didn't want to hear excuses why a grown man couldn't show up to work on time. "It's fine," I lied. I could feel evasiveness in his explanation, though I didn't have the heart to investigate why.

Von sat back down in the chair near the bed, not looking at me. "What do you want me to say?"

My eyes narrowed as I heard people coming up the stairs toward the room. I made sure to keep my voice low so our conversation would be private. "I want you to say you didn't give a crap about my life or what happened to me. I want you to be honest. I want you to admit that I'm being asked to sacrifice everything for your people, while you get to go screw my friend, sleep in and do whatever else you want, like it's all a flipping vacation. I went through the crap of it today, and you were gone." It wasn't a challenge; I just wanted the truth. So many times had Bev told me how much she'd wanted to be there for this school event or that function, but something always came up. It was a lifetime of 'running errands', and I was tired of it.

Von exhaled. "You know that's not true. I just didn't manage my time well. Simple as that."

My hands started to itch, so I gave the backs of them a clumsy scratch. "Alright. You had things to do. We can leave it at that. I'm alive. Bygones. It was good to meet you."

He ran his hand over his face as the bedroom door opened. Danny's eyebrows were pushed together, his expression that of a rhino gearing up for a battle of the horns. "What happened? I told you to follow me after we were done in the hospital when I took Mariang to the car. You can't run yourself into the ground because it'll make you useless the next day! Let me test your reflexes." Danny was shouting as he planted himself directly in front of me. He tapped on my knees, but received no response. I debated between retracting from him and meeting his harsh advance with one of my own. "See? Now you're useless!"

"You don't have to yell at me," I replied, trying to keep my indignation even-toned.

Ezra came in behind Danny with Mason and Mariang. "October Grace, are you hurt?" Ezra had kind aqua eyes that seemed genuinely concerned for my condition. I'd never had a parent worry if I was hurt, or talk to me like they cared. I knew Ezra's agenda was to get me to like him so I didn't cause problems for him and Bev, but every now and then I caught a note of sincerity I couldn't explain away.

On instinct, I retracted from the compassion, afraid of trusting it and then getting bit. "I'm fine. Dazed, but fine. Who's that?" I pointed to a man in a black suit who came in behind Ezra. He had a goatee, was in his late thirties, and looked about zero kinds of fun and nine kinds of serious.

Ezra turned to acknowledge the man. "This is Andy. He'll be added to the security detail I'm assigning you until I can get a handle on things. He's Duwende, so he can pull a little stress from you in a pinch, but he won't be able to take souls from you, since Mason and Von are your Reapers."

"I'm okay without the extra protection," I insisted.

Danny jabbed his finger at me, too angry to be reasoned with. "You can't act all indestructible when one of your Death Reapers is a joke!"

I glared up at him. "I'd like to know who you think you're yelling at. Don't be pissed at me. I didn't do anything wrong. Ya'll are constantly reminding me how down and out Terraway is, but now I'm in trouble because I'm trying to fix the problem faster than you want? Nonsense!"

Danny was instantly fed up. He threw his hands in the

air and backed away. "That's it. I can't deal with her when she's like this. She's being impossible, Ezra!"

Mariang's bell-like voice tried to temper Danny's fury. "Danny, you're shouting! You're scaring her."

I pointed to the door. "Go outside."

"What?"

I stood precariously, grateful that Von offered his arm on my elbow to steady me so I didn't lose my balance. "Go into the hallway and come back when you're good and ready to act like an adult."

Danny's face soured. "Are you serious? You're practically a teenager!"

"And you're an old man who should know better. Someone has to be the adult here, and you sure don't seem up for the task. Now, march!" I lowered my volume. "Go back out and come in with a new attitude, or I don't say a word."

We glared at each other until Danny realized that I held all the cards. He breathed hard through his nose like a bull, then stomped out, slammed the door and came back in with the exact same expression and edge to his tone. "October, how great that you're alive and well. It's great that you woke up when we weren't sure you would! Everything's... great. Say, do you think you could never do that again when you've only got one Puller on you? That would be great."

Von laughed, despite the somber mood. "Oh, that was priceless. Why do I never get these moments on film?"

I gripped the headboard as a residual wave of exhaustion hit me. "Okay, everyone needs to sit down. I'm on the verge of passing out again, so just be cool."

Danny stormed out of the room and came back a few seconds later with a bottle of water, thrusting it in my face and nearly hitting my nose with it. "There. Now can you talk?"

I uncapped the bottle with shaking fingers and tipped the cold liquid to my lips. The refresher felt amazing, reviving me a marginal amount. I wasn't used to my limbs being so out of sorts, and I didn't care for the vulnerability of it. I tilted my head up at Danny, smiling through my loathing. "Did anyone ever tell you that you're a sweetie pie? I mean, you're practically a *My Little Pony* with all your precious little love muffiny goodness. As soon as you grow your hair out, I'm braiding it for you and brushing sparkles in it."

"Ezra!" Danny shouted, pointing at me like a true tattletale. "Deal with her!"

Ezra cut through our bickering with a finality in his tone. "Time to put your childishness aside, you two." He turned his shoulders to address only me, his crisp white oxford shirt not daring to crease at the slight movement. "October, if Von is not with you and Mason, please limit the number of reapings to as many as Mariang can do."

I balked as Von's head whipped in Ezra's direction. "I'm not fired?"

"Though you deserve it, no. It's clear she can do far

more with two Reapers than with one. We need to take our advantage where we can get it. Is that acceptable to you, October Grace?"

"Sure. I don't want to babysit, though. I don't want to have to drag a grown man out of bed or wait for him to show up to work." I scratched the back of my left hand with the plastic cap of my water bottle. "So if you can handle that end of things, I can work with Von just fine."

"That's fair." Ezra placed his hand on Von's shoulder. Though he was not forceful, Von stiffened at the authoritative contact that subtly told him to shape up. "Von, you'll spend every night with Mason and October. There will be no more going out. You cared about this chance at redemption enough to steal the job. Now it's time to actually do your job. Pulling during sleep is quite effective. If she's bent on saving our people at any cost, you'll do everything to make certain the effort doesn't kill her."

"Yes, sir. Thank you, sir." Von's blue and gold eyes were alight with new life at the second chance he had not anticipated. I could tell he was used to being fired.

This was clearly not what Danny wanted to hear. He erupted in a sea of questions and aggressive exclamations, some directed at me, though I was barely upright. I'm not sure what he was expecting me to say. "I'll wait until you're finished," I said when Danny paused for my rebuttal. "I assume you eventually want to hear about the Goblin King's threat when you run out of air?"

Danny's small nose scrunched. "What threat? He's dead."

"Oh, the threat he told me that's already in motion. The one you probably don't want to be yelling at me about. Unless you really do want me to put makeup on you and do your hair up all pretty first. I mean, I assume that's what all the yelling's really been about."

Ezra touched his finger to his forehead, centering himself. "Apologies. Do continue, dear."

It threw me whenever he called me dear or darling, but I breezed over it when Mason sat down next to me on the bed. "It's a family matter, so new guy needs to wait outside." I motioned to Andy, whom Ezra dismissed with a wave of his hand. "Thanks. Titus said that if I didn't cooperate and give him the whole stone, he had spies in the security detail you hired, Ezra, who would target Mason and Von."

"Target how?"

"He threatened me by saying they could feed a few organs not necessary for survival to Sylvia's people. Keep the guys alive, but slice them up. He said he could do the same to Danny if I got attached to him. He said I only needed one Duwende, so if worse came to worst, the plants in security could do away with one of you."

At this, Mariang burst into tears and ran out of the room.

Danny glowered at me. "Did you have to be so graphic? You know she's sensitive."

My head tilted to the side as I looked up at him curiously. "You're really thinking about her when your life's being threatened? Huh. You're sweeter than I thought. That's actually real decent of you, Danny."

Danny started shouting again in exasperation. "Hello! Everything she goes through affects me. I have to clean up every mess. If she's upset, it falls to me to handle."

I nodded at the epiphany. "Ah, gotcha. So you're not worried about her. You're worried about how her loving you is a burden on you. Makes sense. Prince Charming if I ever saw one. I daresay that's a leg up from *My Little Pony*."

Danny turned to Ezra and pointed at me. "Would you deal with her before I lose my temper?"

I gaped at Danny. "This is you keeping your temper? You're yelling like a toddler."

Ezra waved a hand in the air to clear it of our bickering. "Continue with relevant information, October Grace."

"One of the plants in security might try to steal the stone soon to give to some guy named... I think it was Sam?"

"Sama," Danny breathed, his head hanging in defeat. "I was hoping he wouldn't find out about you yet. We need more time before he gets a plan into action."

"Who's Sama?"

Mason fielded this one. "The immortal Mangkukulam."

For my benefit, Von added, "That's sort of like a witch."

"Super," I deadpanned.

Mason continued, "Sama and another mage studied under the last Kapre – that's a giant-like man who loves gems and enchants them with magic. They're extinct now. Have been for like, a century."

Ezra picked up the story for me. "Sama and the other mage stumbled upon the secret to the immortality curse, but the last Kapre punished them for using it. No one knows what became of the second mage, but Sama's been confined to an island no one can get to in Terraway. So he'll live forever alone."

"Then what's the big threat? If Sama can't get to us, who cares if he knows we have the sagrado stone?"

Ezra was patient with my question. "Over the decades, Sama's been perfecting his magic. He can send his spirit out into others now. Weak-minded people are usually his targets, and do his bidding. It's how he negotiates with the rulers of Terraway. He offers rations and relief from the famine, but with Sama, it's never help that should be taken. His help always comes with strings that are most difficult to sever."

Mason rubbed my back, inching closer to my side. "The sagrado stone would make Sama's rations useless. He wants us owing him favors. He wants to be in control of Terraway. Immortality's nothing if you can't lord it over the mortals."

Danny let out a huff of frustration. "All that can wait until later to be discussed. Tell me what Titus said. Was he working for himself, or was he going to hand over the stone to Sama?"

I took another drink of water, prolonging the swallows just to watch Danny creep closer to the edge of exploding again. "Ah. Refreshing. No. It sounded like Titus wanted to keep it for himself. Though I'm not sure if the plants were from just him, or from Sama, or from both."

"Well, that doesn't help us much," Danny grumbled, as if the lack of information that pleased him was my fault. "If the plants in your security are from Titus, they'll go away since he's gone. If they're from Sama, then we still don't know who we can trust."

"Sounded a little like both of them were going to target us for the stone, though I don't think they were working together."

Danny's frown tightened. "Brilliant."

I shrugged, not sure if Danny wanted an apology for something that wasn't my fault. "Titus let it slip that they'll target Mariang next. He said something about her being precious to you, Ezra, and that if you didn't comply with giving the Goblins the stone, they'd start in on her non-vital organs. Now that they have me, they're not as concerned with making sure Mariang stays alive. She's more of a tool to get you to comply."

Ezra gripped the wall, all of a sudden needing it to keep himself upright. "Mariang? Mariang!" he called into the hallway, going from composed king to crazed father. "Mariang!"

Though I didn't expect her to be abducted right then, her answering call was a relief felt around the room. When she entered, tucked in her father's embrace, Danny and Von postured. Mason stood between the door and the group as sentry. I saw just how much she was treasured by the people in her life.

Bev hugged me once that I remember. It was for a mother daughter pageant, and they needed photos of all the mothers with their daughters. I had been wrestled into a red, white and blue leotard with a giant white hoopskirt and white high heels. While I'm sure lots of five-year olds want to wear three-inch high heels, I was not that girl, nor could I walk in them. Bev wore a matching outfit that had been adulted up for the occasion. Her white skirt barely covered her butt, and instead of a leotard, she wore a red halter top that clung to her braless breasts. She shoved those babies in every judge's face she could find. To get me to smile for the picture, she had pinched my arm hard to get me to comply. When she'd drawn blood with her acrylic fingernails, a drop of red had spilled onto my white hoopskirt. I still remember that beating.

Ollie had long since refused to go to any kind of pageanting event, so Allie had been there to chaperone. When I fell onstage because of the high heels I was far too young to handle, Allie held me while I cried for ruining Mama's special day.

After an adolescence of that, I cared probably a little too much about ruining people's days with my feelings, so

I kept them tucked away as much as I was able. I couldn't feel much love in hugs or truth in affection. But looking at Ezra gripping his adult daughter in fear that someone might snatch her away, I almost believed that people could love, and that there didn't have to be a camera present for your parent to hug you.

Ezra explained everything, and Mariang paled further, which I did not think was possible.

"There's more," I said, bringing the scattered attention back to business. "Titus didn't tell me who the spies were, but I assume they're already in place. Point is, if we increase security around Mariang, it's a risk. We don't know who's in Sama's pocket and who's trustworthy. My vote is we only trust each other. Not too many better options than the people in this room."

Ezra clutched his daughter tight, fear etched on his face as the impossible conundrum hung in the air.

5

MY FREAK-OUT BAROMETER

Von sat next to me on the edge of the bed when it was just the two of us left in the room. He leaned his left shoulder against the headboard after the others went downstairs to debate over what measures should be taken. Our legs were slung over the side of the bed, though we kept a few inches of space between us. He slowly lit his cigar and puffed on the end, looking bedraggled and certainly not like he'd slept in.

"Where were you really?" I asked.

"At Katrina's."

"You're a terrible liar, you know. If you were thinking of taking up a career as a double agent for the CIA or something, I'd give the want ads another browse through."

Von eyed me. "Actually, I'm a brilliant liar. Strange that you see through it. Fine. I went over to a friend's in the morning. It got a little messy, and took longer than it should've. By the time I got back, you lot were gone."

"Oh, good. I was worried you'd be cryptic about it. You know, it sucks that you get to keep secrets and I can't."

"What a mess," Von murmured, his eyes downcast. His head hung like there was a weight around his neck. "No offense, but this pulling job's more involved than I realized. No wonder Danny's always such a wanker."

"Yup."

"Ezra gave me the job guarding the mansion only a few months ago. I was trying to turn things around, but of course I mucked it up."

"Oh, I didn't realize you were that new here. What were you doing before this?"

"Nothing I was proud enough to list on a resume."

I winced, remembering Danny's mention of him being a prostitute. I wondered how long ago all of that was.

Von held his right hand up to show it to me, displaying its innocence. "You're ripping your skin, you know. You're going to draw blood, and I'm already feeling it. Can I take a little of the edge off?"

"Oh. I didn't realize I was doing it." I considered his offer and finally nodded, my voice quiet so no one heard my admission of weakness. "Sure. Thanks. Just please don't—"

"I know." Von gently rubbed my back in slow circles. "Don't touch your hands and don't pull too hard. I know."

It took less than a minute for my completely erect spine to slump as Von relaxed me. It was the pulling, sure, but it was also the contact that soothed me. He and Mason offered it so freely and so often – I knew it wouldn't be long before I became a contact junkie, seeking out physical touch for no reason other than luxury, rubbing up against random strangers on the street.

Von slid me closer so I was tucked into his side, my head under his chin as he smoked, blowing out rings over my head that floated down in front of my nose. I didn't mind the minty, masculine smell of Von, nor his cigars. That same magnetic tug in my gut erased my engrained hesitation I would normally feel at being held so close. Von rubbed his thumb down my face, and I closed my eyes. So rarely was I comforted, but the longer Von held me and found new ways to touch me, I was grateful for the kindness. "Rough day, huh."

"What would make you say that?"

Von snorted into my hair. "You called Prince Langgam 'Lang'. Nobody calls him that."

"Well, he's a tool to abduct me. He's lucky I don't call him a vicious blowhole."

"You killed the Goblin King. Do you want to talk about it?"

"I'm not really a talker when it comes to stuff like mass-murder, so I'll pass."

"Fair enough. For the record, I think you were quite brave to use the stone how you did."

"I won't sit back and be a puppet while someone threatens you and Mason. I won't play nice when someone tells me Mariang's next on the list. She's a sweet girl. Doesn't deserve that." I cleared my throat. "But I shouldn't have killed Titus."

Von was quiet a few beats while he held me. If Ollie could see me now, wrapped in a man's arms and not squirming to get away, he wouldn't recognize me. I blame it on the drama of the day. "I'm sorry I wasn't there. I should've been. I wanted to be. I thought I had time to run that errand, but I didn't." He rubbed concentric circles into my back. "How much are you freaking out right now?"

I shrugged. "I dunno. Like, a six? This pulling thing's messing with my barometer, so it's difficult to feel anything in the right amount."

Von's voice was quiet when he spoke. "I spent a fair amount of the time you were asleep studying up on OCD."

I stiffened. "You don't need to do that."

"There are a lot of inconsistencies with what's online and how you are. This right here, this relaxing you're doing in my arms? It's not typical behavior for someone with your condition. Are you quite sure you weren't misdiagnosed? You come off more like an abused kitten than a mental case."

I didn't know whether to shove him for implying I was crazy, or if I should be touched that he actually tried to figure me out by researching OCD online. "I'm relaxed because you're doing your pulling thing. This isn't something I do with other people, unless I have to in order to blend in. Appearing normal is key, I've found."

"But that's just it. The things I've been reading say that you wouldn't be able to blend in, but you somehow find a way. I've seen it. I don't understand."

I closed my eyes and ducked my head. "I dunno. It's as foreign to me as it is to you. Could you do me a favor?"

"You want I should buy you a pony?"

I snorted, leaning my head to his cheek. "Could you hold me like this a little while longer? It's... and I... Today's been... I'm not good at this, but I want to be. Now that I have a chance to be normal? I want that."

I could feel Von's cheek lifting with a precious smile. "A beautiful woman asking me to hold her? What a rough job this is turning out to be."

"Thank you." I cleared my throat and snuggled more firmly into Von's side. "What you were doing this morning after Katrina's, your secret package drop – was it important?"

"It was to me, yes."

"Okay, then. I can move on and be cool about it."

Von stroked his hand down my side. "Thanks, Peach. I promise to plan better next time. I have a thing I have to do every week, and I didn't want to miss my appointment. I'm trying to work out this new schedule, but reaping seems to be pretty all-encompassing."

"You're telling me."

Andy opened the door and walked right in, not knocking or anything. He stood at attention near the exit after checking the windows were secure. His goatee was cut short to his face, and I couldn't decide if it made him look more or less adult. Being that I pegged his age at around thirty-eight, I'm guessing the goatee aged him slightly. "Ezra said you weren't to be out of my sight. Carry on."

Von bristled, his arms still around my malleable form that was growing more rigid by the second. "Hey, I almost got to second base here, mate. Think you could give us a little space?"

My mouth fell open at Von's insinuation that he was trying to put the moves on me. "Huh?" Then I turned to Andy, indignant I'd been assigned yet another babysitter. "I think I'm okay sitting in a room. Von's here. It's Mariang they're targeting, not me."

"Ezra's orders. More Duwende are on the way. You'll be well protected."

I twisted in Von's long arms to look up at him as he took his cigar from his teeth. Making sure to keep my voice to a whisper, I said, "Von, I don't want to do this. I don't want to be here. I told Ezra about the plants. This isn't a good idea."

He held my troubled gaze before kissing the crest of my cheek. "I know."

"I want to go home and back to my regular job."

He pressed his forehead to mine. "I wish you could, but you can't. This is what it is for you, Peach." My face fell, but I kept my mouth shut as the devastation crushed me. He rubbed my back again. "Whoa. That was strong. I felt you crash just then. Hey, it's alright." Von was being sweet to me more than usual, and the funny thing was that I didn't mind it at all. "Do you know how many women would kill to be able to do what you do? You're a national treasure! You're one in ten million. Look! You've got your very own purse holder." He motioned to Andy, who was still standing at attention. "We need you."

I was lost, and didn't want to find myself here in this world. "Can I call my brother? I'm not doing so hot."

"Of course. You can use my phone." He handed me his device, which I only wiped off once, instead of the three times I usually needed to. Von pointed to the phone. "See, the wiping it off's OCD, but that you can use it knowing there are still germs on it isn't OCD. It makes no sense." His eyebrows furrowed as he tried to puzzle through what I'd resigned myself to years ago. My brain was broken, and that's the size of it.

"I don't think I mind your germs," I replied honestly.

The corner of Von's mouth tugged upward, his eyes dancing with that light I adored. "Not in front of Andy, Peach. He's going to get all sorts of sordid mental images of us tangled up in these very sheets."

"Oh, stop being handsome," I scolded him, palming his

face. I tucked my chin downward when my blush crept up at the kiss he placed to the center of my palm. I prayed he wouldn't notice the girlish thrill he injected into a long-dead part of me.

"Not possible." He squeezed me tighter, guiding my free hand to rest in his lap while the phone started ringing.

After two rings, the voice that nearly jerked the tears out of me answered. "Hello?"

"Ollie?"

"Where are you? Why aren't you calling me on your phone? What's wrong?"

I fished around for an acceptable answer. "I'm out with... with Von." I shot Von a look of apology he waved off. "I'm just hanging out with Mariang and all them to get to know our new sister."

"What's wrong? I can hear it in your voice."

"Nothing. I'm fine." My voice caught, and I wished beyond anything that I could be granted the privacy to break down. "I just missed you, is all. I think I might be late coming home. I'll be there, but not for a while." Another swoon hit me, so I gripped Von's knee to keep myself from fainting. I accidentally let out a quiet whimper.

"Where are you at? I'll come to you."

"Ollie, you can't. I'm alright. Go hang out with Gabby. I'll see you tonight."

"No way. I can tell something's wrong. What is it? Did

Bev do something? Is it work? Gabby told me about Beto and Jessica. Is that it?"

"No. And how did she know about them? Why didn't she tell me? Did everyone know but me?" The cut hit me afresh. I closed my eyes and rested my forehead in the crook of Von's neck, where he guided me. His warm skin centered me through my despondency. "Ollie, what am I doing?"

"You're coming home right now. Tell me where you are."

"What am I doing?" I repeated, utterly lost.

Von took the phone from me and made pretty convincing static noises before turning it off. "There, there, darling."

Von's embrace was too comforting, too soothing. Something about the wonderfulness of it all reminded me that I didn't belong in the arms of the hot guy. I didn't belong in anyone's arms, though part of me wished the indulgence would never end. When I stood and stumbled toward the door, Andy intercepted my path. "Where do you think you're going?"

"I can't do this. I'm going home."

"You're not going home. You're staying right here."

Panic welled in my chest, making my heart thump erratically. "I don't live here! I'm not a prisoner! I'll go home when I feel like it, because that's what normal people do. I'm normal!" I insisted, sounding every bit like the crazy person I knew I was.

Andy blocked the doorway. "Sit down, Lady October. Ezra will get more men here to escort you wherever you need to go. Now that we know what your capacity is for reaping, that will be your new daily quota. Terraway will be back on its feet in no time."

"What? No! I was attacked today, and I'm exhausted. I'm going home." Andy was hard to move, and I wasn't sure if I wanted to full-on come to blows with him just yet. "Dude, I need to go home. Shift it!"

Andy reached out and grabbed onto my hands with a punishing grip. Anxiety nudged me when people touched my hands, but when Andy squeezed me without mercy, the fear flooded through my nervous system. "You'll stay and do your duty!" he commanded, shooting waves of submission through me.

I fought with the feeling of calm he tried to inject into me, but the more I tried to fend it off, my fight went straight into Andy, like he was sucking my will through a straw. I felt myself emptying – my fight, my personality, my choices all leaving me the longer Andy gripped my hands. I'd never had much, but I always had myself. Now Andy was taking even that from me. The second I entertained the thought that I truly hated this stranger, the feeling vanished, replaced with a hollow sense of peace I didn't want and didn't need.

"No!" Von was shouting, trying to pry me loose from Andy. "That's not how this is supposed to work! Pulling isn't used for mind control here! And you can't touch her hands. Don't you know anything about your charge? Let go!"

I screamed as my knees went weak and Andy lowered me to the ground. The last thing I saw was Von's cigar hitting the floor as he threw a punch at Andy, and then the world went dark.

6

FAKING THE FLU

 awoke in the back of Terence the Taurus once again. "What? Where? Huh?" was all I could get out. I'd been laying upright with my head on Mason's shoulder. When I pulled away from him, the world spun.

"Easy, tiger. We're on our way to your house." Von had his knees open, taking up too much of the backseat. His blue t-shirt was rumpled and there was a yellow paint stain on the thigh of his jeans. "Here, have something to eat. It's been a while."

Mindlessly I took the burrito Mariang handed back to me from the passenger's seat and bit into it as questions bubbled up inside of me. "What happened?"

Danny spoke over the others. "Andy got himself fired. He barely made it an hour on the job. That's got to be some kind of record."

Mariang turned from the front passenger's seat to face me, placing her frail hand on my knee. "When you tried to leave, Andy pulled your will from you. He blissed you out to keep you in the mansion. That's very much against the rules. They used to do that with the Omens before Dad was instated as the Ambassador to the Topside. That's how they got their numbers so high. They had a few Omens, and they'd work the girls until they dropped. If they tried to escape, the Reapers blissed them out. Then it started all over the next day."

My mouth fell open, horrified. "Are you kidding me?"

Mariang nodded, her gaunt face solemn. "Dad ruled against that practice with me, which is why I'm still alive."

Von's mouth was drawn in a tight line as he went down his row of fingers, cracking them one by one. "Good for production. Bad for, you know, all of humanity. That's how they burned through so many Omens." He chucked my kneecap with his knuckles. "You holding up alright, November?

"I think so. A little dazed. My limbs feel like Jell-O."

Mason's arm around me scooped me closer. I sunk into his side as he rubbed my back, soothing the ache inside me that felt never-ending at this point. I chewed my burrito, smelling the unmistakable lavender scent of my waterless antibacterial hand sanitizer. "Did I wash my hands in my sleep?" I asked him, embarrassed.

Mason chuckled, leaning against the door of the car

and turning his body sideways so I could sit in between his legs, rest against his chest and give Von more room. He raked his fingers through my ponytail as I ate. "Do you often wash your hands in your sleep?"

"Not often. Just a few times." Ollie and Allie had caught me washing my hands several nights till my skin bled in the bathroom.

"No. I did that. Thought you might want any trace of Andy off you when you woke up."

My eyes closed as I tried not to let myself fall apart at the depth of the thoughtfulness in that simple gesture. I reached up and pressed my palm to his trimmed beard, trusting Mason enough to not picture the germs crawling all over him. "Thank you. That was... thank you."

He kissed the inside of my wrist and leaned over my shoulder with his mouth open, as if he was about to take a bite of my burrito. He grinned when I inhaled two giant mouthfuls of bean and cheesy goodness, so he couldn't steal my meal.

"You'd better hurry. I'm coming for the rest of that baby if you don't eat it." There was a casual sweetness to Mason that made me forget how upset I was supposed to be. I knew he wasn't doing excessive pulling; it was simply who he was. He hugged me around the middle, supporting my weight while I relaxed into him. "You don't have to worry about Andy. Ezra will send a replacement out in the morning, and that's that."

Von added, "Danny and I talked Father of the Year out of the small army he wanted to send."

"Not that I think we're safer without the extra protection," Danny muttered. "I can't believe Andy did that. I'm sorry, kid. I should've been there to stop him."

I blinked in Danny's direction, confused at his unexpected humility. "Thanks, Danny. But you weren't even in the room. You couldn't have known."

"I reviewed his test scores. I okayed him to come on the job and shadow me. He shouldn't have done that. The only time Von, Mason or I would ever bliss you out is if you're on the verge of a heart attack or something. I did it once to Mariang by accident when I was new on the job, and felt horrible about it for weeks. It's like, one step off from date rape in my book."

Mariang reached over and stroked his forearm. "It was an accident, Danny Bear. What Andy did was on purpose."

Danny's jaw was set, and I knew that though no one held him accountable for a mistake made years ago, he would not be forgiving himself any time soon. "Point is, Andy's gone. And honestly, I'm not thrilled with just jumping into a replacement tomorrow, knowing any of them could be spies. We've got the three of us watching the two of you. Should be enough for now. That is if *someone* can remember to show up to work on time tomorrow."

"That okay with you?" Von asked me quietly, his eyes insecure, but friendly.

"Can you remember to show up on time tomorrow?"

Von shrugged and shot me a wink. "Probably not."

Danny choked the steering wheel as he turned into my driveway, groaning while Mariang giggled softly.

I only made it into the house upright because Von let me lean on him after Mason turned himself into the gray wolf I loved. Danny was carrying Mariang like a baby. It was sweet, given their intense connection, but I renewed my vow to never let a man carry me like that.

The cicadas were making their evening humming buzz sound that lulled me into thinking sleep might be on the horizon. But when Ollie barked his relief at us, I knew I wouldn't get to rest anytime soon. "Where were you? Do you know how worried I've been?" Ollie was still in his jeans and red polo, even though it was close to ten o'clock at night.

"Hey, Ollie. You didn't have to wait up. I told you I'd be back, and here I am."

"You're barely upright! What happened? You sounded scared on the phone. This guy? Is he the problem?" Ollie jabbed his thumb towards Von, who lowered me gingerly into a chair at the dining room table. The recessed lighting above me highlighted the bags under my eyes, no doubt. Mason sat at my side, his muzzle resting on my knee.

"Why do I always get that?" Von asked, bewildered.

"No, Von's fine. Danny, Mariang and Von are staying over tonight." I motioned to my wan expression. "Flu.

Mariang and I both caught it. Might want a foot of space so I don't get you sick."

Ollie felt my forehead with the back of his hand. "You don't have a fever." He snatched up my keys from where Danny placed them on the table. "I'm taking you to Urgent Care."

My eyes watered as I gazed up into my brother's look of absolute concern. In that simple gesture, I saw Ollie clearly. "You love me," I marveled.

"Why are you saying that like it's some big epiphany? Of course I love you. Let me get you a sweater, then I'm taking you to a doctor." He turned to address Danny, who'd just come back into the kitchen after laying Mariang down on my bed. "You should take her in, too. Mariang didn't look too great. Whatever they have, I'll take care of it. I'm driving."

"I'm fine, Ollie. Just tired. I could use a solid night's sleep. Any chance that's in the day planner?"

Ollie put his keys down and sank into the chair next to mine. "I was worried. You hung up before I knew what was going on. You can't do that. I'm actually here in the state. I can help you now."

I bit my lip, holding back the question I wanted to ask. *How long?* How long would he be here? Just long enough for me to depend on him, and then go back to his home in New York?

I scratched my hands under the table to keep from blubbering all over the place. I was an Omen of death. It was best Ollie go back to his home. Whatever was hunting me, I didn't want it anywhere near him. Mason licked the backs of my hands to remind me to stop punishing myself. I patted his fur that brought me more comfort than most things. "We haven't spent much time together. Sorry I've been out so much this visit."

Ollie rubbed the back of his neck. "Well, that's the thing I wanted to talk to you about. Me coming back wasn't just for Bev." He glanced up at Danny and Von, giving them a look that told them to scram.

Von took the hint. "I'm famished. Any requests for pizza toppings? I'm heading out."

"Olives," Ollie chimed in, pulling out a twenty. "Here. They've got chicken soup at the place in town on 42nd Street and Fraser Boulevard. Could you pick up some soup for October and Mariang? That's where you're going, right?"

Von ignored Ollie's cash, waving the offer away, which I knew earned Von a little respect in Ollie's book. Von paused his exit to rub my back and pull a portion of my stress from me. "You'll be alright while I'm gone, November?" He lifted my hand and placed a kiss to the knuckle of my middle finger.

It was sweet, and though I probably should've been snatching my hand back from his entrancing touch, I allowed my blush to take over, turning the corners of my mouth upwards. I leaned into his hip, letting myself relax into his touch for the briefest of moments before bucking up. "I'll be fine. Thanks." I felt Ollie's wide eyes on me, floored that I was so open around the stranger.

After Von made his exit, Danny excused himself to go check on Mariang, though I could tell from his look of longing toward the door that he was starving. Ollie waited until it was just us and my dog to start in on his agenda.

7

A WORLD OF DIFFERENCE

"You're back with Gabby for real this time? Ollie, that's awesome!" I threw my arms around my brother's neck, squeezing with every ounce of energy I still possessed, which actually wasn't all that much.

"Whoa! Well, I didn't expect that reaction. I mean, I knew you'd be happy, but I was worried you'd think we were rushing into things." My brother wrapped his arms around me, patting my back before I released him.

"Yes, rushing into things with the girl you've been dating on and off for ten years. Will you two be moving in here?"

"No. Gabby won't budge from her townhouse. I don't mind." His phone buzzed, and he looked at the caller ID with an expression of tested patience. "It's Bev. She thinks I broke into her trailer and stole her doorstop. Been blowing up my phone all day, threatening to call the cops on me."

I gulped. "Oh, sorry. That was me. I took it."

Ollie gaped at me, and then he let out a loud laugh, clapping his hands together. "Oh, please tell me you stole something that's actually valuable. No, now that I think of it, a rock is the best thing to gank. Why would she care if it's gone? Stealing from Bev. I didn't think you had it in you. You're always so well-behaved. You're the good child."

I shrugged. "I'm all kinds of bad to the bone now. I killed a man in cold blood this morning just for messing with my dog." I tried to confess the truth about Titus to Ollie in my own way that wouldn't let him too near Terraway. Mason sensed the tension under my blasé joke and rested his nose on my thigh. I reached down to stroke his fur.

Ollie laughed, and the levity looked good on him. "You seem happy now. Man, stealing from Bev? Proud of you, kid. And you're not so allergic to human contact. I noticed you leaning into Von."

The hint of tease to his tone needed addressing. "That was nothing. Von's a nice guy. He's like that with everyone. I'm surprised he hasn't given you a lap dance yet."

Ollie cocked his head to the side and donned a sympathetic expression. "Hey, I'm sorry Beto cheated on you. I had a talk with him about it. I had no idea. But now that I'm moving back home, I can keep better tabs on things."

I swallowed my feelings and put on a convincing smile.

"I'm alright. It was for the best. He's happy with Jessica, so I guess that's good."

"So if the air went mysteriously missing out of his tires in the morning and there was sugar in his gas tank, you wouldn't point any fingers at me?"

I giggled at the delinquency I expected of my brother. He wore polos now, but I knew him best as the white t-shirt king who didn't let me get pushed around, even by his bestie. "You don't have to mess with Beto on my behalf. He's your best friend."

"No, *you're* my best friend," he corrected me.

A soft smile touched my lips. "I love you, Ollie."

"I love you, too, kid."

When Von came back with seven pizzas, Ollie was too caught up in the liveliness of the night to examine the oddity of Von, Danny and my dog wolfing down six of the pies.

"Gabby and I've been talking more and more, so when they passed me over for the promotion again at work, I just up and left." He confessed the crime as if only just telling himself what he'd done. "I still can't believe I quit. I mean, all my stuff's still in New York. I'll have to go pack it all up and move it home. As soon as my lease is up, and I'll be coming back to Georgia."

"That's great! That's so great! I mean, think of all the fun we'll have. Staying up late watching movies, going to the park. Oh! And they have a new ice cream shop in town I know you'll love."

"I'll be going back to New York tomorrow early morning with Gabby. She's going to stay with me these next few weeks, help me pack up, and then I'll be moving home. Well, to *her* home, but still. I'll be just ten minutes away now."

We talked animatedly for the duration of the pizza eating contest Von, Mason and Danny seemed to be in. It was only when my eyelids started drooping that I consented to turn in. Ollie took a chance and hugged me one more time before going to his room to sleep. "You hug people without cringing now. I like it on you," he commented.

"I could say the same thing about you. Gabby's a good influence. Loosens you up. Look at us." I tried to stand straighter. "Almost normal."

"Almost. Goodnight, kiddo."

It was only when Danny retreated to my bedroom that I realized I would be sleeping on the pullout sofa. It wasn't that big a deal. It was encased in tight plastic still, so I wasn't terribly worried about the mold spores and germs that might leak out and infest my lungs while I slept. I dragged out three comforters from the hall closet to make a suitable nest on the pullout.

I didn't say a word to Von when he handed over the bathroom to me to shower and change into my pajamas, but I felt the tension building. I didn't sleep with other people in the room. Beto had tried to stay the night a few times, but I'd made him sleep on the couch. Come to think of it, I might have an idea of why we kept breaking up.

The water couldn't get hot enough to cleanse all of Andy's germs off, so I had to rely on my soap doing most of the dirty work. When I emerged from the shower and wrapped my soft pure white towel around me, I felt one-fifth more me, which made a world of difference.

PENNY'S DAD

*V*on wasn't as attuned to my nerves unless he touched me, so the plan was to give him a wide berth. When I came out of the bathroom ready for bed, I found him already stretched out on the pullout under the covers, reading a paperback. His free hand cradled his head as he stared up at the pages with his shirt off. So much for making him sleep on the floor.

I didn't say a word as I climbed onto the creaky sofa's thin mattress. The springy frame made every shift noticeable, so I tried to move as little as possible while I sought out comfort in the two feet of space his much larger body had left me. Mason left us to go take a quick shower. "Whatcha reading?" I asked politely.

Von flipped the cover to me with an expression that was firm, as if he knew something about the book would cause a fight. My eyes widened when they fell on the title.

"*Your Partner's OCD and You*? What the crap is that? Is that a joke?"

Von raised an eyebrow at me. "I'm not having a laugh. This is my job. You don't like to talk about these things, and I didn't want to push the issue. There's a lot I don't understand about you, and I need to if I'm to do my job properly." His face pulled into a frown. "Are you quite sure you weren't misdiagnosed? Some of the things in here aren't lining up to what I've noticed of you. Sometimes it's spot on OCD, and other times you're fully functional. This books makes it seem like you can't turn it on and off, like I've seen you do."

"We already had this conversation. I'm about to make you eat that book, so I'd tread lightly if I were you. How would you feel if I read a book called *Everything that's Wrong with Von*?"

"I'd be a bit embarrassed if there was a chapter about my night with Felicia. Not my best performance, but in my defense, I was stinking drunk. Other than that, I'd be flattered you wanted to understand me. That's all this is."

I blew out a long breath, trying to rein in my temper before it lashed out too much. "Fine. You want to know more? I can do normal things because I have to. I've been through years of therapy. Ollie and Allie were relentless, trying to make me normal. I'm on medication that helps me calm down about big things that other people think are small things. That's how it might not look like your textbook, which should really be titled, *Why October's Going to Die Alone.*"

Though I'd spilled my guts, Von wasn't satisfied. "But this book even addresses people who are on medication and have gotten help. The fact that you are able to do normal things isn't normal. I don't understand it, but I'm trying to." He put the book on the end table and rolled on his side to stroke my arm. "This is me. This is how I am when I care about someone in my life." He brushed a light kiss to my lips and whispered, "Love me as I am, darling."

I deflated, knowing he was right, and that I was very lucky to be in bed with such a thoughtful guy. Though I knew it was meant to be platonic, his precious little kiss sent warmth into my belly and brought color to my cheeks. "Okay. Could you not read that book around me, though? I feel on edge just looking at the title."

"I can do that." He rubbed my bicep, massaging lightly. "And you won't die alone. Mason and I are here until the end – no matter what end."

I don't know why this made my eyes water, the pledge that threatened to wipe away one of my worst fears. "Don't say nice things to me," I warned, my lashes sweeping shut so I didn't have to take in the sincerity that radiated off him.

Von opened his mouth to respond, but his thoughts were interrupted by his phone, which he answered with a steadying sigh on the second ring. "Angela?" My dreamy mood had no effect on the dark cloud that settled over Von as his conversation grew harsher. "What? No! You can't do this. We had an agreement!"

He ripped off the covers and stomped outside in his bare feet, but I could still hear him just fine. I tried not to eavesdrop, but it was impossible.

"She's like a daughter to me! The new job is... They discovered a new Omen, and I was in the right place at the right time. No one else could suck the soul from her, so I did it. Now it's my job... Yes, I'm telling you the truth. I have a new job, and this is it. You can't take Penny away from me because I might miss my day with her! I was there this morning. I've never missed a date. This is a legitimate job, Ange... Must you always yell when you need money?"

It was at that point I decided I knew enough about the situation to make myself useful. I slipped my shoes on and moved out onto the porch where Von was frantically trying to reassure Angela that no, he wasn't a deadbeat dad, and yes, he really was my Reaper. I motioned for the phone, keeping my voice even when Von handed it over. "Hello? Is this Angela?"

The woman's nasal voice went from aggressive to confused. "Who is this?"

"This is October. I'm the new Omen working with Mariang. Is something wrong with moving the date Von sees his daughter? Because we can try to work around your schedule if you can clear it with Ezra. I know Von's just crushed that he might need you to switch dates, but it's not really something we have control over. Maybe if you cleared your schedule with Ezra, we could work something out."

Girlfriend was shocked, which meant she stopped any edge in her voice when she answered me. "I didn't know the kingdom found a new Omen. I mean, there's been no announcement Topside. Forgive me, Lady... I'm sorry. What was your name again?"

"October." I batted at Von's hand to stop him from nervously chewing on his nails. He was on edge while he watched me work the human magic of diplomacy. "You haven't heard of me yet because I'm still in training. Von and Danny have been real helpful, showing me the ropes. I don't know what state the kingdom would be in, were it not for Von stepping up when no one else could. Please make sure Penny knows what an asset her daddy is to the kingdom." I put on my kindest voice.

"Von's not Penny's father," Angela informed me.

My eyebrows drew together in confusion as I looked up at Von for verification. He shrugged noncommittally, which cleared absolutely nothing up. "Okay. Well, thanks for being so understanding with moving your schedule. I know it's hard, and I'm sorry for being a pain to you."

"So the money will keep coming in regularly?" Angela asked tentatively, getting down to the bottom line.

"I don't see why it wouldn't."

"Working for the new Omen, eh? He's really your Reaper? That's gotta pay well. Does it pay better than his gig working security for King Manaul? Will Von be sending more money?"

Ah, there it is. The classiest girl a blowhole who didn't think with his upstairs brain could procreate with. Or not procreate with. I wasn't totally sure what was going on. "I really can't speak to that. I'm still in training, so I haven't been paid anything yet myself. That's something you'll have to work out with Von." I lowered my voice. "But I'll tell you that threatening to take Penny away from him isn't the way to go about getting more money. In fact, if this becomes an issue, I might have to fire him and get myself a whole new Duwende if he's too distracted by family drama to do quality work. I would imagine whatever lesser paying job he has to slum it with after this would give you a lot less to work with." I pushed the issue further, narrowing my eyes at Von in a threat. "Has he ever missed a child support payment before?"

Von shook his head from side to side so fast, I swear his eyeballs rattled.

"No," Angela confirmed. "And it's not child support, but it's not exactly enough money to live on."

I ignored Von's look of anxiety and introduced a bit of edge to my voice, my accent dipping into my southern lilt that sometimes flew out when I was tired or impatient. "Well, I would think that his new steady government job would help with all that. If I were you, I'd be accommodating as a sunshine in July right about now. I'm tired, and if my Duwende can't pull enough stress from me, I'll move onto someone who can. I'm handing you back to Von now, so I'd wrap it up in a pretty little bow that serves Penny's best interest."

I gave the phone to Von, not expecting him to engulf me in a hug that was filled with relief and gratitude. His tone was light, and he gripped me tight as he ended the conversation with a much more amiable Angela.

He shoved the phone into his pocket and squeezed me with both arms, incredulous that he'd escaped losing his daughter. Or not daughter. I still wasn't sure. "That was brilliant! I didn't want to bring you in on the drama, but boy, was that a good time for you to step in. Did Danny tell you about Penny?"

I wrapped my arms around him and rubbed his naked back, smiling at his elation that made him seem like a younger boy in the moonlight. His black hair was messy, and made him look even more adorable than usual. I don't know how guys can roll out of bed with chaotic hair and still look as sexy as a magazine cover. "No, I just put it together from your conversation. For the record, I am sorry I'm making things more complicated for you with Angela and Penny. How old is she?"

"Six going on sixteen."

"Is she your daughter or not? I was getting kind of confused."

Von let out a heavy sigh. "Technically, no. I had a one-night stand with Angela a while back. She told me I got her pregnant, and I believed her without checking the facts. When Penny came, Danny went behind my back and got a paternity test. Turns out she's not mine. Angela just knew I'd step up and help her out with the kid if I thought she was. But it was too late; I got attached."

"This was six years ago, and she's still in your life?"

"Yeah. Angela's not the best at paying bills when there's alcohol to be had. I help out when I can. I never give Angela the cash, of course. The woman's got a gift for turning cash into alcohol."

"That's some magic trick."

"I pay the heat bill and the water bill directly. Same with Penny's school tuition."

I looked up at him with a small smile. "You love Angela. That's very sweet."

Von made a face. "That wench? No. I don't love Angela. I love Penny. Penny's amazing. Best thing that ever happened to me, no contest. I can't believe you... Let me show you pictures!" He took his phone back out and flipped through the photos stored there to show me the best-ofs with his almost-daughter. His arms were still wrapped around me, my temple pressed to his cheek. The funny thing about it all was that I didn't mind it. In fact, I think I kind of liked being held so sweetly by the hot half-naked man.

"So let me get this straight, you're paying the bills for a kid who's not yours?"

"When you say it like that, it sounds off. Penny thinks of me as her father. She doesn't know I'm not. I can't let that die in a little girl so young. Angela asked me to take Penny out once a week so she can get things done. Angela had an emergency and needed me to watch Penny this morning for a few hours. Best part of my week, that girl."

My mouth fell open. I couldn't believe someone could care that much about a child, to protect her and provide a better life for her even though he didn't have to. "That's maybe the nicest thing I've ever heard. Why didn't you tell me that's where you were this morning?"

Von shrugged. "No one asked. I'm fine with people assuming I'm lazy."

My conscience pinged. "I'm sorry I jumped to conclusions."

"We're still getting to know each other. How about you don't apologize for not knowing me when I'm purposefully being evasive?"

"You're too nice. You should be madder at me."

"I'll save my anger for when you insult my cigars." He found a picture that made him smile even wider than the others had. "This one was us making birthday cupcakes for her kindergarten class. Her favorite color that week was green, so I pureed broccoli and added it to the batter to make them match her dress. They were horrid, but she didn't care. She was so proud to take those into school." He chuckled at the photo. "I learned an important lesson in the kitchen that day: if you cover something inedible with chocolate icing, children don't know the difference."

"Aw, she's a cutie. I didn't know you baked."

"Only broccoli cupcakes."

"Well, I hear they're the best kind."

Penny was a pretty little gangly girl. She had a round face and blonde hair, unlike Von's angular model-like facial features and messy black hair. She was tall for her age, and wiry. Totally cute. Von was eager to show her off, as if he was truly her father. "This one's of us at the zoo. She didn't believe me that wombats weren't bats." He showed me one of her next to the wombat exhibit with her eyebrows furrowed in confusion and disappointment.

"She's stinking cute," I commented, and she was. In nearly every photo, Penny was looking at the man holding the camera, or the man in the photo next to her as if he hung the moon. I'd never known a father figure like that, and knew that I had to do whatever it took to keep Penny's idyllic image of her daddy intact. Someone should have a happy ending, and if it couldn't be me, it should probably be the six-year-old with yellow-colored pigtails. She still had a chance at normal. "Come inside. It's getting cold, and I'm beat."

We moved back into the house, seeking warmth under the covers to escape the outdoor chill that reached into our bones. Von stretched his arm under my neck, angling me so I slid into his nook. We held each other in the dark, with only the light from under the door of the bathroom shedding a little illumination on us. Though I couldn't see every detail of his features, I could make out enough to tell that he was on cloud nine. "Thank you so much, Peach. I can't tell you how much I love that girl, and how hard Angela makes things. She only lets me see her if I keep the money coming. Since I have no legal claim, I do what I have to so I can see Penny, and make sure she has a father looking after her. I make sure Angela's remembering to feed her, wash her clothes, take her to the dentist, and things of that sort."

"No problem. I probably shouldn'ta barged in like that, but it seemed like the right thing to do at the time."

He let out a joyous laugh at his good fortune, rubbing warmth into my cold arm as our legs naturally tangled around each other's. I couldn't believe how easy it was to relax around him. "I owe you so much. Tomorrow I'll make you breakfast in bed. I'll make sure Danny isn't such a control freak and lets you pick the radio station. I'll..." He paused to look at me with new appreciation. "I'll do whatever you want. I'll make this work. All of it."

My heart started beating unnaturally, and I didn't trust the unfamiliar rhythm. "Don't say things like that and look at me like that."

"Like what?"

"Like I'm... Don't say things you might not deliver on."

Von's face grew somber. "You have no idea who I was before it all broke."

"Before what all broke?"

He looked at me like he wanted to tell me his secrets, but pursed his lips instead. "Just, before. It's why Danny hates me so much. I used to be the one everyone counted on, the one who got things done for my brothers. Now I'm a half-vamp. Now I'm the one who didn't graduate. I wasn't always such a disappointment. I was top of my class before it all crumbled."

I rubbed his arm, not feeling the germs I knew had to be there somewhere. "Who do you want to be now? Seems like as good a time as any for a fresh start."

Von examined my face as he searched to make sure there was truth in my offer for a new beginning. "I want to be the man who earns a shot at something good, and then takes that chance and does something amazing with it. I want to turn good into amazing. I had that potential before, I think. Lost it along the way."

My gaze softened as I studied the sincerity in his tone, the blazing determination in his eyes. "I think that's well within your control. I mean, not as cool as if you'd said you wanted to be a video game champion, but to each his own. If you want to become a better man, then I guess I'll just have to live with it."

9

NECKING WITH DRACULA

Von smiled with new hope beaming through his dimples. "Tomorrow starts day one of the old Von. The one before it all broke. I liked that bloke. Wait till you see him. I'm thinking he goes commando and needs a new pair of shoes." He winked at me. "How do you think I'll look in something without paint stains on it?"

"You're fine with the paint stains. You already look like a TV teen vampire or something. The paint stains even it out so girls don't fall head over heels too fast. Give us a fighting chance to resist you."

A wicked grin swept over his face at my admission of attraction. "Just say it. You want me for my hot vampire body."

"You know what I mean." I pointed to his wily grin. "Shut that smile down; you know it's up to no good."

Von sat up on his elbow, reached his hand over and

swept my damp hair off my forehead so he could look deep into my eyes. "I'm sorry I didn't show up this morning. I promise I'll—"

"Shh." I shook my head. "Don't promise; just do. If you want to be responsible and earn this job, then do it. Sure, you were at the right place at the right time at Ezra's house, but now make it your business to keep your job. Deserve this job. Penny's worth a dad who can do that. Just tell me when you need to be gone, and we'll work around it. You don't have to keep your life from me."

Von studied the details of my face as if I was something special. "I don't think I'll ever deserve what you did for me tonight."

"Make it your business to earn it, then. I need you to be on your game. Be better than whoever Danny picks out to guard me."

"I will, November." Von softened us both with the use of the nickname I was growing to love. The corner of his mouth drew up in a teasing half-smile. "TV teen vampire, eh? You think I'm sexy."

I scoffed. "You *know* you're sexy. I'm not adding to that inflated ego."

"Whatever. You basically just begged me to suck on your neck." He laughed at my mouth that fell open. "Come here, you succulent little peach!" He grabbed me around the waist to start a war I was too flustered to win right away. He rocked me over until he was on top. He grinned at my squirm while we wrestled for a few minutes, laughing as we played like flirty teenagers who should know better.

No one really played with me like this. It was my fault; I was too uptight to let down my guard so thoroughly. I don't know why it was easier to laugh with Von, but I found I couldn't help the elation that cleared the cobwebbed holes in me I'd long given up on.

It wasn't until he nipped at my neck that things turned. "I vant to suck your blood!" he said in an imitation of Dracula, his lips grazing a sensitive spot on my neck as he bit down lightly.

I squealed as I fought off the waves of attraction I tried not to feel. We had to work together for who knows how long, and it wouldn't help the situation if I developed a crush on the man currently chewing on my neck like a wildebeest. "Shit! Von, you can't... Mm..." My eyes closed as my head tilted back to grant him further access, despite my better judgment. My back arched as his arm snaked under me, pressing my chest to his as I lost myself in a moment I had no right to be in. Heat flooded my belly and spread out through my limbs like a fire that only wanted more – oh, please, please a little bit more.

My hand fisted in Von's hair, making his moan match my wanton pleading for the moment to stretch on for an eternity. His thumb found the dimple in the dip of my hip, working the vulnerable spot as if I was an instrument Von was well-versed in strumming. My whole body hummed the song that was being played between our bare stomachs, the tension tighter than a fiddle's string. Our navels touched without caring about the ramifications.

This was it. It was exactly what Danny warned me about. I would never behave like this with anyone else; it was the Omen-Reaper voodoo that was messing with my mind, making me think there was something that begged to be explored between us.

Between the sheets.

I'm not sure what might've happened, but I knew nothing would when Ollie's door opened and he padded into the living room, horrified at walking in on a half-naked man atop his moaning and writhing sister. He took several steps back, aghast. "October, what are you doing? I heard noises, so I..."

Von rolled off me, only mildly miffed that our playful romp had been interrupted.

I was mortified. I jumped out of the bed, my hands on my crimson cheeks as I searched for anything that might make sense. "We weren't doing anything! We were just goofing around. I swear, Ollie."

"This guy? He's so old!"

"Hello, Beto was eight years older, and you had no problem with him. Von's only seven years older than I am," I protested before catching myself. "We're not hooking up, so it doesn't matter how old Von is."

Von was settled on his back atop the mattress, and held up his hands in surrender. "Nothing going on here, Officer."

Ollie's face was red. "I didn't mean to barge in on whatever that was. I'll go back to bed." He cast me a hurt look that I hadn't told him I had a man in my life.

"It's really not like that," I assured him, chagrinned.

"It's fine. Goodnight, guys."

When Ollie disappeared into his bedroom, I buried my face in my hands. "I can't believe that just happened! You're not a vampire; you're a warlock or something. I'm not usually like that. Black magic, that was."

"You don't usually invite foreign men to suck on your neck? Shame. You really seemed to like it."

"Shut up! I'm so embarrassed!" I shut my eyes tight, wishing I could melt into the carpet and disappear. "This is what Danny warned me about, that I'd start developing feelings or whatever for you or Mason." I blushed all over again, admitting to the thing I didn't want to examine too closely. "That's not going to happen here. I genuinely like you, and I don't want things to get confusing."

Von shrugged in faux confusion. "What's perplexing about a good friend, who was a stranger a week ago, hopping into bed with you and sucking on your neck?" When I responded with an exasperated groan, Von dropped the act. "Okay, okay. I get it. I can be less sexy, less amazing, less addictive. It'll be hard, but I'll manage mediocrity for you." Then he gave me a sincere smile, which made my shoulders relax. "I genuinely like you, too. That stunt you pulled out there, talking Angela down? No one goes to bat for me, but you did without knowing all the details."

I motioned between us. "We're a team." I covered my face with my hands again as the image of me writhing beneath him on the pullout struck me anew. "Oh, and I made it weird by being all flirty. I'm sorry. That's really not me."

"You mentioned. It's the Omen-Reaper bond. I feel it, too." The bedframe creaked as Von rolled to my side of the bed. He stood before me, so close I could smell his deodorant and cigars. He moved my hands away from my face by gently cuffing my wrists. "Hey, there's nothing to be upset about. That was fun, and it doesn't seem like you've had a whole lot of that in your life. I'm all about the fun. I live for it. Happy to impart my knowledge of enjoying one's life onto you. Come to bed, kitten. In the morning, every-thing will be normal."

"I made it all weird now! I really didn't mean anything by the vampire comment. So uncool of me. I don't know why I said it."

"Because I'm dead sexy, obviously." He motioned to his toned form. "You're only human, and apparently, I'm a vampire. You didn't stand a chance." He winked at me and climbed back into the bed. "Come on. Relax. You never relax, and then when you finally do, you apologize over and over for it."

"Really? Just like that?"

"Just like that. Get on in." Von peeled back the covers

and waved me inside the haven. He tugged me down to lay next to him so I didn't have to feel awkward and hug the edge of the narrow bed. My hand rested on his bare chest, and my head found its home on his shoulder. He sighed contentedly. "This is nice. Should've gotten me one of you years ago."

"An Omen?"

"No, a girl friend I'm not having sex with. Sleeping with you? It's the most naked I've let myself get with a woman."

"I'm sure Katrina begs to differ."

"There's nudity and then there's naked."

I pondered Von's comment as I stroked his chest, tangling my fingers in the nonintrusive puffs of hair as I relaxed us both. When I felt eyes on me, I turned to find Mason staring up at us, fresh from his shower, and towel-dried, thank goodness.

"Come on, boy." I patted my pillow, inviting Mason to share my side of the bed. He looked up at me with a note of reluctance in his gray eyes, like he thought three was a crowd or something. He finally hopped up next to me and laid his head down on my pillow. I rolled over to kiss his snout before settling into the thin mattress on my back. I stared up at the ceiling while Mason leaned into my side to warm me.

Von stroked my arm, and I knew he was pulling off thin layers of stress. He was tender with me, like I was something to be treated with gentle hands. I didn't get a lot of that in my normal life. "You're really worked up," he observed with mild concern.

"I'm nervous about tomorrow. The whole threat on everyone's lives thing," I admitted, knowing if I was going to keep Von around, I had to start depending on him. Mason butted closer to my side so I was hedged in between my two pillars of strength.

"You don't have to be scared. I went to school up until my last year. I'm as trained as anybody at the Academy. Just a little out of practice." Von ran his hand down my arm and rested it across my navel, his stomach pressed to my side. "And Mason actually graduated. Plus, he's a well-known badass. Did he tell you about the Amalanhigs?"

"Are those the zombies?"

Von snorted. "Yeah, I guess they kind of are like zombies."

"Yeah, he told me about them."

"Well, he's a wild zombie killer. You've got nothing to worry about. Plus, he's Matruculan. That breed's far stronger than the others if they don't cut their hair. Strength's tied to their hair never being chopped, hence the dreads."

I reached my fingers up and stroked the underside of his jaw, doing the same to Mason with my other hand. "Stop trying to impress me with your five dollar words like 'hence'."

"I can't help myself."

Mason and Von were determined to give me a good

night's sleep. They pulled away my anxiety, my fear and my unnecessary fight. All my OCD was no match for the calm they replaced my neurosis with. While it was taxing sharing my house with four new people, I was grateful for the twisted road that made it possible for me to sleep in a bed with a man. "Thanks for being cool," I murmured. "It's been a long day."

"If I'm here, you don't have to worry."

"You know, you sound like you actually mean that." I hmm'd when he leaned his cheek into my palm, the fondness between us blooming into something sturdier than a passing flirt. It was like I could feel his heartbeat, even though my hand wasn't pressed to his chest anymore.

His eyebrows furrowed, and his hand reached over to scratch his chest, confused at the tug I could feel on my end too. "This Omen-Reaper bond is stronger than I expected. You're deeper in here than I realized. I don't have much experience with... I mean, I have only brothers."

"That's okay. I'm pretty well grown by now. But sure, you can be my backup older brother."

"In case you need a spare?"

"Sure." I closed my eyes, reveling in the freedom I felt at being so open, when I'd lived most of my life keeping my friends at arm's length. Danny had been right; this bond was no joke. "Goodnight, Von."

Von surprised me by kissing my lips for the second time, making my eyes fly open. It was a light brush, a sweet peck, but I didn't have friends who did that. Heck, I barely let them hug me. Von seemed to treat my hang-ups as he did most rules, and simply ignored them. "Goodnight, November," he whispered with a soft smile. His dimples communicated a devotion that resonated with the part of me Beto had never been able to touch. I could feel loyalty in my bones when I caught a glimpse of the real thing, and I saw it that night in Von's eyes as he looked down on me with affection that transcended our many differences.

Mason sneezed, interrupting my over-analysis of the moment.

And just like that, I fell asleep, safe in Von's arms with my wolf by my side.

Hours later, I barely roused when Ollie kissed my forehead. "I'm headed to the airport, October," he whispered. Von shifted against me, his arm that stretched around my waist gave Mason a sweet pat in his sleep. He'd been using my leg as a body pillow, my thigh sandwiched between his knees. Von's nose was burrowed into my cheek, as if he wanted to smell my skin while he slept. It would've been weird if it didn't give me the best feeling in the world.

My voice was scratchy as I struggled to wake myself. "Okay. Let me drive you."

"No, no. I've got to return the rental anyway. Go back to sleep."

I opened my eyes to get a look at my brother's furrowed brows as he leaned over the back of the couch to stare down at us. "What's wrong?"

"Nothing. I'm just having a panicked dad moment.

Seeing you in bed with a guy? I'm not sure I'm ready for that. I'm debating between congratulating you and calling up the McCray brothers to get myself a gun."

"Von's just a friend," I murmured in a whisper, and then my whisper took on a fiery determination. "And don't you dare go to the McCray brothers for a single thing. You'll not ask for so much as a toothpick from them. And if a toothpick or anything shows up on our doorstep from them, you burn it."

Ollie wasn't surprised or put off by my sudden temper flare. "You and that pride. I got over all of it years ago. You should, too. Judge keeps trying to make amends."

"Judge McCray can take a flying leap." I stared up at my brother, whose eyes were on Von, a look of deep consternation on his face. I glanced to Von, who looked angelic in sleep. "Von really is just a friend, Ollie."

Von mumbled with his eyes still shut, "Now, now. Don't lie to the poor bloke. We all know I'm stark raving naked under this blanket."

"Go back to sleep," I scolded Von, casting up an apologetic look at Ollie. "We're not hooking up. I promise." I don't know why I felt the need to assure my brother so many times.

Ollie tilted his head to the side. "You're growing up, kid. I wish I could keep you in training wheels forever."

I cast Ollie a sleepy smile as my eyes drifted shut again. Mason's fur was warm and so very soft, and Von's body wrapped around mine with his forehead resting on my temple gave me a heavy dose of his masculine scent. I could feel both of their inherent rhythms, and found a deep sense of peace, sandwiched between both of their synchronized heartbeats. "Have a safe flight, Ollie. Love you."

"Love you, too."

10

NURSE GRACIE

Quitting the only job I'd ever loved was awful. The look on the warden's round face ensured that the shame of leaving him in the lurch would remain buried deep. I'd allowed Von and Mason to come into the prison with me, but not to the warden's office. When I emerged, my hand slipped into Mason's, and I could feel him pulling at the angst and devastation of leaving my life of choice behind.

Von gripped my shoulder, sensing my sorrow. "Wow. I didn't think anyone liked work as much as you do. You alright? You're actually holding someone's hand of your own volition."

Mason looked down at me, clearly pleased that I was reaching for one of them, silently asking for pulling instead of resisting them every step of the way. He squeezed my fingers three times, letting me know he liked it when I held his hand.

"I'm fine, Von."

"Dollar," Von reminded me of the Denial Jar bet. He was right; I was like, a planet away from fine.

"Well, I'm officially unemployed. So I won't have dollars to spare soon enough."

"Guess you're going to have to stop lying about if you're okay or not." Von quirked his eyebrow at me. "And obviously your new job comes with a salary. You're the national treasure now. I don't think you'll have to worry about money for a while."

"Oh. Well, that's good. I was a little worried about how I was going to pay for things." I swallowed, clinging to Mason's hand as we walked to the infirmary. I had a few things that were mine that I needed to collect before I left. A stethoscope, my mug, and a few items I didn't actually need, but couldn't justify leaving behind. I inhaled deeply, relishing the familiar scent of antiseptic and bandages that mingled in with the waft of concrete from the bare halls. Some people don't care about how clean smells to a girl, but I took another deep drag to make sure the memory stuck deep inside of me.

"Well, if it isn't the girl who's finally late for work," said Brenden with a small smile in his voice. He held out his wrist to show I was a whopping ten minutes late. He looked up from his clipboard, the grin falling off his face in surprise when he saw I came with a male supermodel and a Viking in a polo. "Hello. I don't believe we've met. Brenden McAllister." His brown eyes watched Mason's hand leave mine to shake his.

Brenden touched the slight cleft in his chin and then pushed his black-rimmed glasses further up on his face. They were always sliding down, but his wife loved the frames, so he wore them even though they annoyed him on the job.

"Mason. Nice to meet you. This is Von."

Brenden answered a crackle on the intercom that told him a patient was being escorted up. He glanced at my jeans and lavender t-shirt and frowned. "You're not dressed for work. Don't tell me you're finally making a dent in your vacation days." He shot me a knowing look and smirked at Mason. "Take as many as you need. Good for you, Gracie."

Mason shot me a look of confusion as to why Brenden was calling me by my middle name, but I ignored him. "Actually, I just quit."

Brenden abandoned his clipboard and the patient files that were too many for one person to get through in a day. "Wait, what? Is it because of Pistola? I can treat him without you in the room, if you like."

I scratched the back of my hand, wishing the guys weren't here for this conversation. "Not at all. Believe me, I wish things were different, but it's just time for me to move on."

Brenden's green scrubs seemed less cheery as he visibly drooped. "You can't possibly think I'll be satisfied with that answer. Why? What's wrong? What does Ollie have to say about this?"

I took the insinuation that I needed my brother's permission to make decisions in stride. I kept a pleasant smile on my face and my chin level to the ground. "It's all fine, Brenden."

The buzzer announced a guard was dropping off a prisoner for medical attention. I groaned and threw my arms up when I saw who it was. "Joseph! Again? Honestly, this is your third fight this month. That's gotta be your all-time high."

Joseph had blood dripping from his receding hairline down over his eyebrows and onto his chin. "I didn't start it, Nurse Gracie."

"I think I'd believe that a little more if you didn't say it every single time. Sing me a new song, Joseph."

Brenden sat the bleeding man down on the stool to get a look at his injury. Joseph was a gusher, and a head wound was never the type of injury that held back the gore. His pooched belly left him no lap at all when he sat on the stool. Joseph was in his late forties, and halfway through his ten-year sentence. He was restless, which meant he was prone to starting fights over the slightest insult. It was what Brenden and I liked to call the "halfway itch" the more irritable inmates just loved to scratch.

Even though I wasn't on the clock, I couldn't leave Brenden without help. "Hey, Jerry," I nodded to the guard who was twenty years my senior, but had never once called me "kid". I liked Jerry.

"Good to see you this morning, Nurse Gracie. Come in on your day off?" Jerry asked of my clothes. His dark skin stood out against the blue uniform that Jerry never permitted to wrinkle.

"Something like that." I motioned to two chairs for Von and Mason to sit in while I pulled on a pair of gloves. I could tell Von was trying to play it cool, but was uncomfortable being in the prison at all.

"I don't like this." Mason's full lips were set in a firm line, his fists clenching every now and then at his sides to express his deep displeasure. It was hard not to admire Mason's sheer bulk, especially when his muscles were tensing.

I tossed my hair over my shoulder. "This'll only take a minute." *So dramatic.*

I set to cleaning the wound while Brenden readied the curved suture needle we used for stitching. I counted the sharps, making sure there wasn't anything lying around that Joseph could stab us with. "You've got to stop this," I admonished Joseph as if he was a five-year old (which, given the state of his temper, he pretty much was). "By the time you get out, your face is going to look like a patched shirt, and then what will your wife say?"

Joseph grinned, and some blood dripped into his mouth and dribbled out his cracked lower lip. "Ah, she'll be glad she has someone to kick around again, the bitter old hag." His eyes fell on Von, who I noticed wore a look of rage mingled with sickness, marring his handsome features. Von didn't do a good sexy brooding. I liked him better with that carefree punch-me-in-the-face smile. "And who's this pretty piece?" Joseph asked with a smarmy grin. The blood oozing down his face made him appear truly terrifying. On a normal day, he looked much like your average murdering-mailman-slash-homicidal-husband (dressed in an orange jumper, of course).

"He's a friend. Archibald Hemsworth." I made up a name on the spot that sounded like it could be British. I swiped at the cut on Joseph's lip. "I've got actual friends on the outside. See? It's what you have to look forward to if you have some good behavior to speak of."

"Wasn't my fault. Pistola was going after T again. Poor kid's too dumb to know not to look Pistola in the eye. Or maybe T's got a death wish; I can't decide."

I chewed on my lower lip, tucking that bit of information in my back pocket. I worried about Terence McCray. I'm not sure I'd ever stop worrying about him. "T's not up here getting stitched. Does that mean he's alright?"

"For now."

I caught the guard's eye. "Jerry, would you mind keeping an eye on T? If Pistola's got a temper today, it won't do to have them near each other. I'm not staying, so Brenden will be shorthanded. One less fight for Brenden to clean up, I hope."

Jerry nodded to me. "Of course, Nurse Gracie."

Joseph's eyes swept up and down my form that I usually tried to keep shapeless. Though my V-neck shirt was modest, my breasts stood out like twin beacons. "You're wearing civilian clothes. You dress up just for me, sweetheart?"

"Yes, this is me all gussied up. Jeans is the best I get," I replied with feigned exasperation.

"I could bounce a quarter off that ass."

I scoffed good-naturedly. "Like you have a quarter."

"You always give me something pretty to look at. Almost worth getting into fights if you're on the clock." His harmless flirt made Mason stand from his chair, arms crossed over his broad chest as he stared Joseph down. I could feel both Von and Mason getting worked up, that tug in my chest tightening as their nerves and tempers climbed.

"Lucky me. You're saying I'm prettier than Pistola? Now, that's high praise." I jerked Joseph's chin back so he was looking straight ahead and not at my breasts. "Hold still and repeat after me: I'm going to go back to my cell and think about what I've done." It was hard to get an even stitch when his head kept moving, so I touched his chin to keep him in place while I worked.

Joseph obeyed, and then took a chance with his life and winked at Mason, who raised an eyebrow at the man. Mason was still standing and ready to pounce if Joseph made a false move. "I don't think the big one likes the look of you so close to the scary inmate."

I rolled my eyes. "Stop trying to convince them you're scary. We all know you're a giant puppy."

Joseph made Von jump when he broke out into a mad bark, howling at the men like a crazed dog before he dissolved into laughter while he slapped his knee. He winked at Von. "Now that one? He's a tasty treat. He'd do well in here. Any chance he's your replacement?"

"Yes, Archibald's very pretty. But no, he's not a nurse." I shot Joseph an unimpressed look in answer to his villainous laughter. I knew he loved that he'd gotten under Von's skin. "Enough, you. Quit baiting my friends. Sit still, or Brenden will stitch your eye shut so you'll walk around with a permanent wink. Think of how that'll go over on the yard."

Joseph chuckled, his belly shaking with the deep sound. "Yes, Nurse Gracie."

11

VON'S SACRIFICE

"Okay, you can't go too far over the limit like that. There's a speed trap coming up, and you're going to get us pulled over," I scolded Von, who was white-knuckling my steering wheel.

"I have no words for what I just saw. I can't... How can... Why? Why were you working there? Do you have a death wish?"

"No. I *had* a steady job that didn't involve sucking the life out of people. That back there was actually a step up from what I'm currently doing." My small box of belongings in the passenger's seat rattled as he turned sharply. The clattering of my stethoscope against my mug reminded me that I was unemployed.

"I'm serious, November. And why were they calling you Gracie?"

I looked out the window, watching the businesses and

trees whip by. "Grace is my middle name. October Grace Reese. Allie and Ollie thought it best I didn't use my first name on the job. Too distinctive. This way when the inmates get paroled they don't come looking for me."

"Do you hear yourself? Here's a tip: if you have to change your name at your job, it's a dangerous job!"

"Jeez, you look like you need a Duwende to pull some stress outta you. You want Mason to work his magic on that frown of yours before it becomes permanent?" Mason's hand in mine was gripping too tight to be comforting as we sat together in the backseat.

"No! What other out of your mind completely mental things are you up to? I can't believe your mum let you get a job like that! And what does your brother have to say about this? If I had a sister, no way would I let that fly."

I bristled that he thought I needed anyone's permission to choose my place of employment. "Look, I don't work there anymore, so you can chill. It's a good job. Great pay with tons of overtime. You know that house you woke up in? The bed you slept in? All paid for by my job, Allie's and Ollie's."

"Never again. I mean it. Never again."

"Hello, I just quit. And you don't get to play the father card. Haven't needed one of those my whole life. Not about to start now. You're pissing me off, Von."

Von's frown twisted the face that was much more attractive when it was laughing. "How about I play the big brother card? You seem pretty close with Ollie."

"Because he knows better than to boss me. See this one?" I pointed to Mason. "He knows not to tell me how to be."

Mason held up his other hand like he wanted nothing to do with being on my side. "Ho! Don't go putting me in this. I'm with Von. Joseph talked to your breasts the whole time. I'm trying to keep a low profile Topside so I don't stand out too much, otherwise I would've blacked his eyes for looking at you like that. That bit about the quarter? Please tell me he's never talked to you like that before. Tell me he was only doing it because Von and I were there, and he wanted to get a rise out of us."

When I sensed my argument taking a downward turn, I changed to a less contemptuous tune. "Look, it's nice of you both to care, but I'm fine. It was the only place that would hire someone like me, so I jumped on it."

Von shook his head. "Loads of places would hire someone with OCD. You sold yourself way short."

My teeth ground together as I siphoned the edge off my response. "Not that, jackweed. I was nineteen when I graduated. Not many places were willing to take a chance with me. It's why I have to work extra hard. I always have to prove myself. Make sure they know I was a good hire."

"Nineteen's not all that different from eighteen to graduate from high school. So you got held back a grade." Von's tone softened and he relaxed his death grip on the wheel, sitting back in his seat a little. "Is that why you're so hard on yourself?"

I took in a deep breath and exhaled slowly. "I didn't graduate from high school at nineteen. I got my nursing degree at nineteen."

Von's eyebrows pulled together again as the corners of his sculpted lips tugged downward. "How's that work? I thought those degrees took a couple years."

"Four years, yeah. I took my GED when I was fifteen, then worked my sweet can off at nursing school. The hospitals didn't want to hire a teenager, but the warden was desperate enough to take a chance on me." I hung my head. "He took a chance on me, and I just up and quit on him." I felt horrible, and knew the guilt wouldn't leave easily.

"You graduated high school at fifteen?" Von whistled his appreciation. "Wow. Bev must've been some epic homeschooler."

I snorted at the mental image of Bev teaching me anything other than how to walk down a runway. "Um, no. That was all Allie and Ollie. They taught me everything I know. They homeschooled me so I could test out of high school."

"At fifteen?" Von repeated, astonished.

I rolled my eyes at having to spell out my life for him. "I went to regular school until I finished my freshman year, then we decided I would be done with it. I took my GED, and that's the name of that tune."

"I can't believe they even let you take the test that young."

"I was emancipated when I was fifteen, so legally I was an adult." I exhaled out a bluster of nerves at revealing so much of myself in one go. "Did you also want to know my social security number? My weight?"

Von was quiet for about twenty seconds, and I could practically hear the questions piling up. "You know I've got to ask how bad it was with Bev that a judge emancipated you so young."

"I'll show you Bev's trailer sometime when Danny can watch her," Mason offered. "I told you about it, but seeing is a whole other thing."

"No, you won't." I kept my gaze stalwartly toward the window. "It was bad enough that I don't need to talk about it. Everything worked out fine. Bev has a mental disorder. She wasn't capable of taking care of three kids, so we gave her a break. Nothing more complicated than that."

"And I thought my family was messed up."

"Let's dive into your personal life, shall we?" I enjoyed Von's squirm and rubbed my hands together in anticipation. "Male escort? Kicked out of the Academy in your last year? Angela? Spill it."

"We don't need to get into all of that unpleasantness, do we?"

"Hey, I'm just being a good work wife. If my life's on display, yours is, too."

Von cleared his throat. "You know all about Angela and Penny. And I was kicked out of the Academy for things that don't matter now."

I scoffed. "Are you kidding me with this? No way. Out with it, Von."

Von blew a long breath out through pursed lips. "Fine. I was caught gambling my senior year."

"Huh? That's it?"

"That started my suspension. Then I got into it with the headmaster over something unrelated. He was thinking of penalizing Boston, my younger brother because Boston was with me while I was gambling."

"And?" I waited for the other shoe to drop.

"And I was young and impetuous. I get a little carried away when the people I watch over are threatened. That's all."

Mason rolled his eyes at Von's evasiveness. "He set the headmaster's car on fire. That's what got him kicked out of the Academy." He shrugged at Von's scowl of betrayal. "What? She's right. If her world's on display, ours should be an open book for her, too."

"You set your headmaster's car on fire for trying to penalize your brother for gambling?"

Von's steely eyes met mine in the rearview mirror. "That's right. Boston went with me to Dagat for a little holiday. Dagat's one of the nations in Terraway – the one Captain Finn's from. Boston was my responsibility. Headmaster Chalmers was throwing around the idea of suspending us both, so I dropped out, did a little fire play with his car, and threatened more if he hurt Boston over *my* night of gambling. Turns out, Headmaster Chalmers can be reasoned with. You just have to find the right pressure point. The car fire didn't do it, but when I told him I just might take a fancy to his daughter, he was surprisingly compliant." Von thumbed the steering wheel as if he was trying to rub his problems off of it. "I don't regret one second of it. Boston's a fantastic Puller. He deserved to graduate, and he did."

No one spoke for several minutes until I broke the silence in a quiet voice. "Von?"

"I'll not tell you what color my knickers are. Some things are meant to be private."

I fiddled with a thread on the thigh of my jeans. "I was just thinking that it's a freaky coincidence that I can't do Death Omen detail on Wednesdays. You might have to take the morning off and spend it with Penny."

Von's shoulders relaxed. "I have to, now?"

"Didn't I tell you? I turn into a werewolf once a week like clockwork. I'll tell Danny that I simply can't work then."

"I was planning on sticking by the house Wednesday mornings, actually," Mason offered, squeezing my hand. He leaned forward to cup Von's shoulder in solidarity, linking the three of us together. "I have to check for werewolf hunters around the house, of course. Perfect timing, really. I can reap with her on Wednesdays while you're with Penny."

Von pulled onto my street, his smile taking over his handsome features. "You don't have to do that. You're new to our world, November, so you don't know how much power you hold. *I* work around *your* schedule, not the other way around."

I threw out my hands in feigned exasperation. "This *is* my schedule. I can't control when the moon turns me into a werewolf."

"That's some affliction you've got there. I bet Mason will be pleased at the K9 companionship. True puppy love, that is."

"Call Angela and set something up with Penny for next Wednesday."

Von slowed as he drove Terence the Taurus up into the garage. "I can't leave you unguarded."

"I promise to stay inside and watch movies with Mason after we do the bare minimum of reaping for the day."

Mason thumbed the outer stitching of my jeans on my thigh. "That actually sounds nice. I haven't spent much time Topside. Might enjoy a morning with no plans."

"I vow to be boring and make sure Danny can hear it if I suddenly feel the need for my fainting salts." A wicked smile crossed my lips. "Do you think I can get him to unclog the shower drain for me?"

Von shrugged. "Probably. I've seen him cut Mariang's meat for her before." Von and I both grimaced in unison.

Mason cleared his throat as he dropped my hand. "Danny's a good man. He does what he needs to for Mariang, and we shouldn't look down on him for it."

"Yes, boss," Von said at Mason's mild scolding. "You think our Gracie needs her meat cut for her?"

Mason shot me a devious smile when he took in my horrified expression. "I think she can handle the challenge."

"Oh, shut it you two."

Mason chuckled and reached for my hand again. I wanted to hesitate, to shirk away at the contact that surely came with germs. They would be impossible to scrub off. But the second our hands touched, I could feel him gently pulling the tension from me. My fingers slid through his, threading between his much thicker ones and squeezing. "I see you, *hani*," Mason whispered. "After the sagrado stone is delivered to the nations, things won't be this tense for you."

"Thanks." I ignored Von's raised eyebrows as he watched us from the rearview mirror. I gave Mason's fingers another squeeze before letting myself out of the car and moving into my house. I hated that I missed the contact when our fingers parted, and what that said about me.

12

READING TO ALICIA

"I don't like this," I stated, sounding like a robot. We rounded the corner with our visitor's badges on, but we weren't just here to hand out pink Mylar balloons with a teddy bear on them that said "You're the Beary Best!"

"You don't have to like it. You've been reaping for two whole weeks now," Danny grumbled, leading the way with Mariang on his arm. "Get over the fear of it already."

"I'm not afraid."

"Yeah? Well then give me a rest from your whining."

"Danny!" Mariang scolded him.

There were too many of us to look inconspicuous, what with the additional guards Ezra had added to our fivesome for extra protection. We walked down the winding hospital corridors toward the pediatric cancer ward, and I wished we were anywhere else. Usually the sterile smell and the uncluttered hallways gave me peace. I'd been to a few different hospitals to reap with the crew. Now after two weeks of reaping, I could categorically say that this ward felt the most wrong. It was one thing to treat inmates. It was a completely other set of compartmentalizing to look kids in the eyes, know how hard they'd fought, and that they wouldn't make it another day.

Mariang looked over her shoulder to talk to me, her white knee-length dress making her look like an angel of mercy, not an Omen of death. "It's okay, little sister. I know it's hard, but these children deserve a peaceful passing more than anyone we reap."

"I guess that's true."

Von reached for my hand when I started clawing at the back of it, but one of the Duwende guards Danny had requested touched my back first. He sucked too hard, making me a little tipsy even after I flinched away from him. Von glowered at Rick while Mason shoved him backward. "That's too much. You have no idea what you're doing."

Rick postured. "I graduated from the Academy at the top of my class, unlike some people." He looked down his nose at Von. I was overcome with the urge to flick the tip of Rick's long nose just to aggravate him. I resisted because, you know, adulthood. Adulthood, plus nose germs. *Ick.*

"Mason and I imprinted on her. So everyone else isn't as true a fit. I'm telling you, that was too much. Focus on pulling from nurses and such to get us into the proper rooms without detection."

"I'm trying, okay?" Rick scratched his copper sideburn. He was pale, his fair skin giving his red hair an orangy glow. "Give me a few weeks to get used to her."

I shoved past the group irritably. "I'm not a car, guys. Quit talking about me like I'm not even here. And no one puts their hands on me unless I say so, alright? I'm not a walking basket case, but you're going to turn me into one if you keep touching me at random."

"Apologies, Lady October." Rick bowed – actually bowed – his flaming hair shifting forward to reveal the genesis of a bald spot. He looked a little like a thirty-five-year-old Ron Howard, but without the boyish charm. Rick was one note: business. Nate, Chet and Bill were also on the same dull note, with a hint of Men in Black to them. Every time we turned a sterile corner, they reached for their pockets to make sure their knives wouldn't need to be drawn. It was enough to make the most well-adjusted person tense up.

A tug in my gut directed me to room 407, though I wished it took me anywhere else. "You ready, Mason?" I asked, giving the four lackeys the hint that I didn't want them near me for this. With Sama's spies that could be anywhere, I didn't trust any of the newbies. I didn't much care for the added stress this brought me.

When Chet reached out to touch my shoulder, I shirked away. "Okay, now I feel like everyone's constantly touching me or just all up in my business. If Mason holds my hand, will that earn me two feet of space? Honestly, I feel like I'm being pawed at."

"Apologies, Lady October," Chet replied, though he didn't look the least bit repentant.

I wasn't used to being touched all the time, so never knowing when the hands would be on me was too unnerving for my liking. I'd only just barely gotten used to the physical nature of my budding friendship with Von and Mason. When Mason's fingers entwined through mine, my climbing anxiety stopped its perpetual race to the peak. I knew we looked like a couple, but I didn't much care anymore.

We entered the room together with Von and a Mylar balloon, shutting the rest of the men out in the hall with Mariang, who was more used to an entourage.

Five-year-old Alicia Reynolds was very much awake. She had a bald head, and was painfully bony and pale. Her curious bugged eyes tracked us as I set the balloon on her nightstand. She had an oxygen mask, and each word she pushed out sounded like it cost her more than it was worth. "You... came... to... read?" She pointed her hand to the nightstand, and I took the opportunity and brushed my finger to hers, reaping her soul so the underworld could live another day. Von's gentle massage of my neck was all that I needed to get the icy blast of poison out of my body and feed it into his.

"Um, sure. I can read to you." I picked up her Beatrix

Potter book off the nightstand and flipped it open to the marked page. Allie had read *Jemima Puddleduck* to me when I was a kid. This one was *Peter Rabbit*, which I was embarrassed to admit I'd never read, though I'm pretty sure it was the most famous one. I sat down in the chair next to her bed and began reading.

"You're doing it wrong," Von complained. "You're not doing any voices. You want voices, don't you?" he asked Alicia, who grinned.

I harrumphed. "You'll do it weird, Von. You'll make it all British."

"Hello! Beatrix Potter was one of ours! Give me that, you Yank. Honestly." He confiscated the book and took over, ramping up his British accent to the level of a caricature to make the girl laugh. He was Dick Van Dyke in action, which I've got to tell you, is just about the most attractive a guy can get.

Von was meant for children. He had a different voice for each character, and jumped around the room to give action to the words. I would have been content to sit down if I'd been the one reading. The mundane story with very little twist became harrowing under his care. Alicia and I were cheering him on when he finally bowed at the conclusion of the act, and Mason was smiling – a thing he'd not done enough of since the visit to the prison a couple weeks ago.

Von set the book on Alicia's lap, flashing his best movie

star grin at her. "Let's see anyone beat that. You have a good day, Alicia darling."

When Von reached for my hand this time on the way out the door and into the hallway, there was nothing to pull from me except the remnants of the soul. He had taken a grim situation and made it a fun memory for her last day on earth. "You're kind of amazing," I said quietly as Von snatched another balloon from the stash Chet carried. The hallway was empty, the additional Duwendes having put themselves to use cleaning it out so we wouldn't be caught being where we most certainly weren't allowed.

Von kissed my cheek, and I felt warmth spread through my body, starting from the light blush where his lips pressed to me. "I'm only kind of amazing?"

"A real, solid kind of."

"Maybe I'm not laying on the accent thick enough." His blue and gold eyes found mine, and we paused in the middle of the hallway, ignoring Chet and Nate's dodgy glances to keep security tight. "This is their last day on earth. Let's give these kids a good one, yeah?"

I nodded. "Alright. But in the next room, you get to be the American, and I get to be the Brit. I'm super good at saying 'bangers and mash'."

Von put his hand on Bill's shoulder. "I might need a Puller myself, listening to a Yank crack out a British accent. Steady me, mate."

We shared a laugh that felt easy. It felt right. It felt like... like I was happy.

13

JUDGE AND NEFARIOUS

My hands were clammy when I pulled into the restaurant's parking lot that evening. I'd cut myself off at fifteen reaps so I wasn't completely useless for what I knew I still had to do. The well-lit, beautifully maintained parking lot complete with sculpted topiaries bespoke of the affluence inside the eatery, yelling at me that I certainly didn't belong. I swallowed, refusing to feel ashamed of Terence the Taurus, parked next to various BMWs and Jaguars. I lifted my chin as I put my hand on the door, ready to step out with confidence I'd learned to manufacture on command. "Remember the rules, guys."

Von harrumphed from the backseat. "I don't think you understand that I've actually been in a restaurant before. I've lived a mostly Topside life. I know how to interact with you lot. Though, I can't speak for wolf-man here." He leaned forward and clapped Mason on the shoulder.

Mason looked down, examining his white button-down and green tie I'd had to knot for him. "I don't like that you want us to leave our knives in here."

"I told you, no weapons. I didn't even want to bring you into this, but I can't seem to shake you two. It's just childhood crap that lingered longer than it should've, so be cool." I held out my palm to Mason expectantly. "Give it."

Mason's eyes narrowed in defiance. "I don't know what you're talking about."

"Don't make me frisk you. I know you're hiding a knife in your boot. Hand it over, chief."

Mason rolled his eyes at me. He slid out the contraband and tucked it under the seat with a petulant look on his face. "This is a bad idea."

I straightened the fitted navy blouse that was the most country club thing I owned. It almost looked nice with my beige, pressed dress pants, but I'm sure none of that mattered. I knew I didn't belong in a fancy restaurant like this. People like that could no doubt smell the bad breeding and trash on me. I inhaled deeply, recalling that I could do anything I put my mind to, and this was a thing that had to be done. "No matter what, please just stay quiet and let me handle it. Don't do your overbearing protector thing."

Von caught my eye in the rearview mirror, raising an eyebrow at me. "Believe it or not, this isn't the first time I've been told to shut up and look pretty. Are we making some poor bloke lousy with jealousy? Is that it?"

I frowned up at him. "You really think I'm that petty?"

Mason shifted the knot of his tie for the millionth time in the brief twenty-five minutes he'd had it on. "What are we about to walk into?"

"Something you should've stayed home for. Look, my life is still mine, and while I get that you have to make sure I don't get decapitated tying my shoes, this is something that's really not meant for you to tag along for. It's too much to explain, so either let me do my thing in silence, or wait in the car."

"You're stalling. We won't embarrass you," Mason assured me. I had much to say to the contrary, but Mason got out of the car, putting an end to how much I was permitted to insult them with my building nerves. Mason's hand found the small of my back while Von offered his elbow to me like a gentleman. I was getting better at not letting that feeling of claustrophobia creep up on me when they hovered so close. I wasn't sure if it was a good thing that I was growing, or a bad thing that they were changing parts of my fundamental makeup.

Von in a tie was a sight to see. The hostess couldn't stop ogling him, making it known that, no matter your social status, Von was everyone's taste. The strangest part of it was that he didn't seem to care that he turned many a single and married woman's eye as we walked in. Von was one of those rare breeds who was totally comfortable in his own skin, no matter his surroundings.

Oh, to be a TV vampire hottie and have the world adore you for the bad boy you are.

"Reservations only," the hostess in a black cocktail dress said to me. She wore a tight smile that veiled a silent threat to keep my poor off the good furniture.

"I'm here to see Nefarious and Judge," I explained, keeping my chin up. "Are they at their usual table?"

The woman's eyes widened. Her chin and her voice lowered as she looked at me like I'd just told her I own six elephants. "Judge McCray?"

"That's the one." I knew Darius, the youngest of the notorious McCray brothers, back when he was nicknamed Crayfish, but his street name now was Nefarious. I was here to see good old Darius, since he'd ditched the moniker "Crayfish" ages ago. Nefarious was a dumb nickname, which I refused to use.

"Let me see if he's here," the hostess said evasively. "Who can I say would like to see him?"

Of course Judge would have gatekeepers at his regular restaurant. My lips tightened. "Tell him Baby Girl is coming back to see him in thirty seconds, whether he's ready or not." I didn't know if he was entertaining criminals back there, and didn't want to risk using my real name.

She tapped the Bluetooth in her ear, speaking quietly.

Von nudged me, speaking out of the corner of his

mouth. "I thought you didn't know who your father was. Is it him back there? Is that who we're meeting?"

"No. That's just what Judge calls me. He's known me since I was a baby, and helped Ollie and Allie raise me when things got tight."

The hostess had a far more amiable demeanor after Judge apparently gave his permission for me to join him through her headset. "Judge and Nefarious will see you now. Right this way." Her fingers flitted over the menus, pausing to look up at Mason and Von before leading us into the restaurant. "You should know that we have a no firearms policy in here. That extends to Judge and Nefarious' guests, as well."

I let out a heavy sigh. Of course this was how I would spend my Friday night. "Don't worry. I'm sure Judge will search us."

The hostess plastered on a breezy smile. "Right this way." She led us through the gold bedecked dining area to Judge's table in the backroom of the restaurant. It was closed off from the general public to give Judge the utmost discretion for his many shady business meetings. The carpet was red, like the rest of the restaurant, and the high-backed gold-trimmed chairs had black cushioned seats. The dimmed crystal chandelier hung lower in here, giving you the illusion that this was a cozy place to divulge secrets best left buried. There were no windows, only a fire exit that let out into the unlit alley. Many a drug dealer short on the take had met their maker in that alley. Of the three strangers who were seated with the McCray brothers at the table, I wondered which would bite it first.

If Darius had his way, he'd be at the most visible table in the picture window at the front of the restaurant, so everyone walking by could see his rise to greatness. He'd been a low-to-no income scrappy kid just like Ollie, Allie and me. When Bev had been too violent to go home to, we escaped to Mama McCray's house in the trailer park across the street. Darius' mama used to make hot applesauce and warn her three boys to do their homework so they didn't fall into drugs. Now the McCray brothers were sitting pretty atop the drug, stolen car and who knows what else kind of empire Judge had built from the ground up. Not quite what Mama McCray had envisioned for her boys, may she rest in peace.

Darius stood to greet me with a wide smile that looked like his heart had been aching without it, but Judge held up his ebony hand. The hostess was waved away, and the two hired hands who stood like personality-minus gargoyles on either side of the table moved forward to pat us down. Mason and Von shot me looks of warning, but managed not to get themselves shot.

I held up my hand when the goon I knew as Big Mike moved forward to check me for hidden bazookas, or whatever he assumed me to be carrying. "Touch me, and I'll break every one of your pretty little fingers, Michael." I liked to call Judge's long-time guard by his formal name because I knew it unnerved him. Watching his eyes narrow predictably, but hearing him say nothing to correct me, was one of my small joys. "Darius can do the honors. I know what your hands have been up to, and I don't need them on me, young man." I grinned inwardly at his intake of breath that always happened when I chastised him like a mama would, though he was at least fifteen years my senior. He never knew what to do with me when I stuck a wrench in the one fragile portion of his psyche. *Ah, mind games.* I missed it.

Judge raised his eyebrow at me, sitting back in his chair and sizing up every move I made with a curious expression, as if he needed to figure me out. As if I hadn't told him time and time again what kind of girl I was and what kind I wasn't.

Judge and Darius McCray shared the same midnight eyes, full lips, rounded dark cheeks and long fingers, but the similarities stopped with the physical. Darius was a sweetheart, and Judge's soul had been running on empty for a long time. Judge motioned to his younger brother to get on with it. The three other guests at the table kept their curious glances in my direction to a minimum, which I appreciated. I knew I was interrupting something official and important, but Judge let me, as I knew he would.

Darius squinted one eye at me and did the usual pat down with a smirk at the thought that I would ever be caught with a gun. "She's clean. Good to see you, Bait." His smile bloomed as he bumped my fist and brought me in for a quick one-armed dude hug before releasing me.

Darius always had the prettiest eyelashes – a feature many a girl had been done in by.

Judge came around the table and kissed both my cheeks, touching my chin to control the tilt of my head. I could feel Mason's human hackles raising behind me, though clearly there was no intention to Judge's kiss. I mean, dude was thirty-four. Plus, it was Judge – the big brother figure who'd been the sun and moon in my eyes, back when I was too young to know better. I probably should've explained some of this to Mason and Von before we got here, but couldn't bring myself to drudge up the whole story. "Always good to see you, baby girl. Have a seat." Judge pulled out my chair for me like a gentleman, leaving Mason and Von to stand sentry behind me. Judge conducted himself more professionally than Darius did. He stood straighter, spoke clearer and saw himself as the rest of the world did – a dangerous man with an empire and a plan for more.

Darius was all smiles at the unexpected intermission I provided from the mayhem. I could tell he'd been working too much and dealing with the lowest common denominator of people. "How's Ollie and Allie? Any word from our girl yet?"

Darius had dated Allie once upon a time. She'd left us with no warning a few months after they'd broken it off. Ollie blamed Darius for Allie splitting on us, but I knew Darius had genuinely cared for Allie, so it couldn't have been that.

"Ollie was just in town, actually. I'm sure he'll be glad to hear from you when he comes back for good. Allie's still in California. Though next time I talk to her, I'll tell her you want a rematch from your last dance contest." It was our longstanding joke. Darius was a terrific dancer, and Allie's best (and only) move was the Running Man.

Darius clapped his hands twice and chuckled. Darius had a great laugh that sounded like pure goofiness, and had a hint of a hiccup somewhere in the middle. I hoped (but doubted) that he still exercised it often. "It's good to see you, kid. You still the smartest person I know?"

"Looks like I just might be, if this is the company you keep." I looked around at Big Mike and Ike (I didn't actually know the second guard's name. We'll go with Ike). At the table were Judge, Darius and the three other men who needed a good trip to church. They didn't look thrilled to have a woman at the table.

I knew that if I wanted any credibility, I needed to keep control of the conversation, which meant not speaking to Judge first. There was a weighted silence as I met Judge's gaze and held it with a patient smile, communicating to him that I could do this silent standoff all friggin' day. He shouldn't have taught me so well if he didn't want me to use his own power tactics to piss him off.

Darius wasn't up to that particular challenge, and was the first to crack, the sweetie. "You wanted to see us?"

I pointed to the brothers. "You two, yes, but I don't know these three future inmates. You can keep the guards, but I need to talk to you privately." The man on Judge's left gave an irritated scoff, while the two in the chairs on either side of me scowled.

Judge leaned his elbows on the table, his mocha-colored hands together like he was praying, his lips resting on the tips. His eyes were always studying, always trying to figure me out. "I trust everyone at this table," Judge said to me in a challenge, letting me know he wasn't thrilled I was trying to control the seating configuration.

"I'm happy you've found people you can trust. Me? Not so much. Hazards of the job, I guess." I sat back in the chair and waited, crossing my ankle over my knee to let him know I had all the time in the world. Mason brushed the back of my neck to pull a small amount of anxiety from me. "Trust," I snorted with a soft smile. "That's downright precious."

14

BELIEVING IN CIRCUSES

I knew Judge was unhappy that I'd rearranged his table. It was too much control I'd taken too soon, but again, Judge conceded the decision to me, telling the men to go wait at the bar. "You know, for someone with something to say, you don't have a whole lot I want to hear. You're lucky we go way back."

I tried to sit tall and not let myself feel like a child sitting at the grownups table. I mean, the man had taught me how to tie my shoes, for crying out loud. I cleared my throat. "That's why I came. Family."

Darius clutched his fork, but tried to slice the anxious edge from his voice. "Everything alright with T? How about Fender?"

"Everything's fine with your men in lockup, as far as I know. I came here for a couple reasons. One's that I know Terence is up for parole next year. If he gets out, I want you to make sure he sees a doctor for the growth on his foot. It's benign now, but those things can turn malignant in a heartbeat. Also, he's been around too much gunfire, thanks to you two dummies being up to things you just plain shouldn't. He's lost fifty percent of his hearing in his left ear, but he's too stubborn to let me fit him for a hearing aid. Make sure to talk some sense into him once he gets out."

Judge's eyebrows rose, stunned that this was the big thing I'd finally wanted to meet with him about. "That's... Okay. We can do that. He's alright now though?"

"I saw him last month, so that's as much as I know."

"What about Fender?" Darius inquired.

"Fender's a hot head. I don't have a medical cure for that." I cleared my throat. "If he ever gets out, I wouldn't have him moving merchandise anymore." That was my fancy way of telling them Fender couldn't steal cars without being a liability. "You'll have to get him a new nickname, like Burger Flipper or something. Utter shame. 'Fender' was so covert ops."

Darius gave me a condescending smile. "We all know you have a conscience. What a good little girl you still are. You going to tell me I should be going to church next? You know, no matter how big you get, I still always want to pat you on the head."

I pursed my lips to keep on topic. "I didn't come here to talk about my choices or lecture you on yours. My conscience isn't actually all that stellar these days. I'm telling you not to have Fender moving merchandise because he was in a yard fight a couple months ago. His hand was broken in several places, and as much as we can set something right again, his left hand doesn't have the same functionality and flexibility it used to. I'd put him in physical therapy first thing if he ever gets out, and I wouldn't trust his dexterity to hotwire a toaster. His pride will tell you otherwise, but he'll get caught easily, and end up right back in lockup."

Judge nodded sincerely at me, always taking careful mental notes whenever we met. "Thank you for coming to me with that. I'll see to it."

I cleared my throat, gearing up for the big speech. "Also, I wanted you to hear it from me that I don't work at the prison anymore. I quit, so you can stop dropping hints that you want me to send messages to the inmates from you."

"Those were gifts you were meant to keep, not send back, burned into ash." Judge's hardened eyes softened with a glimmer of guilt. "I'm sure I should be insulted, but I guess I've earned a lifetime of that from you."

Judge had recently sent me a letter offering me a weekend on his (stolen) boat. That little handwritten kindness was returned to him, burned to ash by yours truly and stuffed into a sandwich bag with a "thanks, but screw you" letter of my own. We'd fallen far from the "I'd die for you" credo our families had once held to. I was older now, and part of me blamed Judge for that most heinous of crimes.

I'd been young when his sun shined on my smile. Since he'd turned his back on me, I'd learned just how cold life could be.

"I sent thank you notes along with the gifts when I sent them back to you. You know I can't accept money or toys from you. It's not ethical, and I was trying to keep my job."

"But now you're not. Have you decided to finally accept my gratitude for saving T's life?" He reached into his pocket and pulled out a thick wad of cash.

My gaze darted wildly around the room as if he'd pulled out a gun, and Von gasped. "Would you put that thing away, you jag?" I held up my hand, my cheeks hot. "I accepted your gratitude last year when you told me 'thank you,' and I said 'you're welcome.' That's how normal people do things. What I won't accept are gifts for doing my job. I already get a gift for that. It's called a paycheck."

"But now you're unemployed, so the pesky ethical dilemma I applaud you for is gone now, along with your steady paycheck."

I glowered at Judge, who allowed the corner of his thick lips to twitch upward at my indignation. We shared an affinity for goading each other. "I didn't come here for money, you jackweed. I wouldn't take a dime from you, even if I was starving to death and you were my only hope." Those words had been chosen carefully, and I could tell by his minor flinch that I'd cut him right where I'd wanted to. I straightened, composing myself as much as I could. "I came here to make sure someone looks after Terence when he gets out, and to let you know that I'm not at the prison anymore. I didn't exactly get to say goodbye to Terence, or thank him again for the time he saved me from that fight. If you could pass that along the next time you visit him, I'd appreciate it."

Judge put his obscene amount of cash away and pointed in the direction of the parking lot. "You still like your car?"

"I do."

"Good. I'll have a new one sent over to you in the morning."

I ground my teeth, ignoring Mason's low grumble and Von's small intake of breath at the grand gift. Judge's love had always been grand, but I didn't want anything to do with it anymore. "I won't have this fight with you again. What happened when you tried to surprise me by paying for my car the last time?"

"You had them send the money back, and you paid for it all by your stubborn self. It's a gift, October." He shot me a patronizing look and gave me a slow clap that made my blood boil. "Very good. We all know and respect that you're not five anymore. It's called looking after the people who take care of you."

My teeth clacked together as I fought to keep my composure. "You send over a new car for me, and you'll find it at the bottom of a cliff with a thank you note that says something along the lines of 'Thanks, Judge. Screw you.'" My glare met his, an identical flicker of hurt seeping through us both.

Judge shook his head at me, a flash of anger sharpening his eyes. "You're just being prideful. Pride won't drive you to your next job. Pride doesn't put food on the table."

"It did for you." I tried to choose my words to make sure I didn't set off the wrong stick of dynamite. "Neither of us would respect me if I took money from you for being who I am. In your line of work, respect goes a lot farther than money. If I barely care about your respect, can you imagine how I feel about your money?"

Darius couldn't help but smile at me. "Damn, that was tight. I think you actually stumped him this time, Bait. Man, I miss you."

Judge folded his hands over his stomach. "Smart move, saving your favor for a rainy day. In the meantime, I'll put you on my tab here and at La Luna. I know how much you like to eat there."

I hissed at his roundabout way of letting me know he had me watched on occasion. "I can feed myself. Your food is poison to me," I all but spat, my words filled with too many years of venom. "And don't you dare have me or my house watched again. You don't need to vet me, because I'm not joining your team."

Darius held up his hands. "I told him you and Ollie like to go there. No one's watching you."

"Anymore," Judge amended, making my spine stiffen. I felt Mason and Von step forward, flanking my chair now instead of standing behind it. Judge pulled out his phone and shot out a text, causing a waiter to appear like a rabbit from a magician's hat. The man poured me wine and recited the specials without making eye contact, like a good boy who didn't want to get shot. "Have the porterhouse, baby girl. It's the best thing here, and you're a thin little thing. Always were tiny."

"The wine's enough for me for tonight. Thank you." I took a sip from the wine that I knew would be too good to pass up. The waiter disappeared out the door in the next breath. "I've got to go anyways. Just wanted to get you up to speed."

Darius waved his hand in the air to clear it of the business talk. "Too much seriousness. Tell me whatcha been up to, kid. Why'd you leave the prison?"

"Another job came along that I couldn't pass up." It was the truth. I'd tried to pass on it, but reaping was my life now.

Darius' dark eyes looked tired with too much life, and not enough play. "You still want to run away and join the circus with Allie and me?"

"The running away part? Only every day," I admitted, recalling the hot summer days when he, Allie and me practiced our flips and somersaults on the front lawn at Mama McCray's house. Darius had promised to take me to the circus one day, but I'd told him that I wanted to *join* the circus as a trapeze artist, not just go to watch. I could still see the flicker of play that hadn't been snuffed out of

Darius, but it wasn't enough for him to run away from his bleak responsibilities. I met his gaze, and I could tell we were thinking on the same memory. I offered Darius a tight smile. "If only solving all the problems was as simple as running away. No, I stopped believing in circuses a long time ago, Darius." I didn't hold back the sadness in my voice when I fixed him with eyes that had once trusted his family without question. "Looks like you stopped believing in them, too."

Darius tapped his heart in that same way Ollie did when he was having a brotherly moment. "You're killing me, kid."

Von brushed his fingers across the nape of my neck, pulling a small amount so I could relax and focus. His touch was a soothing balm, and exactly what I needed.

Judge's lips tightened with unmistakable disdain. "No," he said simply, his long finger pointing to Von, warning him not to touch me again.

My eyes narrowed at Judge while Von stroked the side of my neck with his knuckle in defiance. "You don't call the shots on my life. My guards can be nice to me. I wouldn't begrudge you cozying up to Big Mike."

Mason added to the goading by reaching down and holding my hand, staring Judge down while he stroked the slope of my wrist with his thumb. Judge's gaze sharpened, landing on my Viking with a barely controlled snarl. "You, with the death wish. What's your name?" he demanded of Mason.

Things were quickly devolving, so I regained control of the situation. "His name is none of your business." I took another sip of my wine and set the glass down after a few more back and forths with Darius about the good old days, before his hands got too dirty to remember how to put on sock puppet shows just to make me laugh. "It was good to see you guys. I'll let you get back to selling your Girl Scout cookies and making the world a better place." I stood and let Darius give me a real honest to goodness hug that I didn't even try to shirk out of.

Judge actually stood, tall and leonine, towering over me as he always had. He shook my hand and brought me in for a kiss on both cheeks, his finger on my chin. I permitted him control over the tilt of my head because as big a game as I could talk, part of me swelled and died every time I saw Judge's face. I loved him, and missed the trust that had once come so easily.

My forehead drifted of its own accord to rest against Judge's neck. As if he'd been waiting for my unspoken admission that life was getting to be too harrowing, his hand reached up to cup the back of my head, anchoring me to him so I had a safe place to wait out the storm. "Baby girl," he whispered, pleading with me to talk to him, to trust him with more than just my silence. Judge's other hand wrapped around my back and gripped my elbow, holding me in place. I let him have this small victory.

I felt Mason and Von's tension, even though they hadn't

moved. "Watch your hands," Mason warned, though I wished he'd stayed silent.

Big Mike was at Judge's side in a hot second, adding to my nerves and making me wish I'd found a way to have this meeting without Mason and Von. When I pulled my head back, Judge's lips pressed to my cheekbone so he could whisper, "One day you'll need my help. Don't let your pride stop you then. You can lean on me, baby girl. You can't punish me forever. That's not how I raised you."

"It's *exactly* how you raised me." I brought my hand up and touched Judge's cheek tenderly, not breathing when he leaned into my palm. My heart rate picked up when I smelled his cologne, the familiar scent taking me back to the days I used to fall asleep on his lap after he'd read me book after book until I passed out. It was a dangerous dance I did, being so near the viper. But the viper trusted me not to bite too hard, not to tear apart the tender pieces of him that only I still knew were in there. "Be a good boy," I warned him with a kiss to his cheek, and then turned to Darius. "You too, sweetie."

15

ROUND ONE - OCTOBER

My hands were shaking when we got to the car. I fumbled with the keys, hissing when they dropped to the pavement with a clatter that announced my nerves to the whole of the parking lot.

"How about I drive, yeah?" Von suggested as he bent to retrieve the keys.

"Okay, thanks."

Instead of walking around to the passenger's seat, Mason corralled me to the back, sliding in beside me. He loosened his tie the very second the door shut, turning on me with thunder in his scowl. "What was that?" His voice was gruff, angry at me, though I couldn't tell you why. I dug my lavender-scented hand sanitizer from my purse and was cleaning off the germs that felt stuck to me like flypaper. Judge didn't used to have germs when I'd been a kid, but I could feel them now that I was an adult.

Von started up the car and peeled out of the space, pounding the flat of his hand to the steering wheel. "That was brilliant, is what that was! I wouldn't have believed it if I hadn't seen it with my own two eyes. The way you held the power. I mean, Terraway lucked out that we found a second Omen, but that you can hold your own? Mariang's never been able to stand up to the council. That was... Well, it was terrifying in spots, but brilliant. Truly amazing, Peach."

My eyes fell on the passenger's seat, noticing a bag sitting there with the restaurant's logo on it. "Stop the car!" I demanded, snapping forward when Von hit the brakes too hard. We were almost out of the parking lot, but I pointed to the restaurant. "Keep the engine running. I'll be right back."

"Oh, no you won't." Mason's hand cuffed my shoulder, holding me in place. "Drive home, Von."

"You don't understand. Judge had Ike break into my car and put food here."

"So?" Von leaned over and peeked into the bag curiously, inhaling the wafting scents of the porterhouse I knew was probably inside. "Cheers to him for the free dinner. I could go for a steak."

"You don't understand how his game works. Stop the car." I hopped out when Von pulled into a new parking spot, ignoring Mason's bark to get back into the vehicle.

I didn't much feel like explaining what I was doing when I got down on all fours behind Terence the Taurus, tipping my head under the bumper to look for what I knew had to be there. It took me a couple minutes of searching, but eventually my fingers landed on a small rectangular box that had a little green light shining out from it. I swore loudly, not responding to the many questions Von and Mason hurled at me when they got out of the car.

When I displayed the tracking device, Von gasped, but Mason merely shrugged, not understanding what it was. "Wait here." I gently moved the guys out of the way, placed the device under my back tire, shut myself in the driver's seat with a huff, and backed over the thing, shattering Judge's chances at having one of his men follow me around. Without a word, I got out and retrieved the smashed apparatus, my upper lip snarling with satisfaction that *something* in my life was controllable by me. Not Judge. Not Terraway. Me. "I'll be right back, guys."

I grabbed the meals from the passenger's seat and stomped into the restaurant, not bothering to greet the hostess with a polite smile. "The order Judge had made for me? I'd like to place an order for the exact same thing for myself. And if you could put a rush on it, I'd be grateful." I could feel Von and Mason behind me, and I wished they'd stayed in the parking lot. "Not a word, guys," I warned, ignoring Von's wary expression and Mason's clenched jaw.

Without waiting for a response, I lifted my chin and marched through the restaurant, past all the diners and into the backroom to Judge's table. The anger in my eyes made Big Mike stand closer to the brothers. The three shady guests had rejoined them. Ike moved to stand between me and the table until Judge clicked his fingers to wave him off. "Did you think of some way I could repay you finally?" he asked, his calculating eyes unperturbed.

I hefted the oversized takeout bag onto the middle of the table and slammed the smashed device atop it. "I got your little present."

He glanced over my shoulders at Mason and Von. "I was just testing your security. I like to make sure you're kept safe."

"My safety is zero of your concern. And my security didn't find it, I did, you condescending jackwagon. And you can stop it with the gifts. It's beneath both of us. I already accepted your thank you, and that's enough for me. Stop trying to make me less than I am. I don't know why you do that. It's childish."

Judge had the nerve to smile at my scolding, like he'd set up the trap hoping I'd diffuse it. "You've still got that fire. It's hard to look away."

I bristled, but didn't dare smack Judge across the face, like my palm was itching to. Big Mike and Ike were most likely armed, and I knew Darius never went anywhere without his trusty 1911, though I couldn't picture him pulling it on me. I jabbed my finger, reprimanding Judge like he was a child. "I'm ashamed of you two. Darius, I can't believe you let your brother put a tracker on my car." I straightened, brushing my hand down my blouse to collect myself. "Now if you'll excuse me, I'll go wait for my order. I hear the porterhouse is so good, I just can't go home without it." I spun on my heel toward the silent Mason and Von, and stomped away from the table.

I only made it halfway to the door before Judge was out of his seat. He caught my arm and turned me around to face him. "Wait a second."

Mason's snarl was ominous. "I thought I told you to watch your hands around her."

Judge glared at Mason, but only spoke to me. "No one tampered with the food. I would never do that to you." His tone softened with a note of sadness.

Mason and Von closed in on my sides from behind, letting everyone know that I travelled with two menaces. "I've got this, guys." When Von's hand moved to the small of my back, and Mason looked like he might pounce if Judge breathed wrong, I straightened, my tone firm but quiet. "Stand down."

Von's hand didn't move from my back, but Mason obliged me and took a step away, his eyes never leaving Judge.

There were people eating and enjoying their over-priced dinners just outside the backroom. I so wanted to be one of them right now, instead of caught up in the web I had never managed to escape. Judge's hand tightened on my arm, his eyes pleading for the understanding I'd run out of years ago. He was debasing himself in front of his three colleagues this time though, which was new. His voice was quiet and earnest. "Every time I see you, all I see are your ribs and those pigtails. You were such a little thing. I feel bad about how it all went down. All those times you, Ollie and Allie came by the house, I knew you were starving. I knew Bev wasn't looking after you."

I couldn't believe he was bringing this crap out now, of all the times to slice through the veil and get to the heart of our dysfunction.

My tart reply had a slow seethe to it. Von's hand on my back suddenly turned into an anchor that kept me from lunging at Judge. "You knew, and then you cut us off when you decided you didn't want us coming around anymore for no good reason. You didn't like Darius hanging out with Ollie, so you threw us away." Emotion crept into my voice, and I wished Von and Mason weren't gaping at me, hearing every word. "I loved your mama, Judge! I loved you! They needed a whole new word better than 'love' to describe how much you meant to me. How could you kick us out like that? You knew we had nothing." Von's hand tightened around my waist, offering solidarity, since comfort was beyond my comprehension in the moment.

I still remembered the day Ollie, Allie and me had made our way, bedraggled and filthy to Mama McCray's house. Ollie had a standing arrangement to mow her lawn and do yard work, while Allie did the laundry for both families in exchange for dinner five nights a week. Some days, that was our only meal. I still remember running up the driveway to greet my Judge, confused when he didn't hoist me into the air, like he always did. Confusion that hurt worse than mere tears spread through my small body when Judge wouldn't even let us inside. There was illegal business being done in the house while Mama McCray was out, and we weren't to come back, on threat of much unfixable violence. Violence against us, who'd been like family to the McCrays. Violence against me, who'd colored Judge a picture every week just to make his hardened eyes smile. I'd always known how to make Judge smile. He'd hung my art with pride on the McCray refrigerator, like I was something special.

I'd loved their family, and Judge had been that hero to me that every little girl needs when she doesn't have a dad. I hadn't understood then when he'd cussed Ollie out, ignored Allie's sobs and knelt down to wipe away my stunned tears with his long thumb. I couldn't understand why my Judge didn't love me anymore. Why I couldn't be his special helper. He'd kissed my face and held me one last time that day. He told me that he couldn't look after me anymore, and never to come back. Mama McCray died not long after that, and I never got the chance to say goodbye.

Fifteen years later, and it still stung. He'd broken my world that day. I stopped coloring after that. We didn't have a fridge for my art to hang on anyway.

My voice trembled in the stillness of the backroom, quiet as it was. "The time to buy me a steak was ages ago. Don't try easing your conscience now that I'm grown enough to get a job and look after myself. I was seven years old and starving, and you knew it. We got our food dumpster diving after you cut us off, and I'd rather go right back into the trash for my meals than take a shiny new steak from you. I know exactly how dark your soul is."

Judge's cool expression was utterly destroyed. There was a flicker of horror and regret that haunted his eyes now, touching a part of me I'd long cut off from him. "Take the food. Really, baby girl. It's my olive branch."

Fury burned in my expression as I jerked my arm from his grip. I stomped back to his table and snatched up the tracker. I waved the smashed device in his face, making the unnamed dealer to my right grunt in surprise. "Olive branch? Really? Then what's this supposed to be? Your white flag? Don't piss me off, Judge. I'm this close to taking a baseball bat to your windshield again."

"I can help with that," Mason said, his eyes studying Judge like a lion calculating the agility of a limping gazelle.

This time Judge met me with that amused smile I wanted to knock off his face. "You know I only use bullet-proof glass on my cars. Though I wouldn't mind watching you exhausting yourself trying to make a dent. If you would've let me buy you your car, it would've been delivered with the same protection. I'm actually on your side."

"Not possible," I argued, knowing it was childish to want to have the last word. "Your mama didn't raise you to be like this. She wanted better for you. It's why you always waited until she was out of the house to do your shady deals."

"Spitfire, as usual. That's my baby girl."

It took everything in me not to reach out and punch him in the throat. I could get away with a great many things with Judge, but knew that one would be pushing his patience too far. I was already dancing on the edge by defying him in front of the three men at the table.

I composed myself and narrowed my eyes at the trio of unnamed men I didn't need to know. "If you gentlemen haven't found the trackers on your cars before you landed yourself here, then either he's not bothering to vet you, which means I'd get your wills in order, or you trusted Judge too easily. Pretty deadly mistake, and might I add, a rookie mistake as well. Judge doesn't trust rookies, and trust is the only currency that matters at a table like this. I don't care how much he's promised you." I shot Judge with the most venomous glare I had in me. "Judge only feeds people who don't need to eat."

"That's enough," Judge ordered, his tone firm.

I reached down and took a sip of the wine I'd abandoned, returning Judge's glare as I set it back down. "Enjoy the drinks, guys. If you haven't already found your tracker, it just might be your last one. Judge has a lot of flaws, but his taste in red wine isn't one of them." I spun on my heel and stalked past Von and Mason to the hostess stand, where I kept my back resolutely to their table, my hands in my pockets to keep the trembling unnoticed.

16

ROUND TWO - JUDGE

*V*on and Mason said not a word, but they both had opinions, I could tell. Mason was tight-jawed and glaring at me, while Von rubbed sweet circles across my back to soothe my jumbled nerves. Mason snatched up the bag when it came, wanting to get out of there as fast as we could. I pulled out my wallet, ready to bite the bullet that came when you wanted luxuries like pride. The hostess shook her head. "The bill's been taken care of."

"No, it hasn't," I replied, grinding my teeth. "Please reverse the charges and put it on this card."

"But Mr. McCray said…"

"Judge says a lot of things he shouldn't. Charge the carryout to this card, please."

"Yes, ma'am." She looked at my outfit dubiously and lowered her voice. "The total's $265.75 for the food. Are you sure you don't want me to charge it to his account? He insisted."

I groaned internally, but kept my chin raised and my bland expression in place. It was only money. Money wasn't worth as much as my dignity. "Use my card, please." A smile swept over me as my shoulders rolled back. "And can you add a round of desserts for Judge's table on my card, too? Crème brûlée for five. Let him know it's from his favorite trapeze artist."

"Absolutely." She rang me up for the largest dinner bill I'd ever paid for, and after the food came, I was on my way.

Von pulled the car around, and Mason all but shoved me in back. The second the door shut, he went off on a tirade. "Are you suicidal, or just insane? You can't go tempting fate like that." Mason shook his head at me. "So he wants to do something nice to thank you for saving someone he cares about. There's nothing wrong with that, October. Your stubborn streak is going to get you killed someday."

He kept going, but I wasn't really listening. Mason didn't know my world. My attention returned when Mason finally ran out of steam. "Von, you reason with her. Clearly nothing I'm saying is getting through."

Von belted out a laugh I could tell he'd been holding in as he merged onto the freeway. "That was brilliant! I've never seen anything better. It was like living out a mafia movie. And forgive me Mason, but Peach? That was dead sexy. If you weren't my dedicated little sister, I'd be taking you to my place right about now."

Mason glowered at Von. "That was very helpful, Von. Thanks."

When we reached the house, the smell of the porterhouse steaks had filled up the car, making us all ravenous. Mason was still angry, but I knew a beautiful piece of meat would help with that. Von got out the plates while Mason put a few beers on the table and poured me a glass of water. They waited until my call to Ollie ended before pulling out the food and diving in.

I was all ready to sit down and let the events of the evening go until Von opened a bottle of red wine from the bag that I knew hadn't been in the first order Judge sneaked into my car. I ripped the receipt out of my pocket and skimmed it, swearing so loud I made Von jump when my eyes couldn't find the wine anywhere on the list. "No! I had him. I so had him this time!"

"He sneak the bottle of wine in?"

I held out my hand expectantly. "Give me the keys. It has to go back."

Von quirked an eyebrow at me as he poured a glass. "It's already opened, love. You can't take it back."

I clenched my fist at his solid logic. "He thinks he can just..."

"Just buy you the nicest bottle of wine there?" Von sniffed the glass before handing it to me. "It's the same stuff you drank at his table. He got it for you because he knew you liked it."

"He's trying to buy me so I can help him. I can't believe I lost this time!"

"No one lost this round," Von chuckled, tugging me toward him so he could kiss my cheek. "You bought him and his mates pudding. You're even."

Mason was irate. "I can't even enjoy this steak because of all the talk about that Judge guy. I swear, October. I never want you meeting with him again. He's dangerous. Now everyone sit down and pick a new topic before I lose my temper."

I huffed as I dropped down into my chair. I folded my arms across my chest to have a Mexican standoff with my glass of wine, debating whether or not I could have a drink without Judge thinking he'd won.

17

REASONS AND REASON

$\mathcal{A}$ week later, and Mason still hadn't let the Judge thing go, though at least he'd kept his unhappiness about it to a minimum while we worked.

Twenty reaps in three different hospital wings later, and I was ready for a nap. It was nearing evening, but that fact was harder to tell in the hospital, since many of the rooms we went to were windowless.

Mariang was barely upright after her four reaps, so Danny secured a wheelchair for her to rest in. She looked so small, so fragile. I wondered if I would similarly diminish someday, and shuddered at the thought. I vowed to eat a whole meal when we broke for dinner, no matter how queasy my stomach felt.

"She's done," Danny ruled after coming back with a cup of juice for Mariang. It was the only time he'd left her side all day. "She should've been done an hour ago, but there were so many here. We never got to cover this much ground before you came along."

I guess that was a compliment, but Danny doled those out so infrequently, I couldn't be sure. "I can do a few more. Why don't you guys go back to the car? We'll meet you there."

Rick volunteered to stay with us, while the other three guards went with Danny. "You sure you're not too tired for this?" Mason asked me as we walked to the next door my gut pulled me toward.

"I'm fine." I huffed and rolled my eyes at myself. "I know, Von. I own the dollar another jar," I yawned, not caring that I'd jumbled my sentence.

"That's eleven dollars just today. I think you have a problem, love."

I leaned on Mason more heavily than I had at the day's start. My limbs were weighted and moved out of sync from their proper working order. My lungs felt like they weren't taking in any air that rejuvenated me.

The room was empty when we walked in, which I did not expect. We left Rick in the hallway to guard against... I forget. Something bad. "Well, that sucks. My gut led me to this room. It's still tugging me to this spot. How could there be nobody here?"

"I smell something. Something sweet." Von knocked on the bathroom door, which was halfway shut. "Hello? Anybody here?" He opened it all the way and switched on the light, then he gave out a fearful, "Ho!"

"What?" I moved toward him, but he shot out of the bathroom and shut the door behind him, his eyes wide and panicked as he tried to breathe through his mouth without inhaling the scent that was driving him crazy. I knew that look; he'd been chugging blood bags that looked like juice pouches and sucking on bottles of honey every day we had to reap in a medical facility. There was fresh blood in that bathroom. Though my half-breed blood was the most difficult flavor to resist, a full-human's blood was still a temptation. Honey helped to curb the cravings in a pinch. "Von, what's wrong? Breathe, sweetie. Breathe through it."

Von's fangs that I tried never to notice now gleamed at me. I tried to give him a smile that told him I believed in his ability not to vamp out and drain me. My forced bravery gave him faith in his self-control, and after a few more breaths through his mouth, his shoulders relaxed. "It's uh, just something for Rick to see. Go fetch Rick, will you?"

"You're scaring me. What's in there?"

Mason moved past me into the bathroom and quickly backed out. "Get Rick. Now." He pointed to the door, keeping his body between me and whatever lie in the bathroom that shocked him so.

I poked my head out into the hallway. "Rick? The guys need you in the bathroom." *Yeah, that sounded weird.*

Ever the professional, Rick wasted no time with questions. Von waited in the hallway while Mason let him into the bathroom. I heard shouts of confusion and upset as Rick called someone on his phone. Then Rick and Mason were arguing, which finally culminated in Von coming back into the room, a half-drained blood pouch in his fist. His free hand rubbed my triceps to soothe me as he spoke. "There's a man in there who's on the verge of being dead. I need you to reap him quickly, and then we get the bloody hell out of here, yeah?"

"No." Mason was firm as he stepped out of the bathroom. "She doesn't need to see that."

"It's not about her, Mason. That man needs a peaceful death, what with the way he was attacked. We can give him at least that."

"I can do it, Mason. It's fine." I wasn't sure what to expect when I walked in and saw a man in his fifties bound, gagged and beaten to within an inch of his life. I let out a tiny shriek at the bloody mess that was his body. Leg twisted unnaturally, multiple fresh stab wounds, and a bewildered look on his pale face that told me the pain had deranged him to the point where he couldn't feel anything anymore. He exhaled labored gasps into his cloth gag, begging me with his eyes to get a doctor.

Mason kept one arm banded around my waist when I bent down to reap the soul that was too close to the surface. I barely had to touch him for it to leap into me, and then settle into Mason. The man's body deflated, his pain leaving him in an instant. "Okay, out we go," Mason instructed. "Go into the hallway and wait with Von."

I hadn't noticed it when I first entered. I guess the sight of the dying man was a bit distracting. On the mirror above the sink there was a message written in blood.

KING MANAUL,

If you don't meet your quota, I'll give you more souls to reap than you'll know what to do with. Sama's on the move. I'll protect our people if you can't.

Last warning.

"WHAT THE..." I WAS OUT OF APPROPRIATE WORDS, AND definitely out of sanity. I pulled out my phone and took a picture of the mirror, and then one of the body, just in case. "It's starting. One of the councilmembers is trying to control us. Titus warned it was coming. I just didn't think whoever would do this would start in on civilians. Don't they know we're ahead of the daily quota?"

Von shook his head. "That doesn't matter yet. We're still trying to make up for the months Mariang came up short. We haven't broken even yet. We're not even close."

When two nurses passed by and gave me a curious look, Von's hand brushed to them and did a mild pull. I knew he was taking away a little of their curiosity, so they didn't ask questions, didn't care that we were roaming about the hospital, and wouldn't stop us. It's how we were able to walk in and out of rooms with nothing more than a visitor's pass.

Von met my eye and nodded. "Let's go. Rick's going to wait for our people to show up. He'll keep the staff away from the room until our guys can clean it up."

My hands were trembling, and my knees could barely support me after the long day of life-draining work mixed with the sheer terror from seeing the dying man mangled on the floor. "Could we have helped him? We're in a hospital. Could we have saved him?"

"Once the soul is that close to the surface, it's ready to leave the body. He's dying no matter what. Hey, you okay?" Mason asked when I doubled over to catch my breath.

I probably looked ridiculous, but I didn't have the stamina to stand properly, much less care what other people thought about it. I leaned on Mason. "I'm fine. Just a little... you know. Stupid hazards of the job."

"You want me to fetch you a wheelchair?" Von asked. My answering venom-laced glare told him never to suggest that to me again. "Alright, how about I carry you?"

"How about you carry Mason? I'm not Mariang. I don't need someone to... I don't..." That last reaping was one too many. My vision was starting to blur, and my grip on Mason grew more desperate.

I didn't mean to collapse. There was so much I didn't mean to have happen in that moment. I expected a painful crash, but I was too tired to care. It never came, though.

Mason caught me before I hurt myself and swept me up in his arms.

I didn't want to feel safe. I didn't want to feel anything. I couldn't pull out my list of all the reasons I had where this sort of codependent behavior wasn't for me. In that moment, I lost my list, my reasons and my reason, resting against Mason while he carried me like a princess to the parking structure.

18

THE SAME ANIMAL

awoke in my bed sometime after the sun had set. The curtains were drawn, but I could see a sliver of the glowing moon peeking through, since the guys hadn't shut my shades properly.

I glanced at the space next to me on the bed, relieved to find that Von was not there. I felt the steady breathing of Mason behind me. His warm and naked side was nudged up against my back, his hard human body not quite as snuggly as his wolf form. I made sure to keep silent, so as not to wake him. Since there were no witnesses and my childishness would not be known, I let the tears I'd had on standby well in my eyes and spill down my cheeks. It had been a lot of life change I'd been forced to endure in a short amount of time. I wasn't sure if the worst part was leaving my job or taking a tortured man's soul from him, but whatever horror pushed me over the edge, I was both thankful and resentful it got me there. I shut my eyes as I lay on my side and covered my mouth so no sound would alert the others who were squatting at my house that I was breaking down.

When I felt a large hand brush a few locks of auburn hair from the nape of my neck, I hissed and did my best to steady out my inaudible sobs. "Sorry. Did I wake you?"

"You're crying." Mason touched the tears on my face when I rolled onto my back to look up at him. He was bare-chested and wearing only a pair of jogging shorts, which I decided was my favorite thing on a guy.

Mason was a gorgeous man, and I was a childish wreck. *Perfect.*

"You don't have to point it out. At least let me pretend I still have a little dignity." I sniffled, trying to get myself under wraps. "Where are the new guards? It's so quiet in here."

"They're outside watching the house." He wrapped one of his zombie-crushing arms under my neck and leaned down to press his lips to my eyelashes, blessing my eyes one at a time. "There's dignity in everything you do. Leaving the job you loved to save a world you know little about? Working so hard to save them that you passed out from exhaustion? Everything you do amazes me. And not once did you ask what's in it for you."

"I already know what's in it for me." I held up my fingers in a big zero. "Could you not be nice to me right now? I'm a mess."

Mason's eyebrows tented. "You want me to be mean to you?"

"I want you to never have seen me break down. I already feel too babied. Don't want to add tears to the mix." I swiped at my cheeks. "Seriously. Don't look at me like that."

My humiliation did not deter Mason from studying my face. "You're like me." He pressed his fist to his chest. "You understand taking care of people who can't take care of themselves. It's why you can't forgive Judge." He traced the curve of my cheek. "You're good at taking care of people. That's what you're doing when you grant them a peaceful death, you know."

"No. I'm nothing like as brave as you. You don't cry like a baby at night. You don't need someone to carry you to the c-car. That's so embarrassing!"

"You don't think there've been days I cried?" He traced the outline of my face, looking at me like... like... Beto had never looked at me with such reverence. "*Hani*, we're the same animal."

I wiped away an errant tear. "Where'd Von escape to?"

"He went to visit Penny for the evening. Now he's out picking up another shipment of blood. He'll be back."

"So we're alone?"

"Looks to be that way."

I wasn't sure what I was thinking, only that for once in my life, I wasn't. My hand grew a mind of its own and reached up to touch the full lips I only ever wanted a closer look at. Mason was beautiful in that rugged way I couldn't help but be attracted to. He wasn't polished and didn't quite fit anywhere, but somehow he fit perfectly in my bed next to me. "Mason?" I whispered, unsure how the dangerous ground I was walking on might hold me when the world shook us, as it inevitably would.

The adoring gaze mingled slowly with a lust for conquest in his stormy eyes as he snatched at my wrist. There was a shift between us I could almost grab onto, so thick was the connection that pulled me in. Alarms went off inside my head, warning me of the dangers of kissing someone I worked so closely with.

I ignored the alarm. I ignored the danger. I ignored Terraway and my world as I leaned up and stroked my lips to his. The second I made contact, heat flushed through my body like a jolt of something new and colorful. The incredible ripple unfolded throughout my whole body. I couldn't just feel his lips on mine – I felt his lips everywhere. A million kisses effervesced all over my skin, peppering me in sensation from head to toe. I wanted more, desperately more. His lips were deliciously soft beneath the prickle of his facial hair – soft and unresponsive.

The stunned look on Mason's face scared me when I pulled back, though I needed more of whatever that was. Had I read the situation all wrong? He blinked down at me with wide eyes that held so many conflicting emotions; I couldn't pick just one to judge his mood with.

"I'm sorry. I probably shouldn't have done that." When he didn't correct me, horror washed through my body, ice replacing the buttery heat. "Oh, man! What did I just do? I'm sorry. I wasn't thinking." I covered my face with my hands and rolled away from his half embrace, wishing for a genie to make what I'd done disappear. "I, um, I'm tired. I didn't mean it." I got up from the bed and all but ran into the bathroom like the inexperienced kid I was.

I should've expected the knock, slow and steady, but I jumped at the sound that broke the paced rhythm of my chagrinned heartbeat. I scraped at my hands with self-loathing.

"*Hani*? Open the door."

"Please just go. Could we pretend like nothing happened? Because if we can't, I'm not leaving this bathroom. I swear to you, I'll bolt the door shut and straight up live in here."

"You surprised me, is all. Open the door."

"Please, Mason! I said I was sorry. We don't have to talk about it."

"I don't want to talk about it. Honest. Come on out."

"Promise?"

"Sure." He tapped his fingers on the barrier between us. "You know, I could break this door down easy enough. You have no idea how strong I am. I'm only knocking to be polite."

"Oh, fine. But I don't want to hear a word about what didn't happen out there." I counted to ten before unlocking the door. When I saw Mason staring at me with wild eyes as he gripped the doorframe, I made to shut the door again. "You're thinking about it!"

Mason caught the door and bunched his fist in the front of my t-shirt, dragging me out of the bathroom and into the empty living room before I could dart away. "Do it again," he said, his voice low and gravelly.

Von was away, the guards were outside, and Danny and Mariang were in Ollie's room. I wasn't sure who we were hiding from, but his guarded cadence and body language told me he was on high alert.

"What?"

"That kiss. I felt it everywhere. Is that what it's like to kiss a human? Or was that us?"

I melted at the state of his confusion. "You felt it too?"

Mason nodded, and I could see the entire whites of his eyes as he muscled his way through his own personal freak-out. "One more time. Please. I've never..."

I leaned up on my toes and kissed him again before I could chicken out. My hands cupped his face and stroked the scruff on his jaw. That same unreal bubbling sensation washed through my veins like a lust-filled energy drink. Beneath my closed eyelids I saw colors – actual reds and yellows that danced while flutes started playing, encouraging more and still more.

Three times I kissed him before his lips started to move with mine, giving up on resisting the passion that trickled in and slowly began to fill us both. As soon as his lips came to life, they picked up the pace like a feverish wave I saw coming but was powerless to run from.

I didn't want to run. For the first time, I felt like I was ready for the more I'd been living without. I wanted it, grabbed it by the naked shoulders, jumped up and wrapped my legs around it. The colors urged me onward, pushing my body to his.

I blame it all on the colors and the flutes that diluted my reality. It couldn't be attraction or real, live feelings that whipped our LSD-laced makeout into a frenzy. It just plain couldn't. I wasn't a passionate kisser usually, but a nervous one who pulled away before I could get swept up in a moment too big for me to duck out of.

I lost myself completely in the kiss that I couldn't help but crave still more of. His lips captured mine, drawing out a pathetic bleat from me that he swallowed. Then he begged for another. I melted into his kiss, falling hard and fast as the attraction swirled in both of us like a tornado, daring us to unleash its full wrecking force. I'd never made such scared and impassioned noises when kissing Beto. This was different. This was my Viking king who moon-lighted as a zombie-slayer. Mason had desire deep in his bones. My legs were wrapped around him to hold him in place so I could indulge in more of whatever he had to offer.

Mason was my coworker. I knew I shouldn't be attracted to him. I knew I should run.

But I stayed. I stayed and spoiled myself in foolishness.

I'd skipped most of my opportunity to be a teenager, and it seemed with every kiss, I was devolving into a confused mess of hormones and emotions.

And hormones, if I didn't mention those before. Holy cannoli, the hormones. I could feel the attraction rippling through me, unable to curb my passion to a more acceptable first kiss level.

"Do you feel this?" he breathed between kisses. The sound was husky and positively erotic. "It's never felt like this for me before."

"Me neither." I gripped his skin, scraping his back with my nails. I caught his lower lip between my teeth and tugged. We were the same feral animal, indeed.

Something happened then that I couldn't explain. My head started to swim and my senses started to scramble yet further. I tasted his lips, and they were colorful on my tongue. That same red and yellow danced in my mouth, painting our palettes with a cool sensation that set off more flutes, which played in varying octaves. My senses scrambled, and I found that I could taste color. I quickly learned that red had the flavor of Mason to it, and it was deliciously addictive. When his tongue teased mine, I felt it everywhere, like he had a thousand tongues to torture me with, and I had all day to let him.

My breathing hitched as the euphoria built up inside of me. Mason slammed my back into the wall, his hunger for my lips turning up the volume of the imagined music. His soft moans were now forceful growls that lit in both our bellies and fueled the best kiss of my life. We were ablaze with a red and yellow fire we had no hope of controlling.

He had one hand beneath me, supporting my weight so I could remain pinned to the wall while we ravished each other. His fingers tangled in my hair, tilting my head to deepen the kiss. He uttered erratic, manly noises under his breath that made my heart bang around in my chest like an alarm, cluing me in that something significant was happening. I couldn't turn back from it; I'm not sure I wanted to. Though I knew it was too early to make such grand declarations, I realized that I felt right with Mason. I wanted exactly this moment and dozens more like it. His kiss was heady, and I let it confuse my higher reasoning that otherwise would have told me to run from the crazy mountain man who didn't even know how to drive a car.

Of course Von chose that exact moment to return from his shopping trip. "Ho! Put a sock on the door next time you're snogging, kids."

Mason slowed his passion for me, meeting my lips with gentleness he had not possessed mere seconds ago. We both slowly deflated like overfull balloons a week after a party. He cupped my face with his large, rough hand, caressing the contours of my cheek like he was stroking silk he was afraid to muddy. "So beautiful," he murmured. I could tell from the slight tremble in his voice that he was just as shaken as I was at the kiss.

I heard Von drop his things in the kitchen and head back out to the car for the next round.

Mason lowered my legs to the floor, gripping my thigh with trembling fingers on the way down. He dropped his hands and shook his head, as if trying to snap himself out of the spell we were casting on each other. "Is that what it is to kiss a human? Or is it because you're an Omen? You're my first of either, so I don't know why it feels like this." He wiped his hand over his lips with wide eyes, blinking rapidly to clear his head.

"I think I kiss pretty normal for a human." *I hope.*

He shook his head slowly as he processed the beauty of what we'd just experienced. "No, *hani.* That was anything but normal. I can feel that in my whole body." He flexed his forearms and shivered.

"What does *hani* mean?" I asked quietly. I'd been curious since he first used the term, but had been too chicken to ask.

His lidded eyes found my hazel. "It means 'honey' or 'darling'. It means you're mine."

I reached out and touched his fingers, wondering if we could recreate that same crazed magic, or if it was all a fluke. It was in the name of science that I pulled him forward to kiss him again. Of course that was why. Science. This time I twined my fingers through his as we drew out the painfully slow passion that built like a fire in my chest. The red and the yellow streaks and sparks danced around the edges of my vision, staying with me even after my eyelashes fluttered shut. Part of me was screaming at myself to run from the permanence I could feel settling in my chest.

But I didn't run. I held on for dear life. The significance of me reaching out to grip Mason's hands wasn't lost on me. I couldn't even feel my OCD battling inside of my brain, yelling at me about germs and the doomed intimacy that came with holding hands. Finally the conflict I always warred with stopped. I'd never been able to hold Beto's hand, and here I was, reaching out for more of Mason.

Of course Von came back in through the door, and of course he slammed it loud enough to rouse Danny, who came out to grouse at the intrusion.

Of course Mason and I hadn't kissed enough to satiate either one of us. Mason leaned in to kiss me once more, ignoring the gasp and whistle from his two best friends.

19

MARRYING ME OFF

Danny let out a loud curse when we finally broke apart. Mason and I could do nothing more than stare at each other with mirrored expressions of shock. "Great. So you know?"

"Know what? You knew about this?" Von asked, putting the rest of his bags down in the kitchen. "I mean, I knew they were getting gooey for each other, but I didn't know it'd exploded into humping against a wall. I might need a cold shower after that one. Well done, Mason. And November? Who knew you had *that* in you?"

My face turned crimson as the reality of the most amazing kiss of my life came crashing down on my head. "Oh, gross. Sorry, guys. I should've been more discreet." I'd never been a public display kind of girl, but that one had taken me by storm.

Von held up his hands. "Don't hold back on my account. Happy for you, mate." He slapped Mason on the back a little harder than I thought he should've. Then Von winked at me just to tease my growing discomfort. "Humping in the living room. Sounds like a band name, yeah?"

I paled. "I'm sorry. I got caught up, and I... Totally uncool of me." I couldn't face Von's teasing grin. I flew into the bathroom, locking myself inside with my embarrassment. When a knock came to the door, I begged for them to go away.

Danny's voice was calm to counter my thumping heart. "October, come on out. I've got to explain a few things to you. Did you see colors? Hear music?"

Mason and I both replied with a confused, "How did you know?"

"It's what happens when an awakened Omen gets it on with someone from Terraway. Not many people know about it because it's a pretty private thing, but it happens. Did you hallucinate? Like, did you see anything more specific than just the abstract colors?"

"I did," Mason answered when I cracked open the door.

I shook my head. "I didn't, but something happened that was weird." I covered my face with my hands, wishing I didn't have to talk about something private with Danny, of all people. "When we were... you know, I swear something happened to my senses. It was like I could taste color or something." My nose crinkled as I shook my head. "I'm not explaining it right."

Danny nodded, moving to the couch to decrease the heightened climate of the room. "That's about right. You didn't hallucinate, though? You saw colors, but no specific images or visions?"

"No. Was I supposed to?" I shoved the throw pillow back into place on the other end of the couch from Danny, and sat down so it would support my back.

"Not necessarily. Everything's normal for who you two are. Intense, yeah? People don't get how Mariang and I are the way we are, but imagine years of that. It never gets boring. It never gets less."

Mason perked up at this, shoving his shirt over his head and slumping on the couch to cool down (This, incidentally did nothing to cool me down. Dude was ripped). "Incredible. You never told me it was like that. I've never... not even with Kara."

I grimaced at being compared to his dead wife, though I knew that was an inevitability. "Anything else we should know about?"

Danny's elbows rested on his knees as if gearing up for the birds and the bees. "October, when you start to see hallucinations, let me know. I mean, first thing. Understand?"

"Now I'm worried. What will that mean?"

"Nothing bad, but I'll give you the rest of the sex talk then. There are things you should know, but not yet. You two barely know each other still. And you've got Von to factor into it all."

"Anybody order a third wheel?" Von joked. "I'm kidding. We're making you overanalyze what should be good old fun. Enjoy it. I can make myself scarce with Katrina or whoever.

"Oh my gosh! It's nothing like that. We only just kissed, you guys. Stop marrying me off."

"I have to talk to you!" Mason blurted out at Danny, standing abruptly.

Danny gripped Mason's shoulder and then slapped him on the back with unconcealed pride. "Sure, mate. Let's go for a walk."

20

PRECIOUS

Von waited for the front door to close before he cast me a mischievous grin. "You're a minx, you are. I wonder what would've happened if we hadn't interrupted. Virgin, indeed. Your legs and hips seemed to know the dance well enough. You'll be an absolute tomcat when your time comes."

"Shut up."

"Hold on. Let me get your first aid kit."

"Bathroom. Under the sink."

"I know," he said, glancing at me over his shoulder as he turned toward the bathroom. "I live here too, now. I know where things are." I wasn't sure how to feel about that. The guys had moved in a few weeks ago. Like, *moved in*. Some days it felt like home to have them in my space with me, but other days it felt... I don't know, like, *get out of my space.*

Von returned a minute later with the red box. "Exactly where I knew it would be." I worried at the state of the contents of that cupboard, which he no doubt shifted in the extraction of the kit.

"You alright?" I asked him. "Did you cut yourself?"

"No, daft girl. You did. Give me your hands."

He turned the living room's end table lamp on to get a better look at the damage. I tried to hide my shame from him, and clasped my hands between my knees as I shifted on the couch. "I'm fine, Von. It's not a big deal."

He gently parted my knees and pried my hands out, rubbing them with a warm washcloth that was now totally ruined. He was quiet when he disinfected the cuts, breathing through his teeth as he eyed my blood droplets with lust he tried to conceal. "Did Mason... Was he... How did... Was he nice to you?"

I refused to look at him. "Yes. He was great. It was all pretty intense. I've never kissed anyone like that."

"Talk to me, Peach. Pretend I'm a brother," he reminded me. "I think that'll suit our threesome just fine."

"Really?" I softened at his use of the nickname I cherished.

"Really." The dimple appeared in his left cheek, so I started to relax.

"It was nice. Special, even." My first instinct was to stuff it all down, but under the regime of Von being more of a brother than anything else, I guessed there was no real reason to hold back. "I think I like him. But there's the whole two different worlds thing."

"Small obstacle," Von teased, a smirk tugging up the corner of his mouth.

I kept my eyes trained on Von's dark green t-shirt, wondering when the last time he washed it was. "It was exciting and new. I've only ever kissed Beto. This was different. Like speaking a new language I never even knew existed, but somehow I woke up fluent in it." I shook my head. "I don't know. I'm explaining it wrong."

"Go on."

"I heard flutes playing." The urge to scratch my hands was heady, but I did my best to resist as Von wrapped a bandage around each one. He did a substandard wrap job, but it was the sweetest thing anyone had done for me in a long time. It was the sweetest thing I'd *let* someone do for me in a long time. Somewhere in an unmarked place along our journey, I was starting to trust Von.

"You heard flute music while you were snogging? Like, in your mind?"

"Yeah. That's really how it is for Danny with Mariang? Did you know?"

Von chuckled. "That you think Danny and I talk about anything personal tells me how little you know about us. I have no idea on that front. He's a pretty private person when it comes to Mariang."

"Well, whatever it is, it was intense." I grinned at him, breathing easier as my nerves started to dissipate. "Thanks for letting me girlfriend all over you. I don't really talk about this kind of stuff with anyone."

"I had you pegged as the girl who takes her time to weigh her options. Imagine my surprise when one of the most untamed outcasts in Terraway is plotting his way to your all-access theme park right under my nose. I've been falling down on the big brothering job, no doubt."

My face soured. "For the record, my virginity is not a theme park."

"Then clearly he's doing it wrong." Von placed the kit on the coffee table and sat next to me on the couch, his knees falling open as they did when he was trying to relax.

"You going to Katrina's?"

He shook his head, kicking off his shoes. "No. I'm staying here tonight. And probably most nights, come to think of it. You know Ezra prefers it this way. You and Penny get to be the two women in my life for a while."

I don't know why that made me blush, so I kept my head down until my cheeks turned back to their normal shade of adulthood. "That's a sweet thing to say."

He jerked his head toward my bedroom and pulled me up off the couch. "Why don't you and Mason take up in your bed? Something tells me Mason won't want to sleep in his wolf form tonight, and none of these beds or the pullout is really big enough for three. I've grown quite fond of the couch." Von winked at me. "You're welcome."

My neck started itching, so I scratched a line down my throat to alleviate my growing apprehension. "Von, I don't know. I mean, that's too serious. Sleeping alone together after our first kiss? That's too fast."

"You're just going to have to cry yourself to sleep tonight thinking how much you miss me. You'll think on how fortunate you were when you used to sleep next to the most perfect man you've ever laid eyes on. Tough break, Mason. Best to dash his hopes gently."

I raised my eyebrow at his bluster. "Seriously. I don't want to block you from enjoying your night. Go out with Katrina. There's plenty of security around the house."

Von yanked on my arm and led me into my bedroom. "Lay down," he instructed, shutting the door. He climbed into the bed next to me and pulled the covers up around us, settling down on the pillow to my left. It felt like we were kids in a fort, and I loved him for trying to ratchet down the tension that never seemed all that far away. "Until Danny and Mason figure out this Omen-Reaper business, you're not out of my sight. I'm serious. Now that you and Mason are starting things up, I don't want to get edged out of a job. I need this, November."

I rolled on my side to face him, able to make out just the outline of his features. He was handsome in the barely there moonlight that slid through the half-inch gap in my thick taupe curtains. "First off, I'm not starting things up. It was a kiss, Von. A great kiss, but don't make it weird. Even if something down the road ever did start up, this whole Death Omen thing works far better with two Reapers. Your job's safe. You and Danny can stay out of my love life."

Von pecked my lips with a smirk. "Cute that you think that's true. Think of it as an HR issue. If you hooked up with Brenden, the higher ups might have something to say about it, yeah?"

"I guess. Gross analogy, though. Brenden's like, over thirty."

"Hello! I'm two blinks away from thirty!" He shook his head at me. "Mason's thirty-one, you know."

"Then *you* can date Brenden." I nuzzled my nose to his and whispered, "Old man."

Von's mouth fell open. "I can't believe you just said that. I'm in my prime, I'll have you know."

"I might have something of Ollie's for joint pain if you need it in your old age."

His hand found my waist under the covers and squeezed, finding my ticklish spot and working it right good. We rolled around for a solid minute in a fit of giggles, making a perfect mess of the sheets.

He froze above me, shifting with sudden caution as we stared into each other's eyes. There were things there that didn't have words to match, so we didn't say them. Von slowly closed the gap between us to deliver another simple peck to my lips, making my cheeks turn pink with its sweetness. "You went and made it all precious," I scolded him through my blush. "That was adorable. Now get off me. Mason's going to get the wrong idea."

Von rolled off and laid on his back next to me, resting his heavy leg atop my thigh just for the contact. "You are precious. If Mason starts treating you like you're not, it's time to move on. Understood?"

"Understood." I fiddled with the hem of my yellow t-shirt. "You're not a bad guy, you know."

He turned his head to look at me, his handsome face examining the sincerity of mine. "If you could not spread that around, I'd appreciate it. You'll utterly destroy my loose cannon reputation."

"We can't have that."

Von tossed me a teasing grin. "I'll see you in the morning, love. When you're dreaming about me, try to work up a decent code name, so Mason doesn't feel too put out. Mason gets to be the man in your bed, but I'll always be the man of your dreams."

"You should really work on building up your self-esteem. You're too humble."

"Goodnight, dream girl." He rolled out of the bed and left the room.

I waited for Mason, but after half an hour, I was too exhausted to wait any longer. I made myself at home in my bed, anchoring my body to the center of the mattress – my favorite spot. I hadn't slept by myself in too many nights, and though I wished Mason wasn't avoiding me, I took my rare breath of alone time where I could get it and closed my eyes.

I think I muttered some kind of unladylike reply when Mason slid into the bed next to me however long later. He rolled me over so he could spoon me, kissing the back of my shoulder, as if we did that sort of thing all the time. Which, I guess we sort of did. Though, it felt more intimate when it was just the two of us. Mason didn't need to talk about the kiss, and I was grateful to have escaped the big emotional recap of it all.

Von followed in a few minutes later, uncomfortable as he sat on my other side. "I tried to take the couch, mates, but Danny vetoed it. I want to give you your space, but with all the extra reaping you're doing, Danny thinks you need double the pulling at night. I'm sorry."

Mason made a half-awake noise that meant "Whatever, dude. Just lay down and shut up. I'm almost asleep." I reached out in the darkness and tugged Von down next to me, unwilling to let the threesome I had landed myself in get all weird. "Goodnight, big brother."

Von pulled the comforter up to his chin and whispered, "Goodnight, little peach." His lips were drawn forward, brushing me with a light goodnight kiss that brought a sleepy smile to my face. My shorts left my kneecap exposed for Von to tickle the sensitive flesh there, just to make me squirm. He slid his hand between mine to keep me from scratching while I slept.

That night I closed my eyes with Mason's hand around my ribs and a fraction of peace in my heart that had not been there before. I was learning to soften in small amounts, and the shift felt like the kind of breathing that normal people do. I don't know why I'd wasted so much time afraid to draw in that breath. With tranquility in my lungs, I knew that no matter what sort of warfare greeted us when we woke, Von and Mason would be there. Von was the big brother who wouldn't leave before I was ready. Mason was the... the thing I wasn't ready to examine just yet. But one fact was sure: I wouldn't have to pretend that being alone was what I wanted.

HALLUCINATION HARLOT

I had never been a deep sleeper. In fact, I'd been a frequent tosser and turner before I'd started going to bed with my Reapers. When my eyes closed in Mason and Von's arms, I inhaled what finally felt like fresh air to my soul. Even though we were inside my house, tucked in my bed, the freshness found me. It was new possibilities, new hope. I had been surviving on my own for so long in a world where I was constantly too young, too poor and too... just too much and still never enough.

Somehow in Mason's arms, I felt like the too much I always assumed myself to be wasn't scary or overwhelming at all. I wasn't too much for Mason, the zombie-slayer. It was a thought so peaceful, I never dared to think that a life like this could be mine.

Mason had his larger hand palming my ribs while he spooned me with his much taller body. Every inch I shifted, he compensated for, even in sleep. I knew so little about him, but this Duwende bond was bonkers. His level breathing calmed me, and though there was a lot of sexual tension between us, I relaxed against his hairy chest. Von's steady minty cigar breath tickled my nose, making me smile as I mused that even in sleep, Von was precious to me.

So peaceful was I that I almost didn't see the yellow caterpillar. I almost didn't catch the miniscule movement as it inched across the nightstand.

My tiny intake of breath was quickly countered by my eyes shutting tight, so as not to give away that I'd made Prince Langgam's spy. My house had been breached, if I understood the implications correctly.

"Von," I whispered, my eyes still shut. When he didn't stir, I nudged the leg he had looped between my knees. "Von, could you get me a glass of water?"

"What? Not now, baby. I'm sleeping."

I pursed my lips at his too flirty slip, blaming it on the late hour. "Von, I really need a glass of water. Come to think of it, I'm hungry. Could we go get something to eat?" The guys had been threatened by Titus, the Goblin King. Though he was dead, I didn't know who his allies were. I'm guessing since Lang was spying on me, I couldn't count him among the list of *my* allies. Then there was the mysterious slasher-of-humans enemy who was impatiently waiting for me to go back to work. The anonymous villain who'd murdered the man in the hospital wanted me to reap till I dropped day after day, while he killed civilians to motivate me, the jerk. I hoped that wasn't Prince Langgam's doing, but I knew it could be any person on the council. I wouldn't let anyone take Mason or Von and slice them up for parts. My veins went cold when I thought of the casual way Titus had mentioned abducting Mariang.

But I'd been cooperating. Didn't they see? Why was Lang spying on me now?

I rolled over and whispered in Mason's ear, "Mason, I need you to wake up."

My lips brushed his facial hair and tickled his ear, rousing him only halfway. He turned his head and pressed his puckered lips to mine. Despite my growing determination to get everyone out without alerting Lang, the kiss jerked me into the tryst that had been interrupted earlier. Though it was dark in my room, I started seeing little bursts of the familiar red and yellow as our lips moved together. He smelled like glittering red – I'm not sure how else to describe it. I breathed in each of his exhales as if it was the sweetest, most erotic scent, letting out a moan when he bit my lip. The flutes started their song of seduction, and I was a goner.

"Not cool, mates. I'll take the couch." Von made to sit up, but my arm shot out and dragged him down.

I whispered into his ear, "Pack up the car and get Mariang and Danny to the garage. Lang's spy is watching us."

"Huh?"

Mason was kissing my neck, and I nearly lost my grasp on the English language. My back arched as I released Von. "Do it," I squeaked out. Mason's hand slid down under the covers and gripped my hip possessively.

Von shot out of bed and made a scene of packing a few bags and leaving because of our totally inappropriate display. Not sure how much of an act that was, really. I tried to clue Mason in to the audience we still had, but I could barely locate my body when he kissed my lips again, this time with renewed passion. Von was gone, and we had a whole bed to sow our regrets into. His hands intuited where to move along my body to advance to the next step and the next. It was obvious he'd been married and was used to reaching the end of the dance I'd only just been invited to.

When I heard him murmur "Kara" under his breath, it was just the cold shower I needed. I pulled back, the colors and the flutes deserting me as if they never existed. "What did you just call me?"

Mason looked high as he rolled on top of me, kissing with yet more passion that tugged and ripped at my insides. What had felt the best kind of incredible before was now a jumbled mess. It felt like I was juggling a ball of nails that couldn't help but cut me.

"Mason, we have to stop. We have to..." When his lips didn't part from mine, I slammed my foot on the brakes, rolling away from him and toward the caterpillar I tried not to see. I looked up and saw in the dim moonlight that

Mason's hands were still reaching for me. I wasn't sure what I wanted right then, but I knew for certain I was getting off this ride before I became a roller coaster road-kill statistic. "No more!"

"I need to see her!"

"Stop!" My outstretched hand commanded him clearly, now that his hallucination was beginning to lift. His breath came out in almost animalistic snorts, and I wondered if he was about to transition into a wolf or something. "I'm serious! We need to get some air. This is too fast. It's too much!"

Mason nodded once, his hand slapping his cheek a few times to send a little lucidity into his haze. Then dread twisted his features as he backed off the bed, moving to the opposite side of the room. "What just happened?! What was that? I saw her when I kissed you just then. I wasn't sure the first time, but I definitely saw her!"

"Who? Your wife?"

"Yes! I saw Kara!" he exclaimed, his eyes wide in shock, and then wider still at the horror he'd unwittingly slammed into me.

"You saw your wife? I didn't see anyone, and you saw your wife? You kiss me, and you see another woman?"

"I, um, I didn't mean it like that."

"How exactly did you mean it?"

"October, I wasn't trying to think of her. It's the hallucinations! I can't control what I see. Ask Danny."

I was thunderstruck, and totally beyond being able to

pick my jaw up off the floor. "Get some air. This isn't good. I..." I searched around for anything that would get him to go into the other room with Von. "I need a glass of water."

Mason stood from the bed, shaking his head to right himself as he stumbled out of the room with me. He was clearly upset I was pushing him away from a connection too powerful for either of us to handle without sturdy gloves and bulletproof vests. "Are you mad? I'm so sorry. I shouldn't have blurted it out like that."

"Just shelve it for now." The lights were off in the living room, and I wondered if Von actually had gone to sleep on the sofa. The whispered shouts coming from Ollie's bedroom clued me in to his whereabouts.

Danny all but ran out of the bedroom with his duffel and a bag for Mariang. "I'm going to get a pizza. Anyone hungry?" Danny called through the house.

"I am." Mason raised a finger. "Can't we turn on the lights?"

"Mariang's got a migraine, so just deal with the darkness. Mason, go get in the car." Danny was frustrated that Mason clearly had no clue what was going on.

I pushed past them, casting Danny a knowing look in the dark. The fear that painted Danny was starting to seep into me. I bolted into my bedroom and fished through my things for the essentials, keeping my head down so Wilbur the yellow caterpillar didn't alert his boss. "I'm so cold," I commented, so it looked like I was searching for a change of warmer clothes rather than packing a few days' worth of my things, Mason's and Von's.

Von was onboard and alert, dashing to the kitchen to retrieve his stash of blood. Danny and I had everyone packed in a matter of minutes. My heart was pounding like footsteps of doom stalking toward an untimely demise. Middle of the night escapes weren't part of the job description, yet here we were.

I didn't like Danny touching the small of my back, but it was either that or let him hold my hand. The very notion of people touching my hands gave me the icks, and I sensed we didn't have time for habitual handwashing right now.

My curtains were only half-shut, and my hands grew clammy when I worried one of the guards might peer in and see me. I didn't much care for being a fugitive in my own home, but that was the feeling that crept over me like so many spiders tapping me on the shoulder.

"Stop!" I whispered. "I forgot something."

"It can all be replaced. We have to go now!" Danny's hand on my back wrapped around me and gripped my side.

I felt only medium bad for shoving him as I broke away and darted into the kitchen. Quick as I could, I reached up into the cupboard I kept my medication in. I snatched down the bottle and buried the prescription in my messenger bag I had slung over my shoulder. I knew there were twenty-two pills remaining. That's twenty-two days I had left before I needed to get my prescription filled again. Hopefully this mess would be sorted long before that.

Von met us by the door to the attached garage with Mariang, his finger pressed to his lips. Mariang was in tears on her surrogate brother's arm, clinging to Von while she tried to hold herself together in the dark. We'd escaped Wilbur in my bedroom, but there were the outside guards to contend with, so we moved in silence through the dark in the garage as best we could.

"Keys," Danny demanded of me in a whisper. When I hesitated, he explained, "Your car can handle a chase better than mine if it comes to it. Plus, you've got more trunk space. You three can squeeze in the trunk until we get to Ezra's." He shot Von an apologetic look. "I don't think I could fit in there, and I know Mason can't. He's having trouble shapeshifting."

I wanted to argue as panic welled up in me, but we all sensed the urgency of not getting out at all if we hemmed and hawed over seating arrangements. I slipped back into the house, ran down the hallway and yanked Ollie's comforter off the bed. Mariang was so fragile looking, I didn't want to think what could happen to her dainty bones if Danny hit a pothole too hard.

The garage was spotless and free of clutter, since I scrubbed it once a month. My box of surgical gloves and gym gear were put in the backseat. Von and Danny shoved as many things as they could under the seat and inside the spare tire storage area under the floor of my trunk. I spread out the comforter, making sure to cover every spot we would be laying on, so we didn't bang anything too hard.

"You first," I instructed Von in a whisper as I scratched at my hands. "There's the most room toward the back, so we can stack up that way."

When Von was flattened in the furthest corner of the trunk, Danny and I exchanged worried glances at how little space there was left. "You really can't shift?"

Mason's slate eyes were panicked, not quite sure what was going on. "I don't know what's wrong with me! Something's not working right!"

Danny took control. "Get in the passenger's seat, Mason. If Langgam's spy made it past security... We have to get out of here now, preferably without alerting the guards. You and I are going on a pizza run. Everyone else is asleep inside."

I let Danny steady me with his hand on my elbow as I stepped inside the trunk. When I'd picked out Terence, I certainly didn't base my purchase on how many bodies would fit inside. It was too tight for comfort, and too small not to conjure up old fears I'd tried to bury long ago. Images of my childhood I'd rather never think about flooded up in me. They choked me with claustrophobia, and let me know I would never fully move on from the trauma.

There wasn't enough room next to me left for Mariang, so Danny picked her up like a child and laid her atop me, my hands doing their best to fasten around her like a seatbelt.

Mariang was tiny. I mean, I knew it by looking at her that she was barely a size two, but feeling her feather-like weight atop me made me want to force-feed her pure lard just so she didn't get knocked over by a stiff breeze. She was a couple inches taller than me, but she felt so much smaller. I moved her hair out of her eyes, feeling the wet from her tears. "It's okay, sister. Just pretend we're going camping, okay? Normal families do that. That's all this is. Just going camping." I kissed her temple, catching Danny's eye. He nodded to me, grateful he could trust his most valuable treasure with me for an hour.

Danny tucked a duffel filled with clothes next to my feet. The rest would have to go on the floor in the backseat while we crossed our fingers in hopes that the guards wouldn't notice. Danny brushed his hand over Mariang's face, and she cried harder, though still silently. He leaned his head into the trunk and brushed his lips against hers. "Hey. It's alright. Have I ever not taken care of you?"

She reached out and gripped his hand. It was a simple gesture, but the intensity of their connection manifested itself in an unmistakable beam between them that could not be severed.

Danny gingerly shut the trunk, encasing us in the dark as I swallowed my scream.

22

SHOVED IN A TRUNK

ev had a hard time keeping promises, which was why I didn't ask her for many. Ollie and Allie had it in them that adults should be held accountable for the things they said to kids, but that expectation only lent to more fighting between them and Bev, and more hiding from me. Totally not worth it.

Ollie, Allie and I shared the smaller of the two rooms in the trailer Bev had overrun with stuff she couldn't part with. Sharing a room with your sisters probably wasn't Ollie's ideal living situation, but he made it work. Allie was seven years older than me, and took the mantle of momming me when I needed it. We had bunk beds, and the rule was that Bev could junk up the rest of the house, so long as the bathroom and our bedroom were left alone.

It didn't take long for the bathroom to become unusable. No matter how often the three of us cleaned it and moved stuff out, Bev only saw opportunity for conquest in every inch made available. So Ollie made an arrangement with the trailer two down from ours. He never told us what it cost him, but he rigged it so that the three of us could shower there every morning in Mrs. Kitsa's bathroom. She was a nice old sweetie who sometimes set homemade blueberry muffins on the counter for us in the mornings. She loved to pinch my cheeks and pat the top of my head. Often she confused me with her daughter and called me Heather. She fed me, so I let her call me whatever she liked, since it seemed to make her happy. I'm not sure she ever knew my actual name.

The trailer park had a communal public bathroom near the play yard for us to use the toilet. The bathroom in our trailer was filled to capacity a week after we'd laid down our no-junk-in-the-bathroom edict, and I haven't seen the toilet since. I'm thinking it was ivory.

The fragile system was functional until the great Helzermann's closeout deal. Helzermann's was an odds and ends store not too far from us. It had craft supplies, books, a small non-perishables section and basic home goods throughout. When the store went under, everything was discounted to the hilt, which meant it was open season for Bev.

I didn't even look in the bags that were stacked around our bedroom when I came home from school that afternoon. One look, and I knew it would be World War III between Ollie, Allie and Bev. When the two entered in after me, the yelling started.

I don't remember much about the fight between them. I was only six at the time. All I knew was that I had to get out of there. Using the carefully honed method of moving through the overcrowded home, I scampered away from their fight, burrowing myself in one of the piles of clothes. The mountain of Bev's outfits stretched all the way to the ceiling. She didn't like wearing the same thing too many times. Her brightly colored garments were my safe place where I could tuck myself away until the fighting stopped. Some of the shirts were so new, they didn't even smell like cat urine yet.

It was a long fight, and eventually I fell asleep in the pile. When Ollie's shouts turned fearful and the sound of Allie's tearful beckoning reached me, it was evening, and dark in that part of the house. I tried to climb out of the mountain and run to them, but I was disoriented and took the wrong route to our room. I ran smack into the wall of garbage, which also reached to the ceiling.

I still remember stepping onto something sticky, and then something sharp. Then the mountain fell, burying me in refuse and maggots. I don't remember the things they screamed at Bev that night, but I remember the feel of a maggot sliding into my ear when I was pinned down and couldn't hoist the chaos off myself. Something heavy hit me in the head, and I passed right out. It took Ollie and Allie too many minutes to unearth me, all while Bev freaked out that I had ruined her "special things" that she'd had arranged just the way she liked them.

I had a thing about tight spaces after that.

Ollie and Allie had already taken on the role of being my mama and dad, but after that, security was heightened. I still remember Allie suturing my foot with no anesthesia, while Ollie held me still as I screamed. Not the best way to realize I wanted to be a nurse when I grew up, but whatever.

Allie kept crying, scared at the thought that they'd lost me in the garbage. That was a rough night I still didn't have the words to talk about. I recall them pulling the mattresses off the bunk bed so the three of us could sleep together on the floor with me sandwiched in the middle. I was afraid, but I had Ollie and Allie with me, so I knew that somehow everything would be alright. There was no one but me to hold them through the trauma they'd had to endure, so they were somewhat less hopeful.

Mariang's small body on mine began to feel like a two-ton weight atop my chest. I let out a small whine when the garage door opened. The car started up and we moved down the driveway out into the night.

Von wrapped his arm over Mariang to hold her more securely in place. He cleared his throat. "Two beautiful women who can't get enough of little old me? Not a bad way to go." I knew he could feel my impending freak-out, and was making a joke to cut my building anxiety. His fingers brushed my shoulder, and I felt him pull a layer of

Dear-Lord-get-me-out-of-here. "Hey, it's alright, love. Danny's going at a normal speed, which means they aren't following us."

"It's not that. I..." I didn't know how to voice such a sore subject without going into detail. If I let myself get too upset, I knew the maggots would find me again. One had fallen into my mouth when I screamed for Ollie after I came to. I still recall the horror of them tickling my ears to make my body their new home. I swallowed hard and tried to rein in my crazy. "I have a thing about tight spaces. I can't... I have to get out of here!" The air felt thin, and I sucked in guttural gasps, like someone was choking me. My leg started kicking without my consent. My body jerked as the maggots gunned for me with purpose.

Mariang spoke up through her tears. "Von, is there room for me to lay on you instead? That way October can have some breathing room."

My hands itched like they had trails of Lang's ants crawling up them. "Ollie!" I begged my brother to find me as my chest heaved unnaturally. I knew better than to cry for Allie anymore. She'd stopped answering when we called. I couldn't blame her. She'd given up her adolescence to take care of us. She deserved not to see my face and be reminded of all she missed out on. I couldn't give her much, but I could at least give her that. Tears squeezed out of my eyes, and I was grateful for the pitch black. "Allie, Allie," I sobbed, utterly woebegone. I wished I never needed anything, but in that moment, I desperately needed my sister to find me in the refuse and save me from the avalanche of garbage that crushed down upon me.

Von shifted so he was laying on his back. I breathed afresh when Mariang crawled over atop him. I knew she'd felt a few of my tears, and they'd both heard my choked sobs. The embarrassment clutched me around the throat.

"Close your eyes," Von instructed me in a soothing voice. "Now roll on your side and cuddle up to me. Pretend we're back in your bed and there's loads of space. We just don't need it because we like to sleep close."

"I'm freaking out!" I confessed, finally able to claw at my hands and arms to relieve the trauma, now that Mariang was off of me. My legs were still twitching, unable to find a shred of calm to steady them. I tried arching my back to alleviate some of the suffocating fear that raked at my insides. "I can't do this for a whole hour! The bugs! Get the maggots off me!"

Von shushed me. "We'll be there in five minutes," he lied. "You can do anything for five minutes. I'm here." He drew in an exaggerated breath. "Take a deep one and let it out." His tone changed to something darker that made my spine tingle. "Oh, no. I smell blood! It's fresh. Oh, it's fresh."

"October, you have to stop scratching yourself!" Mariang cried.

I tried to fight against hyperventilation, but the phantom maggots found me in my psychosis. I raked at my cheeks, thrashing around to get them off me. "I can't! I can't!"

I don't know how they did it, but somehow Von rolled Mariang to the very back of the trunk so he could slide on top of me. He boxed me in as he breathed through clenched teeth, his forearms trembling with yearning. "The blood! I need it!" He buried his face in the crook of my neck and howled his desire as I squirmed beneath him. "Just a little taste. I can control myself! Just one taste, and I'll stop."

My limbs were floundering beneath him as I lost myself to two kinds of panic I couldn't logic my way out of. I screamed when Von licked the back of my hand, scared of the sexual groans he made when he tasted the tiny scrapes that were too fresh for him to resist. "No, Von!" His tongue laved between my knuckles, his pelvis rocking against mine. He cried out in self-loathing as he turned back to my neck, licking the skin and sucking too hard. His lips weren't gentle, but they covered his teeth that wanted to puncture and drain me. He was holding himself back from biting down on the veins that had terror and unbidden lust racing through them just below the surface. He sucked hard, and unlike the playful nips he'd teased me with when Ollie had walked in on us, I could tell Von was bruising my skin. "Von, stop!"

"No!" Mariang screamed and pounded on the roof of the trunk. "Danny! Danny! Help!"

23

PUSHED TO THE LIMIT

Danny pulled the car over about a million years into the trip. When the trunk popped open, I choked on my relief in the moonlight. Mason ripped Von off of me and wrestled him to the ground with a look of "holy crap, this just got real" filling his wide slate eyes. Von's teeth were bared and his arms swung out to snatch at me like a wild animal.

Danny wasn't a person I generally looked to for comfort, but when he lifted me out of the trunk, my face sweaty and my hands red from me clawing at them in the dark, I collapsed in his arms. He let out a noise of surprise that I was clinging to him, but I didn't care. "Don't make me go back in there!" I begged, gripping his brown t-shirt like a crazy person. "I can't do it! Don't make me! Ollie! I need my brother. Call Ollie!"

Danny's forced calm was the same soothing balm he

used on Mariang, and I knew his arms around me were pulling the panic out. He was getting better at gently stripping away the layers, even though he hadn't imprinted on me, but I could still feel the jolt as opposed to the slow trickle I experienced when Mason or Von pulled the stress from me. "Hey, it's okay. Calm down."

My knees buckled, but Danny caught me before I hit the ground. "It's not okay! It'll never be okay!" I was beside myself, and completely immune to rational thinking.

"Shh. Hey, I'm here," Danny assured me, waiting until my frantic eyes met his. There was something hard in Danny's gaze that didn't know how to soften, but I could see him trying. "If I'm here, you don't have to worry." For a second, my confusion at his sweetness almost lulled me out of my panic. Almost. "We got enough of a head start. I told the guards I was going to pick up some food. I said it would be best for them to stay out of the house so you three could get some sleep. You can ride in the car for the rest of the trip. Just keep your head down."

"Thank you," I breathed with great relief, the night air filling me with a smidgen of clarity. I smelled pine, and looked around the empty parking lot to find we were parked at a nine-to-five doctor's office lit by a single street lamp half a block down the road.

My knees felt like they'd lost the bones inside as I tried in vain to support my weight. Danny led me to the backseat and sat me down, examining my unnatural panic with his calculating stare. "Claustrophobia?"

I nodded, wishing for a paper bag or something to calm my jumpy breathing. "I'm fine. Thanks for... Let's just go."

"First let me look at you. Did Von bite you?"

"No." I don't know why I covered my neck with my hand, as if Danny couldn't see the obvious tell. I was embarrassed and scared, and wasn't thinking clearly. "I scratched my hands open, and he smelled the blood. He l-licked my h-hands a l-little, but he c-c-c-controlled himself."

Danny tipped my chin up and pried my hand away from my throat, hissing when he took in the damage. "Bollocks. This one's on me. I should never have locked you in a trunk with a vampire. Von always seems so normal until he's pushed to his limit. This was my fault."

I turned from his inspection and reached for my travel first aid kit I saw poking out from under the passenger's seat. I dropped it twice before I finally pulled it onto my lap, my nerves utterly shot and my pride obliterated. Tears fell down my cheeks without my permission, telling Danny more about my weak spots than I had the words for. "Let me fix this f-first. Then we can go."

Danny took the kit from me and bandaged up my trembling hands without a word, probably knowing that his acerbic personality would choose the wrong ones.

"Did you know?" I asked through my hiccupping sobs. I tried to get a hold of myself, but the maggots still felt too near. "The hallucinations. Did you know Mason was s-seeing her when he k-kissed me?"

Danny leaned closer to be sure he heard me right. "What? Seeing who? He told me he saw someone far in the distance on a beach, but he couldn't tell who it was. Did you kiss again? I told him it was probably you."

I eyed Danny through my watery gaze to make sure he wasn't lying to me. "You really don't know?"

"October, if you're trying to tell me something, you're doing a horrid job."

"Nothing. It's nothing. I just wanted to know if you've been hiding things from me that I should know about." I ground my teeth and closed my eyes. "I stored up a few days with all that extra reaping. Could I hop on a plane and go see Ollie?"

Danny watched me closely. "No. You've got to take the sagrado stone to the nations before you can think about taking some time off. After that's done, the burden on us will go down a bit. Then you can go on holiday and see your brother."

I bit my lower lip, debating between fight and flight. "Okay. Go help Mariang. I think I scared her."

Danny nodded, and went to pull from Mariang while Mason concentrated on pouring alternating containers of blood and honey down Von's throat to satiate his hunger. Von was shoved back in the trunk when Danny ruled him unsafe to ride in the car with me. I almost offered to take

Von's place so he didn't feel punished, but I knew the claustrophobia would eat away at me.

"Mariang, would it be okay if I rode shotgun for a while? I'm not feeling so hot," I worked out through my sucked up tears. I didn't want to be anywhere near Mason. Or people. Or magical Terraway creatures.

"Of course. Let's go, Danny." She slid into the backseat next to Mason and cuddled into his side so he could pull from her. She shut the door when Danny revved up the engine.

I rolled the window all the way down. I kept my face near the opening like a dog to try and scoop in all the fresh air I could while Danny drove down the street towards the freeway. "You can keep the window down, but you can't have your face visible like that. Pretty soon people will be looking for us, so stay low." Danny's tone wasn't as harsh as it usually was when he was bossing me. He raised his hand between us. "Can I pull a little from you? You look on the verge of a nervous breakdown."

"No," I ruled, scooting away from him. "Thanks, but no. I'm fine."

Mariang leaned forward in her seat, Danny's brown cardigan covering the right side of her face to shield it from any onlookers. "What was that all about? That wasn't normal claustrophobia. You were having a fit before Von lost his mind."

I shook my head, my face glistening with tears in the

moonlight. "It was nothing. I think it's normal not to like being stuffed in a trunk."

"It is, but that's not it." I could feel Mariang staring at the back of my head with her aqua eyes, gunning for the truth this time, unwilling to let me dodge it. "Tell me what happened to you."

I shook my head as silent tears flowed. These people were in now. They were stuck in my life deeper than the Do Not Pass Go sign I kept firmly in place to fend off conversations exactly like these. Danny intercepted my reach when I made to scratch the back of my right hand, so to compensate, I clawed at my leg through my pajama shorts on my right thigh. My nails skidded on my flesh to alleviate a little of the internal sting. "Just claustrophobia."

Mariang was a lot of things, but when she refused to drop it, I saw in her eyes the same thing that resonated in me: she was a fighter. Despite her slight frame and submissive behavior, she had a will that when kindled, would not bend. "We're traveling together now. You climbed into the trunk without telling us you couldn't handle tight spaces. You should've told us. What happened to you? Why do you always try to hurt yourself with your hands like that?"

I closed my eyes and slumped down in my seat to hide from the world. "Because it doesn't hurt. It makes it feel better."

"Makes what feel better?"

I tapped my chest over my heart. "I'm fine. I just want to close my eyes and forget about it for a minute, okay?"

"Mason, pull something from her," Mariang instructed him, scooting to the side so he could reach me. "She's falling to pieces."

I turned to snarl at his hand. "Touch me and I'll straight up punch you, Mason."

Mason hung his head. "October, I'm sorry. I lost my head. I didn't mean to say those things."

"What things?" Danny asked, trying to keep up.

"Nothing," I answered, turning on my side away from them.

"Before we came out of the bedroom, we kissed again, and I saw—"

"Shut it, Mason! I don't need my business spilled out all over the place. It didn't happen, and it'll never happen again, so forget about it. That's what I plan on doing."

Danny watched my temper spike with confusion. "But you're in love with her. October, Mason's in love with you. That's what it means when an Omen kisses someone, and they have hallucinations. You're not there yet, but Mason saw the colors and sounds and all that, coupled with a hallucination. You only see those when you're in love."

I squinched my eyes shut. "I don't think it works like that when the guy hallucinates about being with his wife when he's supposed to be with you."

No one spoke for the rest of the car ride. All we heard were Von's mournful wails coming from the trunk.

24

SLEEPING ON THE FLOOR

anny booked us a room in a hotel not too far from Ezra's house, ruling even the mansion as unsafe. He'd called Ezra on the way for us to meet him at the hotel to discuss what should be done with Lang's spy and possible untrustworthy guards.

The proper man let himself into our room with the key Danny had left at reception for him under a fake name. Ezra brought with him the backpack that held the sagrado stone. It had been stashed in his safe in the basement so no one would try and steal it from me again. The way that Ezra held it like a covetous treasure told me he was afraid to go anywhere without his eye on it.

The men and Mariang spoke in hushed tones while I unrolled the cot I requested. There wasn't any great place to put it, so I set it up between the two beds. There was no way I was sleeping with Mason anytime soon, and though I wasn't upset with Von, I didn't want him to slip again.

Von sat on the bed while the others stood, staring at the drawn curtains, his back to us. He was part of the conversation, but not. He was upset with himself, even more so than Danny was, which I didn't think possible. I felt for the guy, but didn't have it in me to talk him off the ledge. I was perched on that same precarious precipice, and if I had the sanity to talk someone down, I'd use that magic on myself.

I got off the cot after it was decided Ezra couldn't leave to go to his home, since his mansion had been outfitted with guards as well. He called Lynna, who left the mansion to go stay with a friend in the area. I knew Ezra couldn't fit on the queen bed with Von and Mason, especially since Mason was still having trouble transforming into his wolf counterpart.

I grabbed a few towels and made myself a bed on the floor in the far corner of the room up against the locked door. I was so upset about the day that the prospect of feet germs was only a cup of despair to add to my bucket that had long since overflowed. I ignored Mason, Von and Ezra when they each offered to sleep on the floor in the sold-out hotel, clinging to the space I wouldn't give up without a fight. I felt on the downward swing of a pretty significant low, and knew sleeping in a bed wouldn't fix it. At least my sleeplessness could be explained away by the unforgiving floor with its barely there carpet that offered no cushion whatsoever. If I was on the floor, no one would touch me while I slept.

Ezra was the only one with the guts to kneel down beside me and whisper an apology for all that had gone so wrong that night. Danny had filled him in on everything, which only added to my sweeping low. I didn't want to open my mouth, lest more embarrassing blubbering spill out, so I simply nodded and closed my eyes. The backpack with the sagrado stone was slid into my arms for safekeeping, and I cuddled it like it was my teddy bear.

It took a few false starts, but eventually I drifted off to sleep, finding Philip, my dream makeout buddy waiting for me on a desert island. His smile was genuine and spread across his handsome face, making his white-blond hair appear even lighter. "I was hoping you'd come here."

I didn't say anything; I didn't need to. I cleared the space between us and tugged him down by his bare shoulders, kissing him like I was meant to in a dream.

After a few minutes, Philip pulled back with a breathless grin. "You missed me that much?"

"So much." I reached for him again, but he held up his hand to stop me. "What?"

He traced my cheekbone, scrutinizing my face. "Tell me what's wrong. You're upset about something."

"Too many somethings." Too much had happened for me to talk about. Too much was still swirling in confusion in real life. My fantasy life got to be pure fun and escape.

"It's nothing I want to relive in my dreams. Now kiss me, and make me forget it all."

Philip indulged me, though I could tell he wanted the foreplay of chit-chat. I wondered what it said about me that my dream guy was playing hard to get. My fingertips danced across his chest, playing and flirting and teasing as best I could so I didn't have to think about Mason and the whole mess. There were no hallucinations here. No former wives to worry about.

Philip let go of his resolve to get a conversation out of me and moaned softly into my mouth, tasting my tongue as his hands migrated to the swell of my backside. "Tell me where you are," he demanded between kisses.

"I'm here," I whispered. "I'm here on the island with you."

Philip stopped, as if I'd said something exquisite. He held my face, turning what could have been an animalistic moment into something tender. "You don't know how long I've waited to hear a woman say that to me."

"Shut up and kiss me."

He tried a few more prodding questions, but I put his mouth to use kissing him, which as it turned out, was what Philip did best.

I AWOKE ABRUPTLY TO SOMETHING WET DRIPPING ON MY FACE. I wiped it away, but it was replaced by another drop, and another. When I finally was annoyed enough to open my eyes, a man I had not expected to see was towering over me. Dark brown skin, angular jawline, black eyes and a geometric face tattoo stared down at me. "Lang? What the crap?"

"It's time," he whispered. "We've been patient long enough." Before I had my wits about me, Prince Langgam scooped me and the backpack up in his muddy arms and flopped me down on the bed between Von and Mason.

"No! Stop!" I cried, waking up the others. Danny was slow on the uptake, but Ezra leapt from his cot and rushed Lang. The mud prince stretched out his hands, touching Mason, Von and me just before Ezra crashed into him.

On the first half of my scream, I was in the hotel.

By the second, I was sucked under the ground and dumped in a pile of limbs under the light of the harsh morning suns of Terraway.

25

DELICIOUS BAGA ROOT

y head swam as I tried to make sense of my surroundings. Prince Langgam's rude awakening had yet to be addressed, falling in line behind assessing where the crap I was.

I landed in the mud, which now coated my arms and half my bare legs. I shuddered, my OCD creeping through my bones and reminding me with a constant nagging poke that there was no soap or distilled water for me in Sakuna. There was no escape from the ick that seeped into my pores, taunting me with the knowledge that I would never be normal.

I blinked around in the morning light, breathing through the mania that made me want to scream and wash my hands until they bled. I counted back from ten, telling myself with confidence that my bedroom was perfect, with no dirt or germs in it. If my bedroom was clean, then I could deal with the dirt that was inevitable outside my fortress. I blew my nerves out through pursed lips, reminding myself that my medication was still in my system, whereas the last time I'd been here, I'd been off it.

There was mud everywhere, but through parts of the brown I saw a promise of green. New life was sprouting up here and there across the unending expanse of mud-soaked land, broken up only by clusters of rural huts. I even saw dozens of nourishing beige *buhay* shoots forcing their way through the muck. Though I knew it would take more than those to sustain Sakuna and keep them from dying off, it was a start.

My bare foot sunk an inch into the mud when I stood, and I cringed at the slurpy ickiness that coated my knees and shins. No sooner was I on my feet did I get knocked over by the two battling bulls. Mason and Lang were on each other, with Mason being clearly stronger, but Lang used to fighting in such unhelpful terrain.

"You dare take me from my bed in the dead of night?" Mason threw Lang onto the ground and punched him across the jaw.

Lang grabbed a fistful of mud and slapped it into Mason's eyes. "It's time! We need the sagrado stone. We've been patient long enough. My people need help now!"

"We were getting you help by building up the reaped souls!" Mason growled, not needing sight to punch Lang again. Prince Langgam of Sakuna was huge. He had dark brown skin, black feathery hair and muscles like The

Rock. Lang took as many swings as he could get in on Mason, who was livid his sight was so compromised. Mason was Matruculan, which meant that Lang only had a handful of seconds before Mason overpowered him with his superhuman strength that came from his uncut dreads.

Ezra pulled me back up and guided me away from the raging men. "Are you hurt?"

"What the crap is going on? What just happened?"

"Prince Langgam apparently didn't want to wait. It looks like the mission to divide up your sagrado stone among the seven nations starts tonight."

"Six nations," I corrected him. "You forget I'm a mass-murderer. Thanks to me, the Goblins don't exist anymore." I still couldn't shake that, no matter how often Ezra tried to tell me it was all somehow kosher.

Ezra looked around, and I watched as his tension deflated slightly. "Prince Langgam didn't bring Mariang or Danny down here. That's good. They'll be safer up there. I know Danny will be sore he's missing out, but my daughter's not well enough for the journey."

Von came up behind us. His gym shorts and dark green t-shirt were spattered with mud, but somehow he looked like he was the model for the outfit, and it was supposed to come off the line looking exactly like that. He was the perfect magazine ad for a line of soccer apparel. He had a few dots of mud across his angular jawline, but it only made him more handsome. I don't know how he did it. Maybe it was a vampire thing. We were all barefoot, and I was wearing the same purple cotton shorts and snug yellow t-shirt I'd gone to sleep in.

Mason had Prince Langgam in a spine-twisting hold on the ground. I looked around at the land that was mud, covered in more mud. "Let them duke it out. I don't much care. Can I just break off a piece of the stone now and put it anywhere?"

"No, dear. We'll keep the stone hidden as much as we can until we get to the castle. In the courtyard, there's a well that feeds the people. We sink it down into the well, and the rock will forever cure the main supply of water of any imperfections. Then the crops will grow more easily and the water will remain safe for drinking as long as that stone is there." Ezra pulled out a handkerchief from his pocket, but it was stained with mud. "Oh, sorry. I meant for you to be able to wipe off your face if you wanted, but it appears I'm useless."

"Aw, thanks. I'm alright. And that's a pretty nifty little rock we've got, if can do all that."

"Hold tight, darling. I'll port us all to the surface once Mason's finished punishing Prince Langgam."

I tilted my head up at Ezra, ignoring the burn on the backs of my hands that longed to be scratched. "If we're here, couldn't we just finish the stone bit now? I mean, as fun as it is being abducted, I have a feeling it'll stop once the nations each have their piece."

Ezra stared down at me with compassion and something that looked akin to pride. He stood straighter and rolled his shoulders back. "I think that's a splendid idea."

"How far to the castle?" I grabbed the backpack out of the muck and cringed as I slid it onto my back. I knew one errant touch from the rock, and it would turn anyone but me into stone, so I made sure I was the one who carried it in the backpack, on the rare chance the bag ripped and it accidentally touched the carrier.

"That's the spirit," Ezra cheered. "We can start out toward those mountains over to the north. Those two will catch up when they tire of deciding who will dominate this time around."

"Mason never tires of that battle. It's constant," Von groaned. "Shoes would have been nice. And you know Danny will be in a right state that he got left behind."

Ezra rubbed his forehead as he spoke. "Danny's usually in a state over something. At least this time it's a true fit he can throw." I eyed Ezra appraisingly at having cast out a disparaging remark about the golden boy who guarded his daughter. He shrank noticeably. "Not that I don't admire his judgment. I only meant this time I'm sure his upset will last quite long."

I started walking toward the mountains in the distance that seemed so small on the horizon. I began to wish for comic book hero powers to inhabit the magical creatures I traveled with. If only one of them could snap their fingers and sha-zam us there in a blink. "So none of you can teleport? I mean, Lang got us down here. Couldn't he have gotten us a little closer?"

Ezra was patient with my limited knowledge of all things unicorn. "Only royalty and certain high-ranking officials can port in and out of a country, and we always land in the same spot that welcomes newcomers. You always enter Sakuna right here, for example. The atmosphere's easier to navigate Topside, so we can port anywhere on earth with more precision. Anyone who ports into Sakuna lands themselves right here in this spot of mud, though. But you can port out from anywhere in the land."

"Huh. Alright." I didn't look to see if the others were following me. I wanted to make good time, and knew the wrestling twins weren't going to sort things out any time soon. I was barefoot, covered in mud, braless and in my pajamas. I pretty much wanted to get this first leg of the journey over with as soon as possible. I could drop part of my doorstop in the well in the castle courtyard and head on home. No big deal.

I made it maybe twenty yards before my lungs started to complain that the oxygen felt too thick to drag into my prematurely tiring body. I remembered the last time Lang had abducted me, I'd lasted maybe twenty minutes before nearly passing out. I was a decent runner, but I knew I'd never make it to the mountain in time. "Oh, crap on a stick. Anyone find a solution to me not being able to breathe down here?"

Ezra frowned and turned to the dueling bears, who were now completely covered in thick brown muck. "Gentlemen, if you'll excuse me a moment." He tried to get their attention with his cutie pie British manners, but failed. Von clapped his hands and whistled, but Mason was intent on making Lang suffer for besting us.

I shook my head and stomped over to the men, counting to five before the prison worker in me reared her mud-spattered head. I reached down and snatched at a pressure point on Mason's shoulder and Lang's, cutting their fight short. Or stopping it at intermission. They seemed pretty committed to the takedown that Mason had been clearly winning.

"Ow! Ow! Stop!" they exclaimed, squirming like little boys as I twisted the nerve to leave a sting I knew would last at least a minute.

I had them both on their knees in front of me with all the practiced patience of a kindergarten teacher. "Boys, does anyone have a plan for me breathing down here? Not that I don't love watching Lang try to kick your butt, Mason. And not that I don't love watching Mason humiliate you on your own turf, Lang. But see, over the years I've developed this terrible addiction to breathing."

Lang shook off my hand and rubbed the sore spot between his neck and his shoulder. "I've got the *baga* root. I thought of everything this time."

I reached my hand under his chin, relishing the small window where I had an advantage on his gargantuan height. Lang looked like The Rock, but meaner. The Rock had that sweetie pie adorableness that got him occasionally cast in kids' movies. Lang possessed no such softness. I thumbed his face tattoo, surprised he let me play with his skin without a fight as he knelt before me. "You took me without my shoes, a change of clothes or even checking that a full stock of souls was stored up. Not that I don't appreciate you wanting to help your people, but darlin', you didn't think this plan through."

Lang didn't apologize. His eyes darkened with gravity that fell like a gavel of doom. "Father made good on his word."

It took me a solid three seconds before it clicked what Lang meant. My intake of breath probably wasn't wise, given the rationing I would soon have to do with my oxygen, but it was involuntary. "He made the pregnant women give up their babies? When? But I've been reaping overtime! I made sure there were enough souls so that wouldn't have to happen!"

"It was already in motion. Father ground up *patayin* root and threw it into the river. All the pregnant women lost their young."

Ezra and Von both gasped, their hands covering their mouths.

Lang pressed on. "Next will be the prisoners if another drought happens. There's no waiting anymore. Father said he'd kill everyone in his prison on the first day the suns waver this time."

"Then the elderly," I recalled, finishing his thought for him as I ignored the angry growl from Mason. "Gerda. She'll die if I drop the ball." I softened as I glimpsed the note of fear in Lang's black eyes as he nodded. It was then that I saw that he wasn't trying to be a monster by taking me in the middle of the night. He was desperate for help. He loved the old woman who softened him and looked after him well into adulthood. She'd been kind to me, too. "You're scared for her."

"Yes. That's why I couldn't wait any longer. When Titus attacked, I knew I had to take you first before anyone else did. We need that stone. I won't let her die." Lang leaned into my touch, looking up at me with suddenly earnest black eyes that had more vulnerability than I'd anticipated. "I waited until you had at least a week's worth of souls. That's more than enough time for you to deliver the sagrado piece to my land."

"A week doesn't mean a thing if I can't breathe."

Mason stood and watched me thumb the prince's chin with a firm look of dismay tugging down the corners of his mouth into his muddy beard. "October, what you're doing is inappropriate. He's a prince, and things are quite different between men and women down here."

"You don't talk to me," I said quietly, reminding him he didn't have a leg to stand on with me. I'd trusted Mason, let my guard down enough to sleep in his arms, allowed him to sleep in mine. He was the second man I'd ever kissed, and he used the rare hallucinogenic effect that kissing an

Omen has on a civilian of Terraway to see his long deceased wife. I'm not sure how many levels that was allowed to hurt me on, but I'm guessing nine levels of pain wasn't too many for the sting to still feel fresh.

"She can do with me what she wants, if only she'll save my people." Lang was sincere, which softened me further. It was getting difficult to breathe, but I spent a few seconds watching his face for signs of falsity. I was generally pretty good at spotting blatant lies. "Please, Lady October. I can't take you back until my people are safe. We need this."

I'm not sure why it made me feel powerful to make a man behave like a boy, but when Lang's hand covered mine as he looked up into my eyes, I found I couldn't maintain my anger. I knew I could either throw a fit that he'd acted impulsively, or I could suck it up.

Guess what I'm the queen of.

"On your feet, soldiers," I said as I flicked Lang's earlobe, releasing us both from the almost moment. When Lang stood, his six and a half feet of towering half-naked muscle made my bossiness laughable, but I went with it anyway. "Let's move it, boys."

Lang pulled a gnarled piece of ginger out of his pocket and extended his filthy hand to me. "Here. Eat this, and you'll be able to breathe for about a day. I've got more than enough for the journey."

"Oh, cool. Thanks. How do I... Do I peel it? Doesn't anyone have any water to wash it off with?" The pocket lint and mud and who knows what other kinds of germs were crawling all over the thumb-sized bit of root I was expected to put in my mouth.

Von gave me a you-can-do-it look complete with a thumbs up. "You just shove it down the hatch, love. We don't have any water on us."

I shot him a look that begged him to be joking, but I knew this was par for the course. My OCD was being tested left and right, and I knew I couldn't punk out with all eyes on me. It was a tough call which one would win out: my OCD or my need to breathe.

Von moved toward me and held his hand out for the root, careful not to touch me. He'd been avoiding me since he'd tasted my blood last night and attacked. I wasn't mad, but I had a healthier fear of him now. I'd been sleeping with a kitten who turned out to be a tiger instead. He'd told me he was a tiger. I don't know why I hadn't believed him.

Von wiped off some of the dirt, trying his best to clean the root for me. "Better?" he asked as he handed me the thing that would save my life down here.

I guess beggars can't be choosers, but we *can* be wusses. A quiet whimper was the only sound that made it out of me when I choked down the root. It was squishy and spongy, like overchewed gum when I bit through the center. It tasted like licorice mixed with a piercing lemon rind that made my eyes water as I choked. "Ack! That's terrible! Oh!" I stuck out my tongue like a cat hoarking up a fur ball.

The germs infested my insides, flooding through me like a thousand ants that wanted to lay eggs in my organs. It was one of the few times I actually wanted a Puller, but neither of mine could be trusted.

Instead, I reached for Ezra, gripping his forearm in distress to keep from screaming and clawing at my body. The sweet man drew me into a hug I couldn't participate in, but desperately needed. It wasn't quite the same magic as pulling, but Ezra's kindness did its best to flush the impurities out of my system, chasing away the plague of ants and replacing it with a fatherly affection I'd tried never to need. "You're safe with me," he promised, not taking offense that I couldn't bring myself to hug him back.

It took more than a few seconds, but eventually I nodded. "Thank you."

Lang broke into the moment of much-needed serenity with a loud, "Are we ready, then?"

I pulled away from Ezra, unable to look him in the eye after being such a baby in his embrace. "Okay, let's go quick. If we can get there in a day, then I won't have to eat any more of that stuff. Oh, man! Gross." I turned sheepishly to Lang. "I mean, thanks for thinking of that. Real nice of you."

"Of course."

It took a few minutes, but as we trekked on I found I could breathe normally again. Ezra and Mason were deep in a conversation about the best way to sink the rock into the well, debating between dropping it in under cover of night and making a big announcement in the daylight.

"If they don't know it's there, no one will try to find it."

"But then we're tossing a needle into a haystack. What if something happens to it?"

Mason shrugged. "I think there's less a chance of that if we let it sink in the well with no one trying to uncover it."

We weren't making great time, so I picked up the pace. The rock in my backpack dug against my lower back, but I tried to ignore the discomfort as I trudged through the sticky and slippery surface. No sooner had I skidded and caught myself did Von's arms go flailing out as he slipped in the mud. "I gotcha!" I cried as my hands went to his hips, steadying him just before he fell.

"Whew! Thanks, Peach." He grinned at me and then caught himself, looking away as he recalled his shame.

"Hey, Von?"

"Yeah?" He walked a healthy distance from me as we took up the lead position in the group, setting the brisk pace.

"We're okay, you know. I mean, as far as I'm concerned. We're cool."

His voice quieted so as not to be overheard by Ezra. "How can you say that? I nearly killed you!"

"But you didn't. If you had killed me, I would've flipped out on you. I would've haunted you right good. Turned out the lights when you're reading, levitate your breakfast, freeze your boxer briefs – the works." I blushed at mentioning the specific kind of underwear he preferred. I wasn't sure how I felt about the fact that I knew such intimate things about Von.

"My evil little ghoul," he sniggered, tiptoeing back into our casual back and forth that neither of us wanted to go the whole journey without. "Are you sure? I know I scared you. I completely understand if you want Mason to pull from you for a while until you're not so frightened of me. I'm really fine now. It's just the fresh human blood that unhinges me. So if you could try not to make yourself bleed and smell like a delicious Christmas feast, I'd be grateful."

"I'll do my best to smell like an old can of tuna."

"Oh, you. Save the sexy talk for when we're alone next. I can't take your slutty little come hithers."

I laughed, and the emotion mingled with the movement of my chest and felt just right. I didn't like being too serious for long. Von was my sexy platonic buddy who was always good for a laugh. "That's much better. I don't like it when we're at odds. Much better when we're just being odd together."

He tossed me a look that was relief mixed with sincerity. "I really am sorry, November. I lost control, but I'm good now."

I lowered my voice when he moved closer. "I don't want Mason pulling from me today. I need some time to bounce back from what happened. Apparently I'd rather be killed by you than used by him."

Von reached his arm around me and squeezed my shoulder, securing me to his side so we walked in step. He was half a foot taller than me, but somehow we fit like pie and ice cream.

I felt Von pull, sighing as he let a little of the air out of my stress balloon.

26

BRUISED PEACH

"There's a river up ahead for those of you in need of a cool-off." Lang pointed to the small body of water in between a series of huts in the distance and a sparse forest butting up against the slow trickle that ran over rocks and logs.

We were all sweating through the heat of the day. We'd tried to keep to the fringes of the land so we wouldn't be stopped by Lang's adoring fans. He was well-liked throughout his father's nation, and was the only one from the royal family of Sakuna who lived among the people and took up their cause before the king. Hometown hero stuff, for sure.

"Be careful not to drink," Lang warned us. "This water's not safe, especially to outsiders. Bathing only."

That put up my red flag. I was now already more than half a day without my medication that kept my crazy at bay. Dipping into a polluted river was just plain outside the realm of possibility for me. I was hot from their two fireball suns that glowed with blue tongues overhead. The humidity was all-encompassing. It felt like the most murderous, sticky summer day, and I really wished for an egg to see if it would fry on one of the rocks. I was also pretty hungry, so I wished for an egg just to eat, too.

Egg salad on rye.

Fried egg on toast with Mama McCray's homemade strawberry rhubarb jam.

A poached egg with warm grits.

My stomach groaned, begging me to think of something else.

Eggs, eggs, eggs.

I watched the men wade into the river up to their chins at the deepest point in the middle. I sat on the embankment, trying to pretend I didn't need to cool down or get some of the mud off me.

"October Grace, are you alright?" Ezra asked, his kind manner always confusing me. He was engaged to Bev, so I kept trying to shift him into the role of father in my life, but the concept was so foreign to me; I didn't quite know how to shove the puzzle piece into the gaping hole I'd grown up having to ignore.

"I'm fine. I don't mind a little mud." At my response, Mason waded toward me, but I held up my hand. "You go enjoy yourself. I said I'm fine."

"You're being stubborn."

I shrugged. "I think I've earned the right to speak my mind and not give a flying pig what you think about it."

"Is something wrong with our waters?" Lang asked, slightly miffed that I was acting like a spoiled princess.

"Is that a trick question? You just told us they weren't safe to drink from." I didn't mean to be a snob; I just couldn't will my feet to move me closer into the river. I could feel the amoebas inching toward me, wanting to seep into my crevices and infect me with their alien germs I wouldn't know how to treat. Plus, I didn't know how to swim, and it looked pretty deep in the middle.

Von came out of the water, shirtless, clean and grinning like the fool I couldn't help but smile at. He extended his hand to me. "Let's go get that mountain, November." I took his hand so I didn't look rude, and felt him shoot waves of tranquility into me, calming my anxiety that always came with shaking someone's hand. He hoisted me to my feet, but before I could grab my backpack off the muddy surface, he surprised me by using the upward momentum to pull me off the ground and throw me over his shoulder. "Change of plans!"

"Von! Put me down!" I squeaked, my protest only just barely heard before he threw me into the river. I landed with a splash between Ezra and Lang.

I screamed under the water until I found my footing. I popped my head out of the water with a murderous glare that was quickly replaced by sheer panic. I tried to run out of the river to escape the germs that were now stuck to me, but Von met me halfway, tackling me backward and plunging us both under. I felt him grab my waist and hit me with another dose of calm-the-crap-down. This time when I surfaced, I clung to him. I wasn't sure what he could do to ward off the germs, but hoped in my desperation that he provided some sort of magical anti-microbial protection. "I can't do this! I can't swim!" I whispered, chattering against him. The water wasn't even all that cold probably, but the extreme heat of the day made the normal temperature of the water feel like a much needed bucket of ice.

Von held me, smiling with his "Of course I can throw people into the river. I'm charming" kind of grin. He squeezed me to him until I finally let go of the tight hold I had on my body. He chuckled when I rested my cheek on his shoulder, my trembling hand clinging to his bare chest. "I bet you can learn to swim. I bet you can do all sorts of things you never thought you could."

I didn't care about decorum; it was Von. My legs and arms were wrapped tight around him as I whispered, "Von, my medication's back with all our stuff in my world. I can hold out a little longer, but in a day or so I won't be doing so hot."

"You want me to stay close? Be your own personal drug?"

I nodded, hating myself for the weakness, but I knew I needed to say something. "Thanks. Don't say anything to the others, okay?"

"It'll be our secret. Though Mason knows all about it. I'm sure Ezra's been filled in by good old Danny, the lousy snitch." He shook his head in feigned disappointment at his brother. "So really you don't need to worry about them finding out your secret. And if you can think about forgiving Mason, we can do a double pull, and it'll make you feel that much better."

"No. I don't need Mason. He'll just stress me out. Only you, if that's okay. Just until we get home." I was buoyant in his arms, despite the fact that my soul felt weighted.

"Well, my little peach, it looks like we just became one of those couples who can't get through life without holding hands." He pried my wrist off his chest and linked his fingers through mine, resting our tangled hands over his heart. Every now and then I had to remind myself that Von didn't want me. He was a hopeless flirt who'd slept with my friend Katrina the first night he'd met her, not half an hour after charming my friend Rachel nice and good. I'd been quarantined to friend zone, which was fine. I had enough drama without indulging in fantasies that would never come true.

"Thanks, Von. You're a good buddy."

"I've been called worse."

A small splashing nearby made me look up to see Ezra swimming toward us with his eyebrows furrowed. "October Grace, what is... Oh! Oh, darling!"

"What?" I was confused when Von dropped my hand

and gasped in disgust. "Why are you looking at me like that?"

"Your neck! I'm a monster. If there was any doubt before, there certainly isn't now. I'm sorry." Von looked sick to his stomach, hurt lacing through his sudden melancholy that tugged at my heart. "I bruised my peach."

"What gives?"

Ezra showed me his hands to prove their innocence before lifting my chin so he could get a better look at my throat. "It doesn't look like he broke the skin, but darling, you've got bruises all over your neck. I mean, it looks like you've been beaten and choked. I guess I didn't see it because of all the mud, but oh, it's dreadful."

Von started wading closer to the edge, making sure my feet could touch the ground. Then he dropped me and all but ran for the shore.

Of course I couldn't look down to see my own neck. "Huh. Well, it doesn't hurt. Von controlled himself, so no one needs to make a big deal about it." I raised my voice to carry to my favorite vampire who was standing at the water's edge, visibly hating himself. "You hear that, Von? Nothing happened, so let it go."

"How can you say that? I nearly killed you! If Danny hadn't pulled me off you, I wouldn't have been able to stop."

I waded toward him until the water only lapped at my ankles. "It's enough. You did great. You got ahold of yourself in time."

Von's mismatched eyes conveyed a multitude of emotions that soaked into my pores to tell me just how devastated he was over this, though he couldn't meet my gaze. "Monsters are dangerous. *I* am dangerous. You need to understand that."

I tried to push out all other thoughts, ignoring our audience as I grabbed his face and pulled it down so he'd have to look at me. In his self-loathing, he closed his eyes. I brought his forehead to rest against mine, inhaling the sweet cigar scent that I was learning to grow a fondness for. "You are not a monster, Von. In the next life, you can be a monster all you like. You can have three heads, horns and forked tail. You can take out whole villages with your fire breath if you want." I took a chance with my daring, reached up and pecked his lips. I was aware of the fangs lurking beneath, but I had to show both of us that Von could be trusted to master the dangerous weapon that he was. My whisper came out fierce as I squeezed my palms to his temples. "But in this life, you don't destroy things. In this life, you heal me."

The hug that gripped me was aggressive and desperate, crushing me to him so tightly, it squeezed a little of the air from my lungs. His strong forearms constricted around me, saying more than words could. I felt his heartbeat and knew that he'd just needed someone to believe in him. He'd needed Ezra to give him a job, purpose, to believe that he'd be able to hold on and remain himself for another month, and another. His lips brushed my ear, making goosebumps erupt on the back of my neck when he whispered, "I adore you." It wasn't a flirt or a statement, but a pledge that tied us more firmly together while we figured life out. "Never ever leave me, November."

"Never," I promised.

We held each other until the others had their fill of bathing in the river. Ezra cleared his throat to snap us out of our moment I could've lived in forever. "Perhaps it's time to return to our journey, yeah?"

Though Von's casual demeanor was dampened after he'd seen my bruises, we linked our fingers as we started walking toward the mountains again. I knew he was pulling stress from me, but I like to think our solidarity was taking a little unease off his plate, as well.

SACRIFICE AND SELF-LOATHING

ason walked behind us, and I felt his eyes on me as Von and I led the way with our brisk pace. My sun-drying shorts hung low on my hips, and the mud caked my bare feet and calves as evening neared.

Lang was our tour guide, so when he spoke, our splinters of conversation died down. "The curfew will be in effect soon, but no need to worry. The sigbins know not to attack members of the royal family." Lang looked overhead to the setting balls of fire in the sky. "Feel that? The heat's already more bearable. The sagrado's only been in our nation less than a day, and the sun's responding. Tomorrow will be more tolerable for the workers. Soon children will be able to play outside again. The crops won't be scorched as soon as they're ready for picking. This is good. This is real good."

I had my debates about the sun being bearable. It looked to be around six o'clock in the evening here, and judging from the sweat rolling down my bruised back from the doorstop banging against me with every step, the temperature was dipping down to just under a hundred degrees. "You know what makes me look so hot?" I asked Von in a faux breathy voice to exaggerate some good old sexy talk.

Von raised an eyebrow at me. "I want to say your ample breasts, but I'm thinking I'm not allowed to guess that without getting slapped."

I pointed north. "The two suns, goof. Because they're hot. I can actually feel the sweat running down my back."

"So I'm not allowed to talk about your breasts, then? No fun."

"Not unless I'm allowed to motorboat you later."

Von let out a loud laugh that lightened the moods of everyone, though no one else knew the details of our conversation, thank goodness. He squeezed my hand, and despite the heat, we walked close, enjoying the friendship that was starting to feel familiar and true. Von's smile mutated to confusion. "I hear something. A pounding, sort of. Give it a second for you less brilliant folk to pick up on it."

"I hear it, too," Mason concurred.

I strained to hear anything different, but all I got were the bugs that buzzed and chirped in the air around us.

They'd given us a wide berth on Lang's command, but it was all still pretty unnerving.

Lang sniffed the air, his frown becoming more pronounced as he pointed to a group of men far off in the distance. "Something's wrong. Those are my father's men, but they're not scheduled to do any rounds in this area tonight." He pointed to a cluster of soldiers running in our direction, his eyebrows pushed together in alarm. He pressed his muddied hand to my shoulder. "Lady October, run with your Reapers to the huts and find shelter until the soldiers pass. Ezra and I can speak with the head of the guard back in his home to get their marching path for the next day, so we don't come across them again on our way to the main city. Hide in the village until I come for you. You can trust the people here. They'll take care of you." His eyes clouded over. "But not with Gerda. Anyone's hut but hers."

I knew he didn't want Gerda brought into anything seedy. "Splitting up? Are you sure that's a good idea?" I wasn't a fan of anything that took me away from my guide who had the backstage pass to Sakuna.

"It's our only choice. We'll meet you at the base of the mountain over there. Once the troops pass this area by, you can head that way." His lips tightened when he examined his hand and slowly slid the gold ring off his finger. He gripped my wrist and turned my arm, pressing his ring into my palm and closing my fingers over it. "Show the people in the village this, and they'll hide you without question. It's my signet ring." He looked hesitant, as if he didn't want to loan me so grand a thing. "Don't lose that."

"Okay. Thanks, but are you sure…"

Lang ignored my pause and reached out to shake Von's free hand like a warning. "Keep her safe."

"You don't have to worry." Von postured, looking heroic and strong. Lang shook Mason's hand in the same fashion, though Mason was used to being seen as big and strong, so he didn't puff his chest at the recognition of being entrusted with something big.

Though I wasn't totally understanding of everything that was going on, I ran with Von and Mason to the cluster of huts inland, clutching Lang's ring tight, since it was too big to fit around my fingers.

We passed the first few huts and ducked into one that had the door open, scaring the two women inside. They shrieked when we entered without knocking, like only entitled buttholes do. I felt terrible. The two women had the same sun-browned skin, were bone thin and had been weaving baskets together before our super rude intrusion.

"Apologies, ladies. I'm Mason of Sombi. I'm traveling with the new Omen." Their gasps broke out at his title, and doubled at mention of me. I didn't know what to do, so I waved lamely, making Von chuckle under his breath. Mason was in full take charge mode, which was good, since I had no idea how to navigate the politics of this country. "She's here to free your people from the famine, but we need to stay hidden until the soldiers pass. Can we hide with you in here?"

To sway them, I opened my fist and displayed Lang's ring, eliciting a gasp from them. I slid it onto my thumb. Though it was very loose, I closed my fist and hoped it would stay in place.

One of the two with a baggier shapeless shift on her bony frame stood. "Of course. Any enemy of the king is a friend of mine."

Without warning, Gerda and a teenaged boy let themselves inside. "You have to hide!" Gerda warned us. Her wide hair shone like snow against her wrinkled brown skin. "The soldiers are coming. They're not just checking the area for extra *buhay*, they're coming into each hut to do a search to see if anyone's hoarding it."

The boy's eyes fell on me with wonder and worry. "If they find the Omen here, they'll take her in for sure!"

Gerda closed the distance between us, scooping up my hands to examine Lang's ring on my thumb. "My boy. Is he alright? I saw you coming to the village. Where is he?"

I tried to be a grownup and not pull my hands from hers. I even went so far as to give her fingers a squeeze to reassure her. "Langgam's gone to talk to the head of the guard. He sent me to hide in here."

Mason postured, and then looked in my direction as if deciding something. "It's too risky to have you holding onto the stone, October. If Geon's men capture you, you'll be delivering the stone right into his hands. You trust this woman?"

I looked to Gerda, meeting her kind eyes. "Lang does. That's enough for me."

Mason slid the backpack off of me, not missing a beat. He met Gerda's eyes. "Whatever you do, don't open this. Inside is the sagrado stone. The king can't know it's in Sakuna, or the rest of Terraway will suffer. It's our job to make sure that doesn't happen." He motioned between himself and the teen, making the young man stand taller with pride at being given such a magnificent goal. "This is a grand quest. Can I trust you to help Gerda with this?"

The teen's eyes steeled and his spine straightened. "On my honor, King Mason."

The corner of Mason's mouth lifted slightly that some people still acknowledged his former title. "Very well. Take this to Prince Langgam. He's on his way to the Captain of the Guard's home, and you must reach him before he gets there. He'll know what to do with it. He's the only one you can trust. Unless you see King Ezra Manaul. He can be trusted, too."

"Sama," the boy said with fear in his bugged eyes.

Gerda clarified. "We've heard rumors that Sama's army is on its way to Sakuna to deliver rations. If Sama's men see the new Omen, they'll kill her for certain! It's why King Geon's men are doing a search of each hut for extra *buhay*. He's going to destroy it all so we have no choice but to take

Sama's rations. It was one of Sama's requirements for taking his help. Total surrender."

The muscles in Mason's neck tightened. "So it's already decided, then? King Geon's sided with Sama?"

The boy nodded gravely. "If they find the Omen, they'll take her and offer her up to Sama." His eyes darted to me in silent apology. "If she can't reap, then Terraway will be completely dependent on Sama and his rations. Then he's got us under his thumb, where he wants us."

My blood ran cold at mention of the jaggoff who wanted to keep Terraway from being cured so he could have the control. Some of the countries already flocked to him for rations. Now that they might not need to? Sama wanted to get his hands on some October Grace ribs right quick so he could get back behind the steering wheel. "Where can we hide?"

The women looked around their completely bare hut that had no closets or beds to duck under. Their straw mattress was on the mud floor. Mason's fists clenched. "I can defend the hut. Ladies, maybe you should take up in a neighboring home so you aren't accomplices."

The woman with the baggier shift stood, determination mingling with malice in her black eyes. "I'll gladly fight with you. King Geon forced the *patayin* root on me, poisoning the water so we'd lose our young." She rubbed her flat belly. "He took my baby from me, so I'll help you take a few men from him with a knife in my hand and a smile on my face." She reached under the bed and pulled out a knife with a crooked blade. It looked ripe for a horror movie, and girlfriend looked all kinds of heroic. She had high cheekbones and that vicious kind of tenacity in her glare that made you believe she was ruthless and capable of destroying an army, even though she was all skin and bones. Though life had stolen from her, she wasn't going to be defeated. Her brown face radiated with unparalleled beauty. She extended her wiry hand to me. "I'll not give you my real name, in case you're captured, but you can call me Malisiya. And this is my sister; you can call her Higanti."

Higanti nodded to us with unwavering determination. She rolled her shoulders back as if her hut was a fortress, and she wouldn't see it ransacked without a fight.

I moved toward the teen boy. He was gangly from malnourishment, but still had two inches on me. His teeth poked out at odd angles, and he looked down on me with reverence that was tainted with a little fear for my safety. "This is it for Sakuna, then. It all rests on you getting this backpack to Prince Langgam. What's your name?"

Gerda shook her head. "We'll find you when this is over. It's best you don't know the boy's real name, or his mother's or aunt's. If they capture you, they'll kill anyone who helped you. Best they can't torture the boy's name out of you."

I gulped, suddenly grasping the severity of my plight. "Um, okay. That's fair. And totally horrifying." I clung to Von's hand, and he made a show of standing straight and donning a breezy smile so I didn't freak out. I couldn't believe his calm confidence was actually starting to work on me.

Higanti moved the baskets to the side and took another knife from behind the water basin that sat in the corner of the barren home. "Son, gather the women. Tell them it's time."

The boy's eyes widened. "Yes, Mama." Then he engulfed his mother in a tight hug of desperation. "In case we're killed today, I'll see you in *Sombi*."

I hadn't been witness to many teen boys hugging their mothers, and realized what a sacred sight it was. Judge, Darius and Terence had hugged Mama McCray plenty of times, and I'd always felt like I'd been watching an episode of the Brady Bunch. I'd walked away feeling warm, fuzzy and wishing that kind of utter acceptance could happen to me.

Ollie and Bev had never hugged in living memory.

I could see the connection between the two in the hut, and wondered if they were so close because they had no clutter or junk between them in the barren space. Perhaps if Bev had cleared out some of her treasures, she could've seen the real stack of gold in Ollie. I made a mental note to learn to be a better hugger by the time I saw him next. I swallowed and wrapped my arms around Von's middle, knowing he'd let me practice on him any old day. Von was good like that.

Von leaned his cheek on the top of my head, whispering his assurances that everything would be alright, because he was there. "Who could possibly snatch you up while I'm looking all dashing and fearsome? I'm here, darling," he vowed.

"I was just going to say the same thing to you." I wanted to hide in the safety of Von's embrace, to lose my worries completely and tuck my fears under a rock so I could run far, far away without the weariness of my many burdens.

"I love you, my boy," Higanti whispered through her tears to her son. "Now go tell the women to prepare. The soldiers are on their way. They'll not take our food or our Omen." The boy ran next to Gerda with the backpack, and we all watched their escape to make sure no one intercepted them along the way.

I rubbed my forehead into Von's chest that was warm and inviting before pulling away so I could address both guys. "Okay, Von? Mason? We can't hide here. Obviously we can't get these women killed."

"What life do you think this is for them?" Mason countered with a snarl. "Their biggest hope is to meet as undead so *I* can bury them in Sombi. King Geon should know better than to take the babies from the women of his land. He should know better than to surrender to Sama. He has a fight coming to him, and I'll see to it I lead the people of Sakuna in their rebellion."

Higanti stood tall. "I'll stand with my sister. King Geon's spilled enough of our blood. He'll not take another from our home. I know your quality, King Mason of Hayop. You take care of the dead who roam to Sombi." Her eyes steeled against the sadness that rose up in her. "My husband died a few months ago in an accident at the fire pits. The only hope I have for his eternal rest is that maybe you found him and gave him a proper burial. He died and turned before I could collect his body. My sword is yours. The other women will come."

Mason looked like he wanted to argue at involving two skeletal women in his small battalion, but he nodded with gratitude. "Thank you, ladies. I'm Matruculan, so I hope your swords get no use at all. You can help by protecting the Omen. Von and I are her Reapers, so he'll stay with her while I fight."

Malisiya gasped when she noticed Von's one gold eye. "Vampire!" Then she examined Von more closely, no doubt taking in that he was sentient and you know, not rabidly attacking everyone for their blood. "Oh, but you've not transitioned. You stand there like a normal member of Terraway and haven't attacked anyone here." Her eyes migrated from his gold eye to the piercing blue, and then to the bruises on my neck. "The fate of our Omen rests in the hands of a half-vampire? We're all doomed!"

Higanti's eyes glinted toward the door. "All the more reason to fight to the death today, sister."

"I'm resisting the transition," Von assured them. "So the less she bleeds, the better. Really, I think that's a good rule of thumb for an Omen even if I wasn't a vampire."

I moved my body in front of my vampire to shield him from their scrutiny. They had every right to be wary of Von, but my stubborn streak rose up in me all the same, indignant that anyone would look down on my BFF. "Von's incredible. Have you ever known someone to resist the transition for months? Von's lasted almost a year, and he's done it beautifully. If I die, it won't be because of him." When Von's arm wrapped around my middle, I draped my hand over his, our fingers entwining.

"You love me," Von remarked, as though he was shocked anyone was capable of adoring him.

I wished he hadn't put so blatant a label on it, but there it was, reddening my cheeks and making me cringe. "Yeah, yeah. Shut up about it."

I could tell Malisiya's lost baby was still a fire in her soul as she turned to Von and shook her head. "There's bound to be a bloodbath tonight, so drink your fill of the dead. Leave the Omen untouched."

Higanti clutched her neck in fear that Von might be in the mood for an early dinner. I gripped his hand, wishing I could pull some of his stress so he could stand without shame.

THE BEST KIND OF DANGER

Malisiya checked out the pane-less window. "Our boy is safely on his way. Neither Sama nor King Geon will get their hands on the stone tonight." She exhaled a sigh of relief.

I'd never seen a son more at odds with his father's vendetta. Despite my sudden abduction from the hotel, I fostered a deep appreciation for the lengths Lang was willing to go to so his people could survive and stand without Sama. "Geon's a sideways jackfish if he thinks he's going to find the stone." My snarl couldn't be helped.

The women giggled with scandal that I'd insulted their despicable king. "Good. We would sooner die than let the other kings think murdering children is the way to handle a crisis. We won't see any more babies be taken from their wombs." Malisiya took the bedsheet and handed it to her sister, who cut it in two pieces. I watched them work, taking spices off the shelf and rubbing them into the dirty shirt they'd balled up inside the sheet. I didn't know what was going on, but they sure seemed to. "Do you need a blade, King Mason?"

Mason dipped his head to the women, touched that they still considered him a king instead of a deserter to the Hayop throne. "I wouldn't dream of taking a sword from you. I'll grab one off the first soldier I kill."

"Then we'll see you outside," Malisiya said before holding her sister's hand and leaving us to say our good-byes inside the hut.

Mason turned to Von, his voice low and serious. "You'll stay with October until your last breath. Keep her hidden in here, no matter what. There are two of us. Only one of us needs to survive, and the kingdom still has a chance."

My head whipped from one of my Reapers to the other as my pitch rose. "Don't talk like that! Can't Lang just vanish us out of here? Can't you?"

"He could've, but he thought they were doing a perimeter check, not ransacking each hut for *buhay*." Mason clenched his fists a few times in frustration. "And ever since we…" He cleared his throat uncomfortably. "I haven't been able to shift. I tried to port out to get you shoes and decent clothes when we first landed in Sakuna, but I couldn't manage it."

My eyes widened in horror. "Did I like, accidentally break your magic?"

"No, no. This has happened before. Trauma usually

does it. It'll bounce back. Point is, we're stuck here. If we can destroy King Geon's men on our way to delivering the stone, so much the better. You see how thin his people are, but wait until you see the bulk of the soldiers. He doesn't care about his people, only maintaining his power over them."

"Mason, I can't let two women get killed for me! You know I can defend myself. You know I can fight."

Mason moved in front of me, backing me to the corner of the hut so we could speak privately. He touched my face, expecting correctly that I would jerk my chin away from him. "I know you hate me for using you to see my Kara. I can't blame you for that. But if this is my last, I'd like to see her one more time. To say goodbye to both of you."

"No," Von ruled from the center of the hut. "You messed her up, Mason."

My Viking's voice quieted to a whisper as his hands slowly molded around my jaw, cupping my face. "Danny told me you can only see hallucinations when you kiss an Omen if you're in love. I know you don't love me yet, but know without a doubt that I see Kara only because I love you. If I didn't, I would never have been able to see her." His eyes met mine as I slowly turned my gaze up to meet his. "Know that I will fight to the death for you. Hate me if you need to; I understand. Make no mistake, I'm stronger than anyone out there, but there are too many of them and only one of me."

I watched his sincerity, astonished that he could

declare himself so easily and freely to me, knowing how mad I was at him and that, no, I didn't love him how he needed me to. I mean, come on. I was from the real world. I didn't love on a dime. Yet still he was willing to die for me. I couldn't give him my whole heart, but I could grant him his wish to show my gratitude.

I ignored Von's hiss as I stopped scraping at my hands long enough to stroke Mason's prickly jawline. We were huddled in the corner, and for a second, I let myself believe it was just us, alone in the hut. He was risking his life for me, and all he wanted was a little kiss. To say no felt cruel. I could sacrifice a little heartbreak for the man who was going to war to save me.

"Please," Mason whispered.

I didn't have the right words, so I leaned up on my toes and touched my lips to Mason's. My eyes fluttered shut in anticipation of the stomach flip that pulled me under.

The kiss took on a life of its own, ignoring my pain at being so thoroughly placed on second fiddle. Our lips grew frantic as the colors danced behind my closed eyelids, playing a symphony on a thousand flutes that made me swoon and my knees shake. The red tasted like Mason's lips, and the yellow shimmered on his face as I let the kiss go on a few seconds longer than it should.

"Kara!" Mason worked out before his tongue parted my lips. He tasted my mouth and pulled my heart out of my chest when he murmured my middle name, "October. My Grace. Always my grace."

It was too much. It was, again, the best kiss of my life mingled in with the worst. I let it go on for a solid minute, which was exactly sixty-one seconds too long. When I felt his tears, I pulled away. I held his face when his legs buckled and he fell before me onto his knees with a gust of ecstasy. He rested his cheek to my abdomen, holding my butt and squeezing me tight to him. "Thank you," he whispered. "*Hani*, you're the best kind of danger. You make it too easy to love you. Too easy to fall."

I pretended the tears in my eyes were remnants of his that had fallen on me, and wiped them away. "Alright, then. No more, though. I can't... I just can't. It hurts me too much." I stroked his soft dreads that were pulled back in a leather string.

Von cleared his throat. "That's enough mucking about, you two. Mason, I can't tell you how much better than this you should be. Can't you feel how much you just ripped her up? I'm not even touching her and I can feel it from here! Care about her a little more, mate."

Mason stood, casting a look of warning at Von before leaning in to kiss my lips again. The additional lip-lock took me by surprise and jerked out a noise of distress at having to feel things he didn't deserve to be able to get out of me. "Stay safe, Kara." He straightened and coughed twice. "Gracie. Stay safe, October Grace." He said my name with purpose, but as he looked at my face, I could tell he was seeing her, even after the kiss was finished. He shook his head and blinked a few times before backing out of the hut with an apologetic bow of his head.

I wanted to fall apart, but this was a one-room hut with no spare bedroom to lose my shiz in.

Von's arms crossed over his puffed chest. I knew that look. Von was in full-on big brother mode, but sweet as that was, I didn't want to hear it. "You shouldn't let him do that. I can see what it's doing to you." He touched his heart. "I can feel it. That's a new one. I didn't think this much empathy was in the cards for me these days, but man, I can feel your swings."

"Sorry. I can be cool." I cast up a wan smile. "It's really not a big deal. He should be able to see his wife. It's unfair he didn't get enough time with her."

Von shook his head, ignoring the growing commotion outside the hut, his sculpted lips in a tight line. "What are you on about?"

My sarcasm swung a little too heavy. "It's this foreign concept of putting other people's needs ahead of your own discomfort. Weird, right?"

"It's a terrible rule for this situation."

"It's not a rule that applies to only some things and not to others. It's a blanket rule."

"Well, it's stupid, and I bloody hate it."

I scoffed, rolling my eyes. "You're being a child."

"Yeah? Well, you're being a robot. That's not you. Not the you I know, anyway."

"What do you know about me? We met like, barely two months ago."

"I know enough. You shouldn't let him kiss you and think about Kara. That's messed up, that is."

"I totally cherish your unwelcome opinions on my love life. What makes you think I wasn't daydreaming about Bruce Campbell while I was kissing Mason?"

"Because I know you!" His face twisted in distaste. "You know he's a bit older than you, yeah? Your Bruce Campbell fetish goes deeper than I realized."

I sliced my hand through the air, mildly embarrassed. "We're done talking about this."

"You deserve better."

"And how would you know what I deserve? You don't know me. I'm about to sit back and let two women throw themselves in front of a bullet for me. I'm the worst kind of person. Bruce Campbell would be disgusted with me."

"Because we're making you! And Bruce Campbell's an actor, who probably wouldn't want a young girl like your-self fighting on the front lines of a battle." He shook his head at me.

"Let me fight with them!"

Von jerked me to him, his playboy casual nature running from the hut and leaving in its place a hardened man. "You listen to me, and listen good. King Geon can't have you. He takes you, and it's all over for Terraway. You have no idea what a terror Sama is. King Geon will hand you over to Sama, and you'll beg for the days when a man kissing you and seeing another woman was the worst thing in your life."

I shoved Von. "Get off me."

Mason ran into the hut, eyes wide. "You won't believe the plan they've got brewing. Stay in the hut, no matter what. Von, keep her safe and stay away from the window." He tapped his fist to his chest twice, and Von mirrored the action with a tight frown. Then Von's hand slipped into mine, not to comfort, but to keep me in place so I didn't run out to fight.

I was scared, so I held tight to Von and pursed my lips to keep my chin from quivering. If the king wanted me, he'd have to come and friggin' get me.

29

WOMEN AND THEIR BABIES

There were too many pounding footsteps marching in formation toward us. I heard a man I could only picture as cruel shouting, "Move now! Go back to your huts before the curfew hits. If any of you are hoarding *buhay* in your huts, you'll be taken to the king and flogged for your greed."

"Never!" was the resounding cry of the people. I'd assumed the rebels were a dozen or so that could gather on such short notice, but the answer came from hundreds outside the clusters of huts. I could pick out both men and women protesting the march of the soldiers. Now I was sweating from fear, not just the unforgiving suns. I was here, and I wasn't supposed to be.

The people of Sakuna would pay for their rebellion. I heard them clapping in a slow heartbeat using hand and wood on metal, their palms slapping and weapons beating together in one stalwart voice of get-the-flip-off-our-lawn.

"We know the Omen is here with you! Give us the Omen, and no one will get hurt."

I swallowed hard, wondering how they'd found out I was here. Von's grip on my hand tightened. "Stay," he warned. "Giving yourself up kills far more than the lot of them out there. It kills all of Terraway. Remember that."

"He's negotiating," I whispered to Von. "That's got to mean he's a little afraid, right?"

Mason seemed to be thinking the same thing from the battlefield just outside the huts. "Onward!" my Viking shouted from his position out with the people.

Von moved carefully toward the window hole and peeked, motioning me to his side. "What are they doing?"

I looked from our vantage point of seeing the whole battle from the side through our glass-less window. The soldiers of Sakuna were in perfect formation, staring ahead at the front line of civilians. I expected the men to take the more dangerous position at the front, but was shocked when I saw...

Women and their babies?

The women of Sakuna were a hundred strong at least, and I saw more running to stand with their sisters, infants in hand. Each of them cradled swaddled babies with their faces covered to their breasts, and they marched with heads held high and terrifying fury in their brown faces. "I thought the babies were killed. I don't get it."

"They were." Von's brow furrowed as he peeked out the window with me.

We watched as the women marched straight up to the line of soldiers. Then I heard a shrill demand of, "We will see the king! King Geon will answer for our children! He'll come out of his high and mighty castle, get on his knees in the mud and see what he's done to his people!" Malisiya shouted in the captain's face like a woman possessed. I didn't blame her. She'd just lost a baby because of that jackhole king.

It was the baby she was holding in the blanket at her breast.

But she hadn't had a baby. So what was she holding? I recognized the swaddled lump as her bedsheet, trying to put the pieces together before the next move was made.

The captain and his properly fed men were dressed in leather armor with helmets on to meet with the group of women who stood in front of their husbands and teenaged sons. The civilian men were armed with rocks, long pieces of wood and a smattering of knives. I didn't understand why they were sending out their women to get slaughtered first. I saw Mason standing in front of the men, ordering the women forward. I didn't know how he could sacrifice them like that while he stood back with the men. I wanted to cry out to Mason to stop the women, but a small part of me still harbored enough trust in Mason to handle an army. He was the King of Sombi and the former King of Hayop, after all. His expression was hard, his body lithe and ready to pounce – a Viking preparing to go off on a tear.

The army's commander had a large, wide nose and a missing canine tooth that left a gaping hole when he spoke. "The king doesn't answer to slaves!" Then he pulled out his shining sword and ran Malisiya through before anyone could react.

Von's hand muffled my scream at Malisiya's sacrifice. His face was alight with calculation, and then fear. "Those aren't babies. Get back!"

No sooner had I begun to process the horror of what I'd just witnessed did the women break out in a resounding cry of fury that set loose the beginnings of a war. I watched with my mouth hanging open as the babies who'd been cradled to their breasts were launched at the soldiers – straight into the front line and also hurled overhead to the ranks in the middle and the back.

Only the things that flew out of the baby blankets weren't cute and pink and precious. They were clay balls that exploded on impact, sending blown-off limbs of the doomed soldiers flying.

Von ripped me from the window and shoved me into the far corner. "Get down!" he ordered, hefting up the straw mattress and lugging it over to me. He propped it up in between us and the battle, angling it to rest between the walls as he ducked down with me in the corner. The mattress was an adequate shield from errant clay bombs that might throw shrapnel our way through the hole in the wall that served as a window. Still, Von boxed me in the crevice of the corner with his body, his palms pressing to the wall on either side of me. He breathed heavily as his body caged me in to be my human shield. Or vampire-Duwende shield. "Don't be my shield," I begged, trying to somehow get him to switch places with me. "I can't take this, Von."

"This is my job, love. I take your bullets, and your job is to let me."

"I don't want this job. Not one that gets you hurt." I coiled my arms around him, burying my face in his neck. I positioned one hand on his back to shield his heart, and the other to shield one of his lungs. His spine was still exposed, and I didn't trust the straw mattress to keep Von safe, so I wrapped my legs around his waist, pulling myself onto his lap. My calves shielded his kidneys and the base of his spine. It was the best I could do, since he wouldn't trade positions with me.

One of Von's steady hands reached around to cup the back of my head, while his lips migrated to my forehead. "Now, now. We'll be alright." His words were paired with the shrieks of the damned and the angry clanging of too many swords just outside the hut, so I was dubious.

I was shaken to the core, covering my mouth with his neck as I listened to the sounds of men and women screaming just outside the huts. I couldn't tell who was winning; all I knew was that as the minutes ticked by, more and more from each side were dying. As it usually was in a war, no one really won. It seemed that was the whole point of the people standing up to the guards. Though they knew they couldn't win, they were determined to at least make it so that the soldiers didn't win, either.

30

MY PRECIOUS MENACES

The mayhem outside was still evenly matched as far as who was overpowering the other. The soldiers were well-armed, but the people had fury that could fuel a thousand cannons. I tried to make out clear voices, but it was a jumble of shouts until I heard the captain bellow, "Curfew!"

This seemed to invoke renewed fear into the people, and I knew why. Sigbins were cute little animals that had heads like scaly goats, long taloned forearms and short back legs. They ripped out the hearts of the people who roamed about after curfew, and wore them around their necks. They were terrifying.

I was kind of in love with one of them who'd taken a shine to me. When you got down to the heart of it, they were abused animals groomed for one thing – death. I'd always been good with animals. I hadn't known why the pit bull next door growing up tore at burglars but wagged his tail happily for me. When the new additions to my life informed me it was a perk from my Matruculan genetics, the magic of it somehow took away a little of the magic in it. Funny how that works. I'd thought I was good with animals because of how much I loved them. Turns out, anyone with my DNA could do it.

Well, not anyone. Mason had confessed that even though he was Matruculan, he'd never heard of anyone getting a sigbin to purr for me the way my little Edward Scissorteeth had.

"I can help," I told Von, who was still boxing me in with his body.

Von scooped me more firmly to him, his free hand cupping my rear to keep me from running into the battle. "Your job is to get a piece of the sagrado stone to the well. Nothing else, love."

"I can calm the sigbins down!"

"Not a chance. You'll sit here and wait it out."

"Oh, for heaven's sake." I pried myself from Von's grip and stood to peek out the window, horrified at the number of dead bodies from both sides that were lying about underfoot of those still fighting. Mason was clashing... an arm? Yes, he was holding a ripped-off arm of a man he'd stolen and was using it like a sword against six soldiers, besting them all, sword to bone.

The sigbins came bounding up to the carnage, eager to rip, tear, kill. I recognized my sweet little Edward Scissorteeth in the mix by the ugly gash he had across his nose. Von tugged at me, but I let out a short whistle that drew Edward's eye. Just like that, my killer went from a beast to a puppy, bounding over to me and jumping in through the window to lick my face. "Hi, baby!" I cooed as I smoothed my hand over his scales. "I missed you, Edward." Edward nuzzled into my hand, eager for the scratch to calm him down.

I knew that feeling well.

I hugged my puppy that actually looked more like a janky miniature dragon, and kissed the top of his head. "You want to rest? You want to hide out in here? Go get the others, baby. Bring your buddies in here, and you can all hide out."

I don't know how he understood what I was saying, but just like the therapy dog I'd had to see, and the dogs and cats around the trailer park, he seemed to get me. Edward meandered into the fray, letting out a few yips and a howl that had a hiss to it under the layers of animalistic sound.

Von was sweating when all seven sigbins came bounding into the hut, growling and spitting until Edward reasoned with them in his adorable puppy-like way. One by one, they all sat down when I raised my hand, barking like cuties instead of the abused monsters they'd been groomed to be. "Poor babies!" I exclaimed in dismay at the state of their damaged scaly coats. Though a couple had fresh wounds, most of the missing scales and scars were old, indicating years of mistreatment. They moved like a mixture between a cat and a snake with legs, circling and batting their hands over their faces when they realized they didn't want to eat my heart out, but wanted to play coy games instead.

I knelt down in the center of the room, motioning for them to come up to me if they wanted to be loved on. "I won't hurt you," I promised. "Come take a break. You're all much too young and sweet to be out in a battlefield."

There was utter carnage outside, but it was obedience school in the hut. They took impatient turns letting me run my fingers over their scales, admiring the shimmer through the tears in their flesh. The shiny rubbery material had a greenish hue to the silver that glinted when it caught the last vestiges of the twilight poking in through the window. "Come on out," I said to Von. He was kneeling behind the straw mattress, looking like he was torn between wanting to grab me and run out of the hut, or wanting to play with the cool monsters. "They won't hurt you."

"I can't decide if I want to pee myself or join you."

"Join me. Peeing yourself isn't nearly as fun as you're thinking."

Von got down so he wasn't seen through the window and crawled over to me with caution. He sat to my right, eyes wide as he watched the animals flop next to me and over me so they could get a good belly scratch. "I don't understand how you're doing this."

"I'm magic," I replied with a tease in my tone. I picked

up his hand and placed it on the smallest one's belly so he could rub it. "This one's Cindy. She's the littlest. And this is Jan and Marcia." I pointed to Edward, who was by far the largest one. "That's my Edward. You already met him last time. And this is Greg, Mike and Bobby."

"Brady Bunch fan?"

"It's only the greatest show in the world." I switched from bellies to stroking under their chins, giving a good scratch while they whined for more of the love I had no end of. "The Brady Bunch is always happy. They have problems like who gets to play with which toy, and what time Alice is going to make them all dinner. They have a mama and an Alice. They have a dad." I tried to keep the longing out of my voice, but I was a lousy actress.

Von's arm went around me, pulling me tight to his sweaty armpit. "When we get out of here, I'll watch the whole series with you, start to finish. We'll have a marathon and sit there till our eyes bleed. I could use some Brady optimism." He pointed to Marcia. "Looks like this one loves you the most. Sneezes at me when I try to pet her."

"Aw, you'll get the hang of it."

"Who am I? You gave all of them Brady Bunch roles, but what about me? Noisy neighbor? Sexy policeman?"

I smiled, resting my head to his shoulder. "You can be Mr. Brady. He's an architect, which is sort of like an artist, like you."

He kissed the top of my head. "I knew it. You're in love

with me. Already casting me in the role of your perfect television husband."

I pulled Cindy closer, snapping my fingers twice so she gave Von a kiss. I loved when Von laughed. He was built for it. "I'm Alice. I'm the one who takes care of the family. I'm near the family, but not in it. Big difference."

Von squinted down at me. "Well Mrs. Brady, you've just been promoted. You and I are going to raise these little rugrats to be upstanding members of society."

"Is that so? Then I think we should start now." I kissed each of my babies and clapped them to attention, pleased when they all sat before me like precious little soldiers, trying not to wiggle too much. "Okay, love muffins. If you want to stay with Mama and Daddy, you can. If you want to go out there and get back at the people who hurt you, that's fine too. But you can't attack the civilians, under-stood? They need your help. You up for it?"

Edward let out his snarling growl, making the decision for the others. He licked my face and then led the others out to the battlefield, forked tails swishing as they went out like the precious menaces they were.

31

JUST THE WAY YOU ARE

*V*on and I moved back behind the propped-up mattress, sitting on the floor in the corner of the hut. I was tucked in his embrace with my head leaning on his shoulder. I knew he was pulling stress from me, but for a second I let myself pretend it was romantic. Though I knew he was a guy it wasn't a good idea to get attached to, I let myself depend on him to hold me together while the war continued outside. "Promise me you'll hold Katrina like this through a movie someday. This whole raging battle thing? Not as nice as a romantic comedy. She'll love it."

Von scoffed. "I would never hold Katrina like this. Too intimate."

I expected him to pull away from me when it dawned on him that we were being intimate, perhaps too much so, but he only held me tighter. "You're a good friend, Von."

"I'll hold you exactly like this through our Brady Bunch marathon when we get home."

I managed a small smile into his shirt. "Stop saying sexy things to me."

He chuckled at my mild flirt. "It's a date." Von held me when we heard Marcia howl in pain. "Easy, darling," he whispered.

Von kept me in place through Mason's cry of agony when I fought to go to help our Viking on the battlefield. His comfort was gentle, clashing with the war outside. "He'll be alright, love."

Von let go of me only when the door banged open to reveal a large soldier in the king's leather. He looked just as surprised to see us as we were to see him when he tore the mattress away. He called over his injured shoulder, "I found her!"

Von shoved me behind him and rushed the man, ignoring the blade in the soldier's hand. Von was unarmed, but that didn't seem to bother him one bit. Danny had warned me about Von's vicious streak. I'm pretty sure I'd laughed it off at the time. But I saw it in that moment – the calculating glint in his eye, the muscles poised for action, the cool, relaxed shoulders that clashed with the look that had no fear, only sudden conquest. I hadn't understood Danny's wariness of Von's temper, but I began to see traces of the threat. He had fire in his mismatched eyes. He had a lithe, toned body.

He had fangs.

Von was on the man in a hot second, his teeth bared and plunging into the neck of the soldier so quickly, the man scarcely had the wherewithal to fight back. The soldier cried out in pain and what sounded a little like strangled pleasure. He deflated to the ground while Von went to town on his meal. He drained the soldier in three minutes flat, rearing his head back when he finished to let out a contented moan at the feeling of finally being full of the stuff he always craved.

When two more soldiers came to the door in various shades of battle-torn, Von was ready. He pounced and bit so quickly, I barely saw it all happen. The gooey red blood of Terraway coated his face and hands, dripping down his green shirt and pooling on the floor below. He slurped and glutted himself until the intruders were beyond survival. Von was pure animal, making sexual groans, his buttocks clenching as he drank, holding the men beneath him like they were damsels who swooned only for him.

It wasn't until all three grown men were drained in the doorway of the hut that Von slowed. He was on all fours, panting like he'd just run a marathon. He paused only to lick the neck wounds a few more times to catch the last drops. He growled, slapping the floor in frustration. I couldn't tell if he was mad because he'd just killed three men, or if it was because there were only three at his disposal, and he wanted more. He swore loudly before he righted himself. Von stood to drag the bodies from the entryway, trembling as he went. I moved to help him, but he kept his red-stained face bent away from me in shame. "Von? You alright? Like, you're full, right? I don't need to make myself scarce?"

"I won't attack you. I'll get more than enough on the battlefield when it's all over."

We dragged the bodies the rest of the way inside and shut the door, and then I waved him toward me. "Come here."

"No. I can't believe you'd want to be near me after seeing all that. It's not me. I'm not that person. Or rather, I *am* a person, not the monster you just saw."

Using a sword, I cut off the front of one of the dead men's shirts, trying to keep my cool. "Come here, Mr. Brady. You've got something on your face."

He turned to me, looking so lost, my heart sank at the sight of something so beautiful and carefree being weighted by war. I took him by the hand and led him behind the mattress we propped up in the corner, ducking down with him like we were kids in a fort. I slid the sword to the side in case we needed it and reached out to him with the shirt in my hand, dabbing at the shame on his handsome face. He was coated in crimson that stuck to the fabric while I wiped his face clean. "Why are you being nice to me?"

"You saved my life, Von. Making you a napkin is the least I can do. Thank you."

"You're not scared of me?"

"Only if you start singing Phil Collins. He scares me

even if I'm totally zen. Something about a man saying 'Sus-sudio' over and over hits me the wrong way. I don't really understand what that song's about. I think it might be voodoo or something."

Von let out a perfunctory laugh at my conversational diversion. He pulled his ruined shirt over his head and threw it out of our fort. Then he wrapped me in a warm hug that heated my body when he kissed my cheek. I probably wasn't supposed to love the feel of a half-naked Von, but there we were. "I'm sorry you had to see that, Mrs. Brady."

"Are you hurt?"

"Nah. They didn't get in a single hit on me. That's the beauty of not realizing you're fighting a vampire. We're pretty lethal when we're hungry." At the admission of his weakness, he shook his head, disgusted with himself. "This wasn't my plan. I wasn't supposed to get bitten. I was going to graduate from the Academy. I was supposed to get a regular job and complain about taxes and Monday mornings." He clutched me through his admission of pain. "I was the one my brothers came to, and now they look at me like I can't even tie my own shoes. I was supposed to live a long life, and now I'm temporary!"

"Honey," I cooed, my hand trailing down his spine to soothe him.

"I spent most of my life before this being responsible because I thought once my brothers were grown, there would be time for me to muck about and enjoy life a little.

When do I get to be young?" He gripped my body, and I held him together as he fell apart. "Half-vamps usually only make it a few weeks before they transition, if that. Then they get swept up in Terraway by some cruel owner. The second I transition, they'll put me to use as an attack dog." He squeezed me and shouted into my hair, "I'm no one's dog!"

I held Von through his long-overdue breakdown. I took my time stroking his hair, my fear of germs parting from me in the wake of his utter devastation. If I was honest with myself, Von hadn't had germs in weeks, so permanent was his place in my heart. I gave Von time, not willing to insult his pain by trying to cheer him up. When finally I whispered, "I'm here," he slumped in the comfort of my arms. "You're not a dog. And you've made it far more than a few weeks as a half-vamp. I daresay you might just be the exception to the rule – too stubborn to transition." I kissed an errant tear on his cheek, accepting him no matter what state he came to me in. "You've got me now. I'll make sure you don't turn."

"But I'm temporary now. No one can stop the inevitable."

"Then you don't know how stubborn I am. Let me help you. When you're thirsty, tell me; don't hide it. I'll make myself scarce so you're not so miserable. And you don't have to go sneaking off to another room to drink those blood pouches. You can be who you are, and I won't look at you like you're anyone less than the hero who saved my life." I met his eyes and held his face so he could see that I wasn't afraid of him. "We can do this."

He closed his eyes, leaning his forehead to mine as we knelt on the floor of the hut, hidden behind the mattress. When he pecked my lips, my heart did a miniature flutter, spreading a blush onto my cheeks. "Tell me we can complain about the length of the lawn someday. Tell me we can get all fired up about how much junk mail we get, and how no one handwrites letters anymore."

"Maybe in the next life, you'll do exactly that. We'll have to work out a signal so I can recognize you in whatever flabby body you get next time around."

"Flabby?" Von straightened as he pulled out of our hug, sucking in his toned stomach indignantly.

I motioned to his perfect form. "Well, yeah. The universe has to compensate somehow. You're too perfect looking in this life. Prepare yourself for the crushing blow of a beer gut, my friend. See? You peaked too soon. It's all downhill from the top."

He smiled, but the levity was short-lived as he hung his head. "You shouldn't be nice to me. I almost bit you in the trunk of your car."

"But you didn't."

"I didn't used to be like this."

"Oh, honey. I like you just the way you are." I'd been held quite a bit since Von came into my life. He was free with the hugging and the kissing. The sweet pecks he blessed me with forced the rigidity out of me one degree at a time. I knew he needed me to be there for him, so I gave a shot at speaking his language – the language of touch. I pulled him forward as I rocked back to sit on my butt, taking his top half with me. I laid his head down on my lap and ran my fingers through his hair, ignoring the sweat and flecks of mud that made the messy mass slick and greasy. I knew he was also pulling stress from me, which made my OCD bearable. "Take a few minutes and calm down. You saved the day. No one's thinking anything but that." I stroked the side of his face, smiling maternally when he leaned into my touch. "You saved us, Von."

"Look at you, being all nice to me. You're not so uptight anymore."

"Man, you suck at compliments," I laughed. "I guess you and Mason are good for me."

Von frowned. "Can we talk about that? He's clearly using you. I mean, to each her own, but you've got to know you don't have to put up with that."

I shrugged off the sting. "He was only the best kiss of my life. I'm getting something out of it, too."

Von's nose crinkled in distaste. "I'm not one to invest in kissing. Ask Katrina. Didn't kiss her once. She kept going in for my lips, so I finally had to lay down the law. Too intimate."

"Hello, you had sex with Katrina. That's intimate."

"Not really. Not if you don't want it to be. Kissing is face to face. I don't like leaving myself that vulnerable. You should take a page from my book, Peach."

"But you kiss my face when you're happy or flirty just fine." I winced, wishing I could suck those words back into my mouth. I liked when he did those things, and didn't want him to stop if he assumed I was making too much of it.

"It's different. *We're* different. You're turning into my best girlfriend or something. A guy friend, but with a great rack." It was his turn to wince and suck on his poorly chosen words. He cleared his throat. "We sort of have to be intimate on occasion. Nature of the job."

"Just say it," I teased, combing through his hair again. "You're in love with me. You want me for my hot body. You want to buy me presents, take me dancing and wear a tie."

Von chuckled. "Wear a tie. You're funny. Let's put that on the list for our next life. I'll have a beer gut, and you'll be the sexy librarian who helps me find books about weight loss. Our fingers will brush as you're handing me a book, and it'll be kismet. I'll wear a tie for our first date." He tangled his fingers through mine, staring curiously at our entwined hands.

"Promise?"

"On my honor. I'll even let you pick it out." He kissed my knuckles one at a time, running his nose over my scabbed cuts. "Thanks for this. You're like my Puller now."

"I told you, I'm here. We're in this together." I stroked the side of his face until he felt centered enough to sit up. He looped his arm around my shoulders and pressed the outside of his knee to mine.

We sat in our fort, content to cuddle while the world fell to pieces outside our doorstep. Maybe that's a terrible thing, but in that moment, I felt protected. In that protection, I felt something I hadn't experienced a whole lot of in my life.

Von held me, and I felt truly loved.

32

BATTLEFIELD NURSE GRACIE

Mason stalked into the hut on unsteady feet that were clad in boots he'd clearly stolen off a soldier. He had blood oozing from a gash on his arm that Von eyed greedily. In the name of preserving our threesome, he didn't lick Mason's cut before he exited the hut, but went out to get his fill of the soldiers. Their bodies lay scattered on the open space between the mountains in the distance and the cluster of huts.

"Here, lay down a minute. Catch your breath." I pulled down the mattress and lowered Mason onto it so I could get a better look at his two-inch cut. "This is it? This is all you got? Am I missing something?"

Mason sat instead of laying, and leaned forward, resting his forehead in his hands to close his eyes for a moment. "We won, but only just. There were too many casualties to call this a victory. I'm fine. It's the others you should worry about." He jerked his arm from me when my fingers ran over a sore spot. "I said I'm alright."

"Yeah, I don't really feel the need to listen when you lie. Your pulse is crazy and your eyes are dilated. You only breathe heavy like this when you're super worked up."

Mason softened, shooting me an apologetic look at his short tone. "So many died. I'm Matruculan, so I'm far stronger and my bones don't break near as easy. I wish that were true for some of the civilians out there." He shook his head in admiration. "The women. So brave."

"They were amazing. I don't really know how to help them without first aid stuff, though. I mean, I'm in my pajamas still without the basics." I turned when the owner of the hut came inside, her face dotted with blood. Tears ran down her face at the loss of her sister. "Oh! Sweetie, lie down. Do you have anything I can use to help you? Needle and thread? Antiseptic?"

Mason shook his head as Higanti went to get her sewing kit from the box where they stored all their worldly possessions. "They don't have antiseptic, and don't need it like humans do. Needle and thread. That's a good place to start. Don't worry about disinfecting. Once you toss a bit of the sagrado in the well, they can wash their wounds in it, and it'll disinfect perfectly. Trick is to get to the well before any infection starts to set in on the wounded."

"Wow. Seriously? That's pretty awesome."

Higanti handed me her sewing kit, so I set to work on fixing her up first. To her credit, she didn't flinch when the needle tugged at her cheekbone. It was hard to get a good grasp on the wound, what with her blood staining everything and sticking to my fingers. The panic welled up in me at the number of infections I might get from touching bodily fluids without my gloves on, but I choked down my anxiety as best I could. So many had given their lives so I wouldn't be abducted and handed over to Sama. With all the pulling Von had done to steady me, I muscled through my mania for the good of the cause.

When I finished with Higanti, she kissed both my cheeks and sent me on my way. I walked out onto the battlefield with Mason, but he stopped me a few feet from the carnage. "You wait here. Von and I can bring the wounded ones to you. There's nails and bits of steel everywhere out here from the homemade bombs the ladies had." He shook his head. "I still can't believe they did that."

"I about lost my shiz when I thought they were throwing real babies at people."

"They had that plan already in motion after King Geon poisoned them and killed their babies. Just needed a catalyst, which I guess we were. You stay here, though. I mean it. One cut, and Von might lose himself. It won't do for you to survive the battle only to die over a stubbed toe."

"Alright. Send them on over."

I patched up men and women with bruised brown skin, oozing wounds and too many tears to count while Mason, Von and a few of the able-bodied men started digging a mass grave. By the end of their efforts, there were two graves – one for the civilians and one for the soldiers. I tore my eyes from the teen I was treating to look at the rituals Mason was performing in the dark of night that was lit only by torches. The teen boy's arm was cut so deeply, I had to wait for the blood to clot before sewing.

Mason, Von and the men were lifting (not dragging) the bodies of the civilians and laying them face-down in the mass grave after one of the women made an account of who each person was on a piece of paper. I sucked in my breath when Mason took two of the torches and threw one into each of the two graves. The fire went out without catching on more than a few articles of clothing, but whatever purpose the fire served, Mason seemed satisfied.

I tried not to comment on the oddity as I moved on to stitching up a guy's leg who couldn't have been that much older than I was. Many of the people gathered around the grave of their fellow man, holding hands and singing a song with words I didn't understand. It tugged at my heart as I tugged at the man's skin to suture it properly in the flickering torchlight. There was so much weeping, so many bodies.

The two moons' lights weren't giving me much help, and the torches flickered often, leaving much of the wounded area in shadow. It made the last few stitches on the guy's thigh difficult to finish off. I motioned him closer, draping his knee over my outstretched thigh so I could raise and lower his leg as needed. My nose was almost touching his skin as I tried to get the stitching tight enough. There were a few torches, but they weren't near enough to do much good.

Mason made his way over to us, taking a break from the shoveling to stand next to me with a frown. "October, you're drawing quite a few eyes, positioned like that."

"Huh? Do you have a light or something? And where's Von? He doing alright?"

"He hasn't surfaced from his endless supper. Though I do admire that he mainly stuck to feasting on the soldiers." He mopped the sweat from his brow with a forfeited shirt from one of the dead. "Aren't you finished yet?"

"Sheesh, Mason. This isn't exactly easy to do when I can't see much. I'm almost done."

The guy I was treating looked at me with an embarrassed smile. "You're really not from here, are you."

"Nope. And I hope to leave before anything else like that goes down. I'm not all that used to war."

"Take your time," he told me, looking around and waving at a few guy friends who made lewd noises to my left.

Mason sounded exasperated. "You're making him the king of all the men who've got their eyes on you."

"What are you talking about?" It wasn't until that moment I realized I had my head too far down between the guy's legs, making me look like a service girl, and not a battlefield nurse. I picked my head up and did my best to trust my fingers in the dark as I finished the suture as quick as I could.

Mason pulled me up and thumbed my lower lip, giving it a kiss that made me feel like I was being dowsed with cold water. In the dark I started to see bursts of yellow and that familiar red I couldn't blink away whenever he kissed me. "Come back to me," he murmured. My stomach twisted when I realized he was already picturing his wife. It was almost like he loved me, but nothing like it at all. He was lost in the kiss and murmured, "So beautiful."

I pulled out of the euphoria that crashed from such a steep height, leaving me a wreck in the aftermath. "That's enough. People are looking, Mason."

"So?"

"So, know me a little bit. I'm not big into public displays. It's like you're peeing all over me to mark your territory or something."

Mason cleared his throat. "A thousand apologies," he offered, though not without a hint of a bite to his words.

I sucked in a deep breath and tried to be kind. "Kara, she's... she's doing alright? In the vision? She's happy with you?"

Mason looked deep into my eyes with an unfathomable expression. "She is. I was a good husband."

I nodded, trying to be an adult. "Then every now and then, as often as I can muscle through it, we can kiss so you can see her. I'm thinking once a day is a fair amount. I can do that for you." My eyes sharpened. "But not in public, and no more than once a day."

Mason's mouth fell open. "You have no idea what that means to me."

I cleared my throat to change the subject. "That's all I can do for these people. I can't reset a broken arm that has multiple breaks, which is what Felix has over there. I reset as much as I could, but I'd need an actual x-ray to make sure it's all perfectly aligned, which I'm guessing we don't have down here. And Lona needs to stay awake until the possibility of a concussion's been ruled out. Other than that, it's all I can do. I hate that I'm not being more helpful." Two bleeders had died while I'd been frantically stitching people up towards the beginning. That one sat heavy on me and would for a while, I just knew it. I'm not sure I could've saved them, but to not be able to try was a bitter pill I deserved to choke on.

Mason slowly came back to himself. "It's good, *hani.* You did a good job."

His arm on my back was supposed to offer comfort, but it felt wrong there now. I moved away a few steps. "We should go, then. I don't like the idea of sleeping here. Let's keep going in the dark toward the well."

Mason held onto my arm to stop my progression. "The nails," he reminded me. "Wait here for me to finish filling in the grave with the men, then I'll carry you out."

I didn't like that option, but knew if I got even a paper cut, it would make things hard for Von. I sat down and whistled for my dragon puppies, who came bounding up to me eagerly after collecting more hearts from the soldiers they'd helped kill on my command. They nudged closer, trying to edge the others out so they could show me the trophies they were so proud of. Edward laid the top half of his body in my lap, licking my face as I came down from Mason's kiss. He'd jerked me around too much for me to remain stable. I stroked my baby's scales, tsking when I saw a wet gouge that looked fresh from the battle. "Oh, honey. I'm so sorry. I can't even fix it for you, either. Your scales are too thick for my needle. What can I do to help? Tell me, Edward."

The civilians were watching me with mouths agape, but I didn't care. They were shocked the sigbins had fought on their side. They'd been unable to explain the unnatural shift until they saw Edward and me together. I don't know why animals were so much easier to talk to than people, but I was grateful for the release of tension Edward brought me with his unconditional acceptance of all the things I was not, and might never be. My hands were coated in blood, so Edward did me a solid and started licking the crimson off to calm me down.

Edward was good like that.

Von came over with Mason, blood all down his front and covering his contented face. He looked too pleasantly gorged to be ashamed of himself this time. "You ready, Peach?"

"Yup. Are you full?"

"Quite, yes. Do I have something on my face?" He dabbed comically at the corner of his mouth, though his lips, nose, chin and chest were utterly dripping with the red goo.

"You did, but you got it. You're ready for the prom now."

Mason gave the sigbins a wide berth and hoisted me up. He made to carry me like a princess, but I opted for being worn like a backpack to avoid any chance he might kiss me again. Mason smelled like pine, patchouli and sweaty man. It was a deeply masculine allure he had on me, and I tried with every step he took to cross him off my list of men I was attracted to.

Edward followed us even after I sent the other puppies home, leading the way with his forked tail guiding us through the dark that engulfed us all too quickly.

33

SWIMMING AND DROWNING

The night in Sakuna was a black blanket that swept over our trio. We reached the base of the mountain where we were supposed to meet Ezra and Lang. "I don't see them," Von ruled. "And it's at least another day's journey to the castle from here. I vote we get a few hours of shuteye in the woods over there." He pointed to a forest between our mountain and the one on the other side. "The trees can cover us in case King Geon sends any more of his men to find her."

Mason looked like he wanted to argue, but finally consented when he spotted a smattering of trees thick enough to provide us with a little shelter. "Alright. Let's grab a quick nap. So long as we're up and moving by first light, that should be fine." Mason stretched while I started clearing the space he led us to. We were deep inside the thicket of trees, and I knew that when we laid down, we wouldn't be able to be seen by passersby on the road, which was now several stones' throws away.

There were leaves, pebbles and various types of bramble I didn't feel like sleeping on. I took my time clearing it all away for us while the guys eyed my meticulous care with curiosity. I needed the dirt swept in a certain even design, which was hard to get perfect. I knew I was starting to give in to my obsessive tendencies, and dreaded the person I would devolve into by morning.

When the three of us finally laid down, I was sandwiched in the middle, both of them seeking comfort from the traumatic events of the day. Mason spooned me while Von slid his hand between mine to assure us both I wouldn't scratch open my scabs in my sleep. Edward wriggled up in between Von and me, snuggling his head through my elbows and resting his jaw to my breasts. I was endeared to my puppy even more when he looped his forked tail over Von to pull him closer.

Von marveled at the docile beast who loved us, mouthing, "Wicked!" He moved in so Edward's slim body was the only space between us. Von's lips were just inches from mine when he closed his eyes after delivering a sweet kiss to the tip of my nose. "Goodnight, darling."

"Von?" I whispered, my anxiety getting the best of me.

"Yes, love?"

"You know how you don't like people to see you as a monster when you vamp out? How that person isn't the real you?"

Von's eyes focused on mine as he nodded.

"I'm a day off my meds. When I wake up, I might not be able to be myself. I…" I pursed my lips together, hating the words that tumbled out next. "Please don't leave me when I lose myself."

Von's gaze hardened in a vow of solidarity I desperately needed. "Never." He held tight to my hand as he kissed my lips once more, just to assure me that he wasn't afraid of the monster that was always lurking inside of me, shunning people and smiling at hand sanitizer. "Goodnight, Mrs. Brady."

I smiled, giving his hand a squeeze. "Goodnight, Mr. Brady."

I DREAMT I WAS SWIMMING IN A PERFECTLY STERILIZED POOL. The water was a tropical crystal clear with a hint of blue to it. I wore my gold bikini I'd never had the guts to put on in public before. I was alone in the water, my arms cutting the surface as I swam along at my own pace, enjoying the sun overhead for what it was. I didn't know how to swim in real life, but in my dreams, I was a rocket. Or, you know, something that knows how to swim crazy fast.

I looked up and saw a familiar face that had visited my dreams before. My smile greeted him, but he didn't seem to have one for me. "Hi, Philip."

"Where are you?"

I glanced around to the palm trees and orange trees that dotted the yard I was swimming in. "I dunno. Florida? Come on in."

Philip was wearing leather armor over black clothes, much like the soldiers of Sakuna. Only his skin was lighter and his hair still that shocking Billy Idol white-blond. "I'm not going swimming. I have things to do. Where are you really?"

"In real life? I'm not sure. I don't think we're lost, but the guys wouldn't tell me if we were."

"How many guys are you with?"

"The usual amount." I quirked my eyebrow at him. "No offense, but I don't conjure you up in my dreams to chat me up about real life. I come here to escape all that. So either escape it with me or go away. The madness starts all over again once I'm awake."

Philip gave me a hard look, the muscles in his cleft chin flexing as if he wanted to be a jerk, but knew he shouldn't. "If that's what you want, then I'll stay."

"I do. I want." I waded to the edge of the pool, blinking up at him through wet lashes. He was pretty, that's for sure. I didn't like him so frustrated, though. He was much better when he was seducing me.

Without warning, I grew tired in the water. I wasn't sure why, but I couldn't catch my breath. My limbs felt weighted and my brain foggy. "October?" Philip called, wary.

"Can't breathe!" I wasn't underwater, but it felt like

I was.

"Where are you?" He was looking straight at me, his eyes wide as he swore. "Are you in Terraway?"

"Yes! I'm... I can't..." I pressed the flat of my hand to my chest, confused and scared.

"*Baga* root! When was the last time you had any *baga* root?"

"Yesterday morning! No! Has it been twenty-four hours already?"

When I met his panicked gaze with one of my own, he cried out, "It's been more than a day you've been here? The *baga* root might be out of your system?"

I nodded, confused and still short of breath.

"No! This wasn't the plan." He knelt at the edge of the pool and hiked me up over the edge, laying me down on the concrete. I gasped, fighting with the thinning air for a decent breath. I was reaching full-on panic mode, but Philip leaned over me and pressed his mouth to mine, pinching my nose and blowing in air to inflate my lungs.

It bought me a few seconds of life, but then something happened I couldn't explain. The concrete beneath us began to crumble, plummeting us both down into the water below.

My arms began to flail as I felt myself drowning. Down, down, down I sank into the depth, watching the sun through the haze of crystal blue that had seconds ago felt refreshing. I knew in that moment that I would soon die.

I decided I was okay with that.

HAMMER, NOT DAUGHTER

I awoke to chest compressions and old spongy gum in my mouth. I tried to spit it out, but a large hand shoved it back in and closed my mouth so I had to swallow. My hands and feet were vacillating between tingly and numb, and were too heavy to lift to bat away the pressure that was still being pumped into my chest in a rhythm.

I opened my eyes to see Ezra's mouth coming at me, pressing on my unresponsive lips and blowing air into my body. I was so confused in that moment, I didn't know how to pull away or do anything that would end the strange mutation of my dream. Ezra, not Philip. Terraway, not the Florida pool.

I blinked and began to draw breath on my own. In and out, the sweet relief dragged through my lungs. It was fresh air that smelled like dirt and non-pollution. Ezra was shouting, overcome with elation as he slid his arm under my back to lift me up to sit. I couldn't support my weight though, so I sagged against him. Ezra's dirty fingers ran through my hair as he pressed my temple to his breast. His chest shook with emotional release as the world slowly started to filter into its right order again.

The fiery suns were rising through the trees, adding too much heat to the morning. I felt another hand on my back and looked over to find, of all people, Prince Langgam. He was scared, moving his hand with care down my spine. "I'm sorry. I'm so sorry. We've been looking for you all night. I didn't dream we'd be parted for so long."

"Huh?" I tried to lift my arm, but it was too heavy. Everything about me felt weighted and clumsy, so I closed my eyes and hoped when I opened them again, I would be back in my bed – or at the very least, making out with Philip. Ezra's chest was solid, so I leaned into him, relaxing in the paternal shelter I'd been surviving for so long without. I knew he wasn't really my dad and probably never would be, but he was warm and held me with something I let myself pretend was the purest kind of love. In my fantasy, I'd skinned my knee riding my brand new shiny bike (not the rusty one Ollie had found me from the neighbor's trash, and Terence had fixed up). My dad would come running toward me and scoop me up off the ground, not annoyed at all if I cried. There would be no need to suck it up. He was stronger than all the things that broke me.

I felt hot tears slide down my cheeks, followed by a

semi-moist handkerchief wiping the dots of emotion away to salvage what was left of my pride. I was desperate for the shelter I knew I would be pushing away when my eyes opened again.

So I kept my eyes shut tight, leaning on the father I never had. When a little feeling came back into my hands, I clung to Ezra, surprising both of us. I felt his arm slide under my knees, then he rocked back to sit on his butt. He pulled me onto his lap, swaying my body gently to soothe us both. I'd not been held much as a child, and the difference good touch made was indescribable. I was curled up in a grown man's lap like a baby, crying out years of pent-up loneliness coupled with the fear of waking up to suffocation. The sting of my own father never once coming to look for me to see if my knee was skinned poured out onto Ezra's once white undershirt. The quiet song he hummed only to me sliced through the barrier of distance I usually regarded men with. I was broken, and he was gentle with the pieces. It was a surprisingly good fit.

I clung to Ezra, wishing he wouldn't disappear from my life with his superhero dad kind of amazingness, but I knew he and Bev would never last. I ignored my instinct to pull away and bunched my fist into his shirt, hoping my sheer force of will would hold him to this very spot until I pulled myself together and stopped needing a dad. The longing ripped at my heart, so my natural inclination was to rip at the skin on the backs of my hands.

Ezra caught up my left hand in his, holding with a firm

strength that told me I didn't have to handle things by myself. That surviving didn't have to hurt. That my dad would be there, and I could trust him not to leave. He pressed his cheek to my forehead as he rocked me for who knows how long.

I'd been declared an adult by a judge at the age of fifteen, but now at twenty-two, I was finally a child. I hadn't been a child in so very long.

"I'm here, October Grace. I'm here," Ezra whispered, tears dotting his eyes and falling into my hair. "Get that thing out of here, Von. I don't care how much you love it."

"What am I doing?" I asked, not able to mask how very lost I was. I mean, I'd barely woken up and meandered onto a grown man's lap. To say that I was lost was pretty apparent.

"You're breathing. That's all you need to do now. We've been searching all night for you three. We had the *baga* root, and knew you wouldn't last the morning. But we found you." Ezra squeezed me, closing his eyes like a prayer. "The kingdom's safe. The kingdom's safe."

It was like being doused with cold water. Ezra wasn't my dad. He cared about me in the way you care about your hammer. I was a tool to be put to work until my usefulness expired. Ezra loved his kingdom. He'd rushed all night to save my life because I was his hammer. Hammer, not daughter.

I extracted myself from his embrace, only just now realizing I had an audience. There were a few new faces who'd just seen me fall apart like the child I knew I couldn't afford to be. I gave Ezra back his handkerchief and offered him my hand to hoist him up, looking anywhere but into his aqua eyes that made me want to forget I was his hammer. "Hey, so there's new people. Hi." I held up my hand like it was the first day of school. "October."

The man to the right of Lang knelt before me, his towering six and a half feet lowered so his bowed head was level with my abdomen. "Lady October, forgive me. We searched all through the night, but couldn't find you before the root began to wear off. I'm Klark, your servant."

"Uh, what?"

The man to Lang's left bent to one knee as well. "I'm Ruiz, and my sword serves your will."

I took a step back, shaking my head. Lang was patient with my confusion. "These are my most trusted men. Hard to come by trust in Sakuna among my father's soldiers, but these are the ones to bet on. They'll see us to the castle safely."

I was out of my element here, and the bowing wasn't helping any. "Okay, thanks. But please get up. The bowing really isn't for me."

Ruiz and Klark stood, perplexed and concerned. "Have we offended you, milady?"

I looked to Mason, who puffed out his chest to mimic my queenly role and the pride I should take in doling out the pleasure of my mere presence.

No. Just... no.

"That's not how I roll. If we're traveling together, you don't need to act like I need bowing to. I sleep on the ground just like you guys, so we're cool." I chucked Ruiz on the shoulder, smirking at his wide eyes.

Mason groaned at my lack of decorum. "They're addressing you as they should. You're the Queen of Hayop, and they'll respect you as such."

My nose crinkled. "Huh? I'm not a queen. I'm an asset. Big difference. And I've never even set foot in Hayop." Then it dawned on me he was thinking about Kara. She'd been Queen of Hayop when Mason had been granted the crown for the short time he was in power. My correction was quiet, and I tried to keep my inflection kind. "I'm not your wife, Mason."

"Oh. Yes, of course. I know that. Obviously." Mason's cheeks flushed pink, and he turned away to go toward the main road. "They'll still bow to you. I'm firm on that. Omens hold even more clout than kings and queens."

I rolled my eyes to Ruiz and Klark. "Ignore him. He's in a mood."

Ruiz and Klark exchanged uncertain looks when they rose slowly, as if unsure whether I might change my mind and off-with-their-heads them. Lang's two besties both wore brown t-shirts and matching shorts with leather armor over their clothes. I realized they probably dressed to match the mud as camouflage. I looked on the towering men with new appreciation.

Ruiz scratched his five o'clock shadow as he stood with

his chest barreled. "Lady October, it's a day's walk to the castle where the main well is. Are you healthy enough for the journey?"

I was the runt of the group, so I understood his assumption that I was more decorative than useful. "I'm fine, now that I can breathe. Minor detail." I stretched and slid on the backpack I spotted on the ground at Lang's feet. "Oh, cool. I was hoping Gerda and that kid found you with the stone. Trade you." I slid Lang's signet ring off my thumb and dropped it in his palm, grateful I hadn't lost it.

Lang nodded, exhaling with relief as he slid his ring back on his finger. "The boy will be rewarded in secret, so my father knows nothing of his help in hiding the sagrado stone."

I looked around for my favorite smarmy smirk. "Where's Von? And where'd Edward wander to?"

"I assume you mean the sigbin?" Ezra's smile died on his face. "Sigbins are dangerous creatures, dear. I won't have one tailing us through our journey. Von went to go take it to the main road to set it loose."

"Oh, you don't know Edward like I do. He's a puppy."

"Not a puppy. He's a monster, trained to kill on command."

"Edward's fine. Onward, boys." I waved the guys forward and started toward the main road, trusting the others would follow behind if they felt like it. "Von?" I called when I saw his green t-shirt and black hair that stuck out at all angles.

"November?" Von turned with a look of relief on his face. "Hey!" He held out his arms to me with that affectionate casualness he had with everyone. I fell into his embrace, muscling through the panic when it seemed like Von's germs were nearer the surface than usual. I was now on my second day without medication, and I was starting to feel the damning pressure.

Von squeezed me, lifting my feet off the ground. "Aren't you supposed to be resting? I mean, you almost died, Peach. That was terrifying. I woke up to you gasping, and your lips were all blue. Then Mason and I realized the bit about the root, so Edward and I went in search of it. Your dog's dead useful, by the way. He dug up a *baga* root about the same time Prince Langgam and Ezra found us." He set me down, looking at me with ease to mask his worry. "I've never woken up next to a woman who was mid-suffocation before. Let's not do that in our next life, yeah? Make sure you come back as a sexy librarian who's also a marathon runner or deep sea diver. Someone with amazing lung capacity."

"I'll put in a formal request first thing. But we should get going. I don't feel like waking up to not breathing again."

"Demanding little vixen, you are." Edward came back to Von, whining with his tail between his legs as he licked my knuckle. "Go on, Edward. You know Ezra said you can't chum with us."

I clicked my fingers to Edward and started down the

trail toward the mountains. "It's fine. Edward can stay."

Ezra and the others came up behind me and followed down the mud path. It was slightly elevated from the trees and the vast nothingness on the other side, so there were whole patches of dry dirt to walk on. "October Grace, I told you we can't travel with a sigbin. It's dangerous."

I kept walking with Edward on my left and Von on my right, who cast an apologetic glance at Ezra as we walked. "It's fine, Ezra. The first time he eats out someone's heart, I'll start writing that apology note."

"Hilarious. This one seems docile now, but it's not likely he'll stay that way. I have no idea why he's been so compliant. I'm not willing to gamble your safety on the mercy of a monster."

"Edward doesn't deserve to be ostracized. So he didn't grow up with people who loved him. He has me now, and he's not ready to give that up. Von tried to shoo him away, and he wouldn't go. Edward knows who I am. He's cool." I reached down and patted Edward's head, smiling when he ground his muzzle into my leg while I walked.

"This is the exact opposite of what I asked you to do, kids," Ezra said to Von and me with a frown.

Von took the scolding with grace, matching my pace as I started walking faster to make better time. "I tried, Ezra. He wouldn't leave her. Or me, actually. It's not my fault that I'm a fearsome dragon tamer."

I turned toward Ezra, still stinging from his hug that had turned sour. "Look, I appreciate where it's coming from, but I'm not your kid. You care about the welfare of your country, and I get that. Edward is dead useful. He'll make sure I'm safe. If I can keep an eye on him, he should be able to stay."

Ezra frowned. "I care about your safety, as well. You're my daughter, and I think I have to right to be able to tell you not to play with killers."

"Then tell Lang to go on home. Tell Mason he's no longer needed. How about you? How clean are your hands?" I felt a little bad for lashing out at him, but I didn't much like being bossed. "And all due respect, but you're not my dad. I know you're not going through with that marriage, so let it be what it is. You're my co-worker."

Von let out a low whistle, and I felt a ping of guilt at my blatant attitude.

Mason saddled up beside me and placed his hand on my back. "Excuse us for a moment. Sorry, Ezra. My charge doesn't know what she's saying. Go on ahead. We'll catch up after I've had a talk with her."

Ezra nodded, watching as I retracted from Mason and stood to the side with Edward while the others passed by. Mason squared his shoulders to mine and put his hands on my biceps, looking at me as if gearing up for a grounding. "What was that? Ezra's been perfectly nice to you. He saved your life! This is how you thank him?"

"I'm not giving up Edward, and I don't much care for being bossed like I'm his kid. You want to have this same talk with him? You know Edward's not dangerous to me."

Mason studied the defiance in my eyes. "Why are you being like this?"

"You all want me to act like this important person who has all this power, but I'm not allowed to make small decisions, like whether or not I want a dog? How's that measure up?"

"Ezra's a good man."

"I know that."

"He saved your life. He's been searching all night for us with Prince Langgam."

"Yes, I know they need me alive for the safety of the kingdom. It's a real heartwarming father-daughter tale of sending the unsuspecting girl into the lion's den and then getting pissed when the girl makes friends with the lion."

"That's how you see this?"

"It's how it is. Ezra's a good guy, but I don't need him to play the dad card when we all know what this is. I'm here because I drew the short straw from the genetic pool. At least let me keep the ounce of sunshine I found with my dog."

Mason dropped his hands from my arms and stood straighter, looking down his nose at me. "I thought I saw a glimmer of my wife's nobility in you, but I was wrong."

I don't know why I allowed his words to cut me, but they did. "Dude, I'm not your wife. I'm not Ezra's daughter. I'm just me, and that should be enough for anyone who actually cares about me." I clicked my fingers to Edward. "Come on, buddy. We're falling behind."

35

THE PRINCE'S PROPOSAL

I kept my distance from Mason and Ezra as we walked through the day and on into the evening. Mason, Von and I hadn't eaten in almost two days, and it was starting to affect my energy level. I trudged on through the muck in my bare feet, the sagrado stone banging against the small of my back as the backpack shifted with every step I took. When the pointy end hit my spine in just the right way, I slid the pack off and moved off the path so the others could keep going.

Mason took the pack by the strap and set it on the ground as I winced through a stretch. "I'll carry this for a while. Give you a break."

"I can do it. It's just poking my back, is all. I'm afraid it's going to break my skin and Von'll vamp out. Give it here. I know touching the backpack makes you uncomfortable." I held out my hand to retrieve it from him. "I needed a two-second break. I'm good now."

"I'm more uncomfortable at the prospect of you being the only one who's carrying anything heavy. You've done more than your fair share. It's my turn. Now lift up your shirt."

I raised my eyebrow at Mason. "You've gotta know I'm not doing that. Dude, put some grease on it. Spread a little 'you're so beautiful' before asking a girl to take off her shirt, not that I would've anyway."

Mason huffed. "I meant so I can see your back. Just a few inches."

"Oh. That sounds much better. It's fine." I hiked up my yellow t-shirt to show him my lower back, expecting maybe a little red mark or something.

Mason hissed. "Ruiz, do you have any salve in your satchel? We're taking a break." He lowered his voice to me, still holding the backpack as if carrying a bomb. "You should've told me it was hurting you sooner. It's my job to make sure you don't have to go through too much pain in all this."

"My pain?" I looked up at him, too tired to play games. "I crossed you off the list of people who care about my pain as soon as you went in for that second kiss. You care about *your* pain. It's fine. It's Darwinian. Just don't lie about it. I'm not five." I didn't speak with an attitude, just without tact.

Mason's mouth fell open, speechless at the scolding.

Ruiz pulled out a small unmarked tub of cream that was a sickly shade of greenish yellow. The others stretched and sat down to share from Lang's men's canteens. I didn't want to think about the ramifications of putting an unnamed random mud concoction on my skin. I wanted to run from that little tub, but remained in place, not wanting to inflict my neurosis on poor Ruiz, who was only trying to help. I counted back from ten, readying myself to be cool about whatever was slathered on my back.

"Is it bad?" I asked. "I'm not bleeding, right?"

Ruiz frowned when he took in the damage. "No. No blood. But your back is starting to bruise and blister. My ointment will speed the healing, but it can't undo this." Ruiz knelt down behind me, casting a sheepish grin up. His wide nose revealed four freckles I could now see, since he was finally shorter than me. "I apologize for kneeling. There's just no other way for me to see what I'm doing."

"Very well, you may keep your kneecaps," I ruled in my most queenly voice, grateful he chuckled and didn't take me seriously. Edward sniffed Ruiz, who froze upon such close contact with the monster I adored. "It's alright, Edward. He's helping."

"I confess, I've never seen a sigbin so tamed. He even bites Prince Aranya on occasion."

"Who's Prince Aranya?"

"Prince Langgam's older brother. Next in line for the throne, and totally undeserving of it. Most of Sakuna would follow Prince Langgam to the grave." Ruiz paused before putting the germy glop on me. "I apologize. Some of your scrapes are lower on your... I..."

"I gotcha." I rolled down the waist of my shorts an inch, hissing when the cold cream slathered over my skin. "Oh, that's nice." It tingled when the air hit it, sending a hot and cold sensation through my spine. I looked over my shoulder and found Ruiz blowing on my lower back.

"You have to let it dry," he explained apologetically. "The longer the salve stays on your skin, the better."

I nodded, rolling my shirt to be more of a halter. I tied it off below my breasts, while wishing for a sweater to cover my naked skin.

"Nice," Von teased me, pinching my stomach just to make me yelp.

"Knock it off. I wouldn't bother with it if it wasn't actually painful."

"No, I think you look quite fetching." Von took in my discomfort as my eyes shifted from side to side and my arms crossed over my stomach. "In fact, I think I'll copycat that style." He took his emerald t-shirt and rolled it up to reveal his toned midsection, trying to cinch it as I had, but coming up with no luck. "How did you manage that?"

I laughed, and the motion felt amazing. I hadn't laughed in a while. I reached out and tied Von's shirt around his ribs to match me, grinning at his antics done just to lighten my mood. He hadn't even touched me to pull my anxiety, but lifted a portion using only his strange personality. "You're a diva if I ever saw one."

"Oh, you." He motioned to his toned stomach. "But we're looking for drop dead gorgeous. I would also have settled for lust-worthy, sexy beast, Von the Amazing Seducer of Women – just to give you a few ideas for next time you describe me to your girlfriends. I've got my eye on Stacy next. Then Christina. Then maybe I'll give Rachel another go."

"That's quite the list."

"Well, I'm quite the guy." He helped Ruiz to stand and raised his fist in the air. "Onward, soldiers!"

Von looked hilarious with his haltered shirt. I was so distracted by the cuteness that I didn't even mind it when his hand slid into mine. I knew he was pulling from me, but it didn't remind me that I was the basket case among warriors. We were just two goofballs out for a walk in the too-hot summer. Von bumped his hip to mine as we led the way. "Do you mind if I see if Stacy's up for giving me a tour of her bedroom?"

I reminded myself of my firm placement in the friend zone and tried to make myself useful on the sidelines. "I can't imagine she wouldn't be. She's usually up for anything if the guy's cute enough. I recommend wearing exactly this when you hit on her." I chuckled, squeezing his hand. "Oh! Ask her to do her British accent for you. It's hilarious. Honestly, best laugh you'll have for weeks."

"Is she all cockney?"

"No, it's completely Jamaican. I swear, she doesn't even hear the difference."

"Well, that's just wrong." He rolled his shoulders as we walked through the mud. "I'll suffer through the accent mishaps if it takes the edge off for a night. It's been too long. You've domesticated me, love."

"I can't imagine anything more tragic." I tried to let go of his hand, but he only held tighter. "Well, Mr. Brady, you can spend your nights however you like. Just make sure you're home by morning to read your paper at the breakfast table and take our dog for a walk."

"Yes, dear." He leaned over and kissed my nose, grinning when I swiped away the affection. "Wiping my love away, are you? Oh, you're afraid some lone wolf might see and get jealous?"

"No. It's not that."

He looked over his shoulder to confirm we were a safe distance ahead of the others. "Look, date who you want. Mason's a solid bloke usually, and he's been one of my best mates for years. I've got nothing against Mason, but don't let him use you like that anymore. Go make it with some lucky bloke who's not loaded with baggage."

"Who would that be? I've had exactly one guy off and on in my life, and he cheated on me with my friend. I'm just not the dating type."

Von frowned. "When we get back, I'll see to remedying that. I'll find you someone good. Someone really clean who gets off on washing his hands."

"I don't need your help finding a boyfriend."

"Who said anything about a boyfriend? I'm just talking

about a boy to neck with who won't leave welts on you." He motioned to the bruises on my collar with a guilty expression. "Have I said I'm sorry about that?"

"Only every five minutes. I'm really fine. Fine about the neck stuff. Fine without a guy to take me out. I'm more the work type of girl than the dating type of girl."

"Boy, are you lucky I came along. These are your golden years. Use them unwisely." He pinched my stomach again, smiling at my squeak and shove.

"Would you knock it off?"

"You've got this cute little defiant face where you scrunch your nose up. It's like you think you're going to be all scary. Downright adorable."

"Oh, hush."

Ruiz saddled up beside me, giving Edward a wary glance. He held his hands up to prove their innocence. "Excuse me, Lady October. May I ask you a few questions about your world? I've never met a human before."

"Oh, wow. No pressure. Sure. What do you want to know?"

"Is everyone pale, like you? Your skin is so light."

"Oh, well, we've got all different shades up there, from lighter than mine to darker than yours. Just depends on genetics."

"Are they all short, like you and Lady Mariang?"

I pursed my lips at being called short. "I'm not all that short. I'm mid-range for a girl my age. But I'm thinking people from Sakuna naturally run a little taller than us."

"How about terrain?"

Ruiz fired question after question at me, and before long Klark chimed in with his own. I would've thought Lang might have answered some of the basics for his men, but when I thought about it, Lang stood out as a stranger when I'd first met him, so I couldn't be sure how familiar he really was with my world. "When are you planning on moving into the mansion?" Lang inquired, participating in the discussion a little.

"I'm not. I live at my house. You sent a spy to watch me sleep, you wang. You know that."

Von sniggered at my slang.

Lang studied me with a superior eye, his thick lips pursed. "It's not very well guarded. If my spy can get in, any number of things can get at you."

"Well, you stole me first, so here I am. And you infiltrated the mansion easy enough."

"That took weeks of planning, and it wasn't easy at all. Your house? That was easy. If you don't want to get snatched at by the others, you'll move into the mansion."

I blinked up at him, the exhaustion and hunger making me slightly giddy. "Aw, you care about little old me? You want to make sure I'm safe? You're a regular gentleman, you are. I take back the part about you being a wang."

Lang frowned at my joking nature. "If you die, the world dies. Of course I care."

"That's it. It's settled. You're in love with me." I elbowed Von. "You heard it, right?"

Von grinned at the much-needed levity, walking in step with me. "I surely did. You might have to go through Mason, mate. Fair warning. He's got it bad for your sweet November."

Mason glowered at Von. Lang spluttered, touching my arm. "I said nothing like that. I only meant..."

I gasped dramatically at his fingers on my elbow. "Lang! Save something for the honeymoon! I mean, I am a lady." I bristled, and then laughed when his mouth fell open in horror.

"I don't understand your humor," Lang grumbled when he caught on that I was joking. "Are all humans so easily given to this kind of thing? I don't like it."

"What humor? You just got down on your knee, asked me to marry you and told me you were madly in love with me."

"I did no such thing." He turned to Ezra, frowning at the snickers coming from Ruiz and Klark. "Ezra, control your Omen."

I started talking wildly with my hands. "You said, and I quote, 'October Grace Reese, I was half a man before I met you. I cried myself to sleep every night until I saw your sunshine of a face. Now I skip in the meadows and pick flowers all day for you. Marry me, my beauty.'"

"That's what I heard," Von chuckled.

Ezra shook his head in feigned disappointment. "I had

hoped you would've asked for my blessing first, Prince Langgam."

Ruiz and Klark both grinned at the scandal of mocking their prince. Ruiz laughed. "I heard exactly the proposal she described. Wasn't there a song he sang to you, Lady October?"

"There was. I think it was called, 'I never should've abducted you, please let me buy you new shoes.'"

Lang rolled his eyes at being jabbed at like one of the guys. "Fine. I'll buy you new shoes. You know, you can have whatever you want from any of our lands. That's all standard for Omens."

"Really?" This was news to me. "Then I think the first thing I'll want is a big porch swing for the two of us to snuggle in. Can't you just picture it? You and me, swinging while we hold hands and talk about growing old together."

Lang eyed me to make sure I was still joking. Finally, his frown gave way to a smile. "Yeah, alright. Keep it up."

"Oh, I have every intention of making this the longest walk of your life."

"So long as we get there eventually, I can handle that."

"I also want a wombat. Not a real one. That'd be crazy. A stuffed animal one. I've never seen a stuffed animal wombat before, and think they'd be cute. Put that on my list of presents you're going to buy to make this all up to me."

"Sure thing. Keep it coming."

"I think I want to go on a spa weekend so I can get a mud bath. I haven't had enough mud lately."

Von bumped his hip to mine. "Really? A mud bath. I can't picture you doing that."

I raised my nose indignantly. "You're not allowed to picture me in the bath. I'm getting married to Prince Langgam."

"Ah, of course. Apologies, milady," Von said with a sweeping bow.

"So you *can* say my full name and title. I didn't think you capable," Lang groused as he reached down to adjust the lace on his boot, pausing my progression.

"Of course. But I assume you want me to call you something like 'sugar britches' or 'squeezy buns' once we get married." I mimed squeezing Lang's tight backside while Von snorted.

Lang was still on his knee when he touched my arm, gazing up at me with a serious look on his face. "October Grace Reese, I've never taken a wife, but now I see the error of my ways. My beauty, will you do me the great honor of..." And then he interrupted the speech that made my eyes go wide by smearing a fistful of mud on my cheek. "There. Now you can cross mud bath off your list. That present didn't cost me a thing."

"Ack!" After Von gripped my shoulder to pull my impending dirt freak-out from me, I was back to swinging with the levity of the moment. I leaned forward and wiped my cheek on Lang's shirt when he stood, grinning at his laughter that sounded actually joyful. It started from deep inside of him and bubbled out in luxurious waves that bathed everyone in something beautiful. I looked up at him with new appreciation, seeing just how much he'd needed to let go. "There you are," I marveled, as if seeing him for the first time. "I like you much better with a smile. I feel like you might abduct me less."

Lang looked down at me with unconcealed affection for seeing his inner goofball and poking it until it came out. "Sure. Some abduction, but definitely less."

I dropped Von's hand to clap. "He did it! He made a joke! Who knew you were funny? Well done, sugar britches. Well done."

Von held up his finger, his other hand gripping mine to calm my nerves while I breathed through icks of the mud splotches that clung to my face. "Is 'squeezy buns' not on the table, then? That's the one I fancied."

Lang bowed to the peanut gallery, who clapped that he'd made a joke. We continued on our walk, and somewhere between the mud and the laughter, our group of royal misfits were starting to become a team.

36

MY BROKEN MUSIC

As we neared the city, Von, Mason and I walked hand in hand in hand. The sun started to grow just as tired as I was, kissing the horizon and warning us to hurry. As the remnants of my medication left my system, they kept up a constant stream of slow pulling to stop me from regressing.

Ruiz and Klark finally started to lighten up, though they still dipped their heads when speaking to me and referred to me repeatedly as "your grace" or "Lady October". We were starting to inch more toward the feel of old buddies going for a hike, and it was nice. I felt Mason's eyes on me, disapproving of my casual nature that no doubt was nothing like his perfect wife's. I internally shrugged, ruling that it was probably a good thing that Mason was disappointed I wasn't who he wanted me to be.

Ezra was quiet until we neared the main city. "I move

we break off a portion of the rock now for October Grace to hold. I don't want any chance of this going awry."

"Sure. Do we have anything I can use to break it?" I asked, surprising Ezra with my compliance. I cast him a bland smile. I didn't not like the guy. I just didn't like him pretending to be my dad so he could boss me around. I also didn't care for the too vulnerable way I'd let my guard down with him, only to find he was protecting his asset, not his daughter. If he could be a co-worker without muddying the lines, I could play along.

Ezra raised both eyebrows at my non-attitude, and I felt a little bad about that. I really wasn't a jerk; I just didn't like being played. "Um, sure. Of course. Perhaps the hilt of Mason's machete?"

Mason was already unsheathing his sword, though he didn't give it to me. He gave me the backpack as if handing me the Holy Grail, which to them, I guess it was. We moved off the trail further into the woods so we couldn't be seen by passersby. Edward whined when I told him to go stand with Von. "Go on, baby. Go to your daddy. I mean it. I don't want you turning to stone."

Prince Langgam let out a short whistle I could tell Edward didn't like. He snorted and sat at Von's feet while Mason and I went deeper into the woods. His tone wasn't unkind, but it wasn't friendly, either. "Here. Just break off a portion. Remember, we need six pieces, one for each region."

"Got it."

Mason backed up in case any shards broke loose and went flying, watching with trepidation as I unzipped the filthy backpack and slid out the other backpack Danny had used to double-wrap it inside. In that one was the rock, which lit up when I touched it.

I examined the doorstop my family had owned since childhood. It still looked ordinary, like a cheap eighties novelty toy. Judging by Mason's gasp when it lit up, the rock's mundane appearance was part of its charm. I set it on the forest floor and aimed the hilt of Mason's machete to it, taking a few practice blows before whacking. I couldn't decide where to hit it. I divided the stone in my mind into six equal pieces, but the rock was unevenly shaped, so I knew no matter how I hit it, the pieces would be impossible to make perfectly even. "Mason, what if one region gets a slightly bigger piece than another? Would that matter?"

"No. Just a piece of the rock in the water will cure most everything in the region that can be fixed by nature."

"Okay." I aimed at a different spot, hesitating longer than I knew was acceptable. I couldn't get it perfect. The pieces would be uneven.

After a few minutes of waiting patiently, Klark came over to check on our progress. "Do you need something to better break the stone with? I can travel into the city and get you a hammer, if you prefer."

"No. Thanks, though. I'm almost there."

"It's just that we're losing the light."

I nodded, biting my lip as I aimed at the stone. "Sorry. I can do better."

Mason cleared his throat. "Stop a second. Let me pull a little more from you before you try again. I can practically see your insides building up."

I nodded, ashamed at my limitations. I walked over to Mason instead of making him go near the rock. He could have just touched my elbow, but instead he squared his shoulders to me and massaged both my arms, tugging some of my tension out so it didn't take me over. "What's wrong?" he asked me with actual compassion shining through in his eyes. It was the first time in hours he'd looked on me with actual kindness instead of veiled irritation.

"I'm having some trouble," I admitted. "It won't break evenly, no matter how I do it. It won't be perfect."

Mason touched me under my chin and lifted so I was blinking up at him. "*Hani*, nothing's perfect. We just work with what we have."

"But it'll be uneven. Are you sure we can't get a saw or something?"

"I'm sure. Let's break off a piece and be done with it. We'll go straight home and you'll never have to come back to Sakuna ever again."

"Promise?"

"If we hustle, you can be in your shower in less than an hour."

"You've never been more beautiful than when you say

sexy things like that to me." I'd meant it as a joke, but the desire in his stormy gaze was palpable. His focus drifted to my lips as his tongue moistened his.

Mason's grip was firm as he drew me even closer, his mouth an inch from mine. "Let me take you home. Get you out of these clothes." Then before I could brace myself, his lips caressed mine, my stomach banging around as the red and yellow swirled up and painted his face with smears of color. One lonely flute started to play a melancholy Irish tune. Mason was highlighted in a halo of yellow as we kissed, looking like a work of art I wanted to throw my arms around and make out with until we couldn't take it anymore. I also wanted to run away from him. A little bit, I wanted to punch him. It was his one kiss of the day I'd allotted us, and dang, if it didn't take my breath away.

I wanted to forget. I wanted to close the door on Sakuna, Terraway, all the death and even Mason. It was probably counterintuitive to kiss him hoping for a few minutes of forgetting him, but it worked. The lone flute was joined by three more, then four. Then a whole smattering of flutes started drowning out the things that weighed me down.

We were music, and it was a beautiful thing.

The passion came crashing to a halt when his grip migrated to my waist, and he accidentally squeezed the bruises and blisters on my lower back. "Ow! Yeah, that'll do it." I jumped away, my back burning as the music and colors gave way to the brown terrain. I looked up, hoping to see Mason looking at me in that way he did when he thought I was funny, but his eyes were still closed. Then he gripped his heart and stumbled backwards, opening his eyes in wonder as he took in my face.

Only he wasn't seeing me. I could tell that he was seeing his wife.

I should've expected the crash that seemed to accompany being kissed too beautifully, but it always caught me off guard. I walked back to the stone, picked up the machete, selected a corner at random, and set to breaking off a piece. Even after I finally cracked through, Mason was still holding his heart, that dazed grin on his face as he watched me be Kara.

My hands burned with the need to be scratched. I slid the larger portion of the rock back into the first carrier, then into the second backpack, zipping everything up and sliding it on my back with the spare piece clutched in my hand like a baseball. I didn't look at Von as I rejoined the gang, nor did I make eye contact with Ezra, who I could see in my periphery was watching me with unconcealed sadness. "It's done. I've got the piece here in my hand, so no one come near me, okay?"

Von kept a safe distance as we started walking. "You did good, Peach."

"It's not even. I mean, it's not a true sixth. I think it's a little smaller than it should be."

"That's alright." Von watched me warily. "Could you stop that?"

"What?"

"You're scratching your hand again. Please, November. I'm starting to get hungry. I'm doing my best here. You can't scratch yourself. I can't pull from you when you're holding the rock like that."

I slid the baseball-sized chunk into the front zipper pouch, and everyone's stress went down a noticeable degree. Von reached for my hand, but I couldn't touch him. "No. It's the germs. I can't do it. I'm sorry."

Von didn't say anything to my dysfunction. He merely put his hand on my back and rubbed my shoulder as we walked. He was kind to me when I didn't deserve it.

"No, Mason," I heard Ezra say with a stern tone when Mason saddled up on my other side. "You take up the rear. You've carried on enough. You're done now." Ezra had that paternal tone I'd heard dads on TV use when their kid came home late or got in trouble for something or other. I don't know why it softened me, but I began to relax in Von's half-embrace as we walked through the night toward the village. Though I couldn't cure myself, I hoped to have Sakuna cured within the hour.

37

COUNTING

When we reached the city, it was decided I would wait with Von and Mason just outside in the woods. Lang and the guys went with Ezra to throw the stone in the well.

The contents of Ruiz's satchel were emptied into Klark's, and the stone segment was carefully placed in Ruiz's bag. Ruiz took the burden with a grave sense of honor, gripping my shoulder as if we were engaged in some sort of ceremonial passing of the baton. "Thank you, Lady October. Thank you for all you've done for our people. It's been a privilege to journey with you."

"Thanks for keeping me company and showing me around."

"I'll be sure to return your fiancé to you within the hour."

I managed a grin, winking at Lang. "See you soon, squeezy buns."

Lang actually smiled at me, shaking his head at the levity I'd sown that had sprouted into little bits of hope growing into new air. One day I wished for him to enjoy a life without so much secrecy and duty.

Lang stiffened when he addressed Mason and Von. "Take my bride deep into the woods and wait for us there. I'll bring you all to the surface as soon as we finish up."

Mason, Von and I turned back to the woods with Edward as soon as the four left for the city gate. I could see two-story buildings poking out over the stone walls that lined the main city, housing the important people. Toward the back was a large gray stone castle with a tower in the center shooting up to serve as the highest manmade point in the nation. It was hard to think of that being someone's childhood home, but it had been Lang's. It looked cold, and I now knew that just wasn't him.

Von and Mason picked a spot to wait far away from the main road, but I was too keyed up to sit with them. Edward and I wandered a few feet deeper, leaving the backpack with them so I could count the trees. I know that sounds lame, but counting was a habit I fell into on the days I went off my meds. It was soothing, and helped organize my brain when everything seemed too out of place. I was a big fan of even numbers, so I counted by twos, ticking off marks on my arm when I hit the next grouping of fifty. I had a thing about groupings. So soothing.

Von's hand on my shoulder made me jump, so engrossed was I in the counting. "Okay, you have to stop. You're going to break the skin, and I haven't eaten anything all day." His nose wrinkled. "You haven't eaten in two days. That can't be good. Mason's started complaining. What are you going to get on your pizza?"

"You're making me lose count. Now I have to start over." I began counting again, jumping by twos and growing more content while giving in to my anxiety. It was an odd little dichotomy. Counting relaxed me for a time, until the scales tipped and I couldn't stop. I knew I was on what my therapist had called "the path to danger," but as I was already in danger and had a mini dragon as a pet, I figured one more threat to my sanity couldn't hurt all that much.

"What are you counting?"

"The trees."

"You're joking. Why?"

I rubbed my forehead, losing my place again. "I like to count them. Is that alright?"

Von wrapped his arms around my waist from behind and leaned me to his chest. "Okay. Wow. You're overloaded with stress. This is... It's like every time I stop touching you, it starts building up with a vengeance. What are you upset about?"

"I'm not upset. I'm counting."

Von was quiet while he held me, offering his forearm for me to make little ticks on when I reached the next fifty.

His chin rested atop my head as he pulled from me while Edward sniffed by our feet. The outlines of some of the trees in the distance were harder to make out, so I couldn't be sure I was getting an accurate count unless I touched them.

I *needed* to touch them. I lifted my foot to move toward the darkness, but made a quick decision and gripped Von's arm, my panic peaking. "Don't let me touch the trees," I whispered, knowing if I started, I would never stop. The obsessive touching was the tipping point where the counting started being a detriment rather than a soothing balm on my splintered brain.

"What?"

"I want to touch them, but you can't let me. If I start touching them, I won't be able to stop."

"Mason! Get your hairy arse over here." He waited until Mason joined us. "She's cracked. That medication's no joke. She needs it now. I'm pulling, but it's barely making a dent."

Mason lifted my chin up to look into my eyes, but I barely saw him. All I saw were the trees that needed counting. There was no order to them, and I had to be the one to put them right. "If only they'd been planted in neat little rows. That would be perfect. Twenty rows. Twenty rows by one hundred trees. That would be perfect. Maybe even one hundred twenty trees to a row. No, maybe one hundred forty. That would be perfect."

"What's wrong with you?" Mason asked, though he

said it like he was pleading a prayer, begging for answers as to why I couldn't stop counting, and why I sounded like a crazy person.

That's the thing about love. You don't want to believe the person you're kissing could be cracked, but Mason finally understood that part of me was, and might always be.

Mason blocked my view by gripping the back of my head and pressing my face to his chest, but I still saw the trees in my mind's eye. I counted them there, whispering the numbers and putting them in perfect rows like obedient soldiers who didn't need to ever step out of line. Mason whispered a pained, "You have to stop, *hani*. You can't be broken. I need you strong."

I was sandwiched between Mason and Von while Edward whined. He whined three times, which was an odd number. I didn't much care for those.

"Someone's coming," Von whispered. "My spidey senses are tingling."

Not five minutes later, my counting was interrupted by the sound of too many marching feet coming toward us. Then I heard shouts of, "I found them!"

Mason pulled back, his senses on high alert. "Take her deeper into the woods! Run until you don't hear us anymore."

"What? No! We can't split up." I was scared to leave him to fend off an army.

"It's done." Mason pecked my lips, handed me the

backpack and sent us off.

Von and I were barefoot and running through the woods with Edward leading the way. Von hissed when a branch broke the skin on my arm, but he seethed through his teeth and we kept up our pace. We didn't stop for breath. We didn't stop for anything. I couldn't count fast enough, and the number of trees started piling up.

That hardly mattered when the soldiers had boots to charge after us with, making far better time than we could in bare feet. With tears in my eyes, I stopped and wrapped the strap of the backpack around Edward's neck. "Go, Edward! Don't let them get the stone! Run! Take it to Ezra!"

No sooner had Edward bounded on ahead of us did an arrow sink itself into the back of Von's thigh. He turned with a yelp that quickly mutated into a hiss. "Run, Peach!" he ordered. Then he lunged at the dozen men who were hot on our heels. He growled like a rabid animal, and I could tell without looking that his fangs were bared as he attacked, taking them down with his best weapon.

I didn't look to see what was happening; I only knew that three men were still giving chase. Three was an odd number. I didn't much care for those.

I cried out when I felt a greasy hand grip my shoulder, infesting me with a flood of germs. My shouts stopped when he tackled me to the ground.

Then the numbers stopped.

In fact, just about everything stopped when I hit my head on a rock, and the world went dark.

38

CAGED OMEN

I awoke to total darkness, and for a second, I was afraid I'd somehow been blinded. I pawed at the ground, feeling concrete beneath me. The ground was freeze-your-bra cold, and the silence was so thick, I could practically feel it on my skin. My joints felt years older than they were as I pushed myself up off the ground, shivering in my filthy t-shirt and shorts.

I took three steps forward and hit my face on iron bars. As my hands felt each bar, the panic built up in me. I was in a cell.

The irony of a prison nurse being locked in a jail cell was not lost on me. I knew of quite a few inmates who would give up their contraband cigarettes for a picture of this. I rattled the cage and shouted, but it did little good.

I heard footsteps, and I didn't know whether to be relieved or petrified. A door creaked open and the slow cackle of a woman's evil laughter flowed through the room, along with a dozen tiny flapping wings. "This is her? This is the new Omen? She's barely more useful than Mariang, and that girl's on her last leg. And you thought we could get along without Sama's rations. This is why, Langgam. This is why you're not next in line for the throne."

Lang's response was short and clipped, and my heart soared when I heard his voice. It anchored me so I didn't feel like I was drifting in the sea of dark nothingness. "She's new still. The numbers are far better since she's started, Luna. You see our suns are steadier since she was awakened, and the *buhay* has been growing taller. Be a slave to Sama all you want; I won't give up like that. Not when there's hope."

I wanted to rally at the sound of a familiar voice, but I guessed he was keeping his distance to maintain his spy status to his sister. "What do you jackholes want?" I seethed in the darkness.

"She's a feisty one," Luna mused, running her finger over the bar. "Do you want to eat, little Omen?" Her voice was patronizing, like I was a pet.

"I want to go home. Where am I?"

"You're in the Sakuna underground. This is *our* kingdom, not yours." She turned to Lang. "Pretty hair. I can see why you made a fool of yourself trying to get her spared from Sama. But it's her he wants, so it's her he'll get."

Lang made a noise of disinterest, and I wanted to punch him for it. He was turning out to be a terrible fake fiancé. The door opened again, letting in no light to let me know where Von and Mason were.

"Good evening, Lady October," came an unfamiliar voice. "I'm King Geon. My eldest son, Prince Aranya, brought you here on my request."

I said nothing to this. I couldn't even see the man who was addressing me. I wondered if this wasn't one of their tactics – keeping me in the dark to break me down. I'd seen what solitary could do to a man.

"You're unhappy with your lodging? I can't say I blame you." Geon sounded almost kind, welcoming me as if I was a houseguest there on my own free will. "My Aranya had to act quickly to capture you. When Langgam reported back that you'd found the sagrado stone, well, I knew I just had to meet you. Tell me, where did you put the stone?"

I debated between spitting in his direction and not answering at all. The debate went on too long, so silence was the thing I stuck with.

The king continued as if we were sitting down to tea. "I expected as much cooperation. After all, Ezra found you first. Probably poisoned you against me. I merely wanted to see the stone, make sure my people got their fair share. You know we're the first ones the famine affects. When Lady Mariang doesn't meet her quota for the day, we suffer the most. You can imagine how the sagrado stone might be of interest to me." He waited for a response, and continued when I offered nothing. "Sama's promised us many things if we deliver the rest of the stone to him after taking our share." He leaned forward, and though I couldn't see him, his pointed snarly speech let me know he was looking right at me. I made sure not to cower. "Make no mistake, child, I will have that stone."

Again I said nothing, gripping the bars in the utter blackness. I held onto them as if they centered me to the planet, the unending void of darkness sucking at me and making me feel a little off my balance.

Lang spoke up. "Father, Aranya's men didn't find the stone on her. We have no idea if she even has it. It's all still rumor at this point. When I was up there, I didn't actually see the stone. I reported back what the council discussed, not what I saw with my own eyes." My ears perked up as Lang fed me details of the new truth. He'd told Ezra that his spies had seen me with the stone in Bev's trailer, but he'd hidden that gem from his own father. I heard his loyalty ring true, and it was enough to center me while I tried to stay calm. I knew Lang was remaining close so he could help me, but the help didn't seem to be near enough for me to touch just yet.

"No, but I assume Ezra brought her down here to start splitting up the stone and take it to the nations. Why else would she be in our country? If she has it, she no doubt buried it in the woods Aranya's men found her hiding in. If we keep her locked up in here for a few months, the stone stays with us."

"If I'm stuck down here, I can't reap, and the nations will slowly start to starve again!" I blurted out.

I heard the smile in Geon's voice. "So you can speak. Good to know your tongue has use. I'll be sure my men don't pull it out of your head, then." He chuckled, and I guessed he could see my horrified expression in the dark, even though I still couldn't see the details of anything. "You'll keep us company until we have the stone, or until the countries who didn't send enough aid to us start to collapse. Sama will be pleased either way. If we give him the rest of the stone, he'll be happy. If you don't have the stone and we keep you here so the other nations are starved into taking Sama's rations, he'll be thrilled." A glimmer of bitterness sunk into his voice. "He loves being the one that kings answer to. Necessary evil to feed my people."

"You've got to know I won't go along with that."

"I don't need your compliance. I have my cage." The smile in his voice was wicked as he flicked his finger to one of the iron bars. "And I have your Duwendes. I wouldn't have believed it if I didn't see it with my own two eyes. Two Duwendes for one little Omen. No doubt that'll be how all Omens are awakened from now on."

Panic gripped me around the throat. "Where are they? What have you done to them?"

"My men tell me you've been stirring up trouble in our ranks. We lost many in the uprising yesterday. Mason forgets his new place too often for my liking. He could have been welcomed like a king, but he's chosen to live amongst the dead. Now that he's your Reaper? I'll keep him here until my men can knock some sense back into him. They've got sturdy clubs for such things. And Von? Well, he's just good sport. Vampires are an easy mark, especially the stubborn ones who drag out their transition."

I kept my mouth shut, but I was sure the pounding of my heart was audible.

Five small points of light suddenly glowed in front of me, shedding some much-needed illumination on my surroundings. Upon closer inspection, the lights were fingers, casting dimly upon the brown, round Santa-like face of King Geon, who was almost seven feet tall.

My anger was fresh, but sadness controlled my mouth. "Why? Why are you doing this? You'll starve people you've never even met. You know Mariang can't keep up with the demand. And giving Sama more power? You've got to be smarter than this."

"You sound like Ezra. *I* was the first to build a relationship with the Immortal King. *I* let him come in with his aid when the other countries were turning up their noses at his rations. Before you came along, a few others started begging for his help. I'll be rewarded for my faithfulness, coming to him and trusting him first."

I rubbed my temples. "People who want more power rarely share any. Read a book, dumbass."

Evil Santa chuckled, looking to the snotty woman on his right. "Oh, let me have some fun with her first, father." Lang's sister had a pinched nose and tangled brown curly hair down to her waist. She wore gauzy gray wizarding robes and a sneer that looked permanent.

"Let me go," I seethed.

Santa Geon wore brown pants, a ruffled white pirate-looking shirt and a long red robe that touched the floor. The geometric tattoo that curled along the side of his face was much like Lang's, and when Luna came closer, I saw she had one, as well. The gold crown on Geon's head glinted against the darkness, catching on the small pinpricks of light. "Oh, child. How disorganized Ezra must be if he didn't think to educate you on our kind yet. I care nothing of the nations who didn't send enough aid while my people slowly starved. Let them burn. I would've thought the gem who vanquished the entire race of Goblins in a breath would understand that. Don't pretend to grow a conscience now. I liked you better when you were utterly ruthless."

I flinched at the sore spot of my role in the undoing of the Goblin race. Everything in me despised Geon, especially when he laughed at my fuming. I refused to cower, though I was weak, starving and tired. "Why am I in jail? What law did I break?"

Geon tsked me as if I was a petulant child. "Now, now. I have a special guest coming who desperately wants to meet you. His army should be here in a couple days, just as soon as my men can send word after they burn the last of the *buhay*." He pulled out a key that was so filthy, I cringed at the state of the pocket it emerged from. He unlocked the door and let himself into my cell, smiling as I glowered. My fists clenched as I readied for a fight. "I've assured the kingdom that you will cooperate. I trust no more uprisings will be happening in your name. You'll stay here until you either give me the stone, or until Sama himself decides the other countries have suffered enough famine. He can do with the stone as he wishes, so long as we get our piece of it."

I shifted away from him until my back hit the corner of the cage. "I don't know what sort of negotiation this is, but it's sucky. Some king you are if you're locking up fifty percent of your food suppliers. All Sama has to do is stop giving you the rations, and you're in the same boat as everyone else. I didn't bring any stone here, so I can't wait to see how this all plays out." I laid my bluff out for him to inspect, my arms crossed over my chest. "Only this time the severe famine won't be the luck of the draw. It'll be your fault for locking up an Omen. How well do you think Sama's going to be able to protect you when word gets around that this famine's on you? Where's this almighty bringer of doom now? How far away is his aid? Where was he during the uprising when your own people slaughtered your soldiers? So far this Sama jaggoff seems super helpful," I added sarcastically. I let out a scoff filled with probably too much attitude. "You're burning your food in anticipation of rations coming. They're not actually here, you know. You still need me to be reaping. What if Sama changes his mind? What if one of the nations attacks

Sama's army and steals the rations? Your people will die in days because I'm down here, and the stone isn't. You're an idiot."

Geon's amused smile mutated to a sneer. In the next beat, he raised his fist and struck out at me, knocking me across the face before he exited the cage. Maybe I would've been able to defend myself if I'd had a bit more light to work with. My cheekbone throbbed, and I knew I'd have a shiner in the morning.

I'd made Geon lose his temper, which meant I was winning. I needed him to doubt his plan, to think that I truly had never seen the sagrado stone before.

"I'll teach you how to speak to a king! Lock her back up until she learns some respect."

"Fine!" I banged on the bars when Lang secured the iron cell. "Lock me up and let your people die. I can tell you really give a crap about your nation. No wonder you guys are starving. Pride before practicality. It's how all the great nations fell. Whoever gave you a crown clearly believed in nepotism."

Geon cringed, turning to me with a livid glare that was lit by his five fingerlights. "Perhaps you don't care about your own life, the way you throw yourself in front of danger." He turned to Luna. "Should we bring the disgrace to her? Let her see what we've done to her Duwendes?"

Luna let out a deliciously evil laugh that all mean junior high girls had down pat. "Not yet. The guards are having too much fun breaking him down."

I wanted to rage against the bars, but knew that would only confirm they'd hit a sore spot. I was desperate to get Mason and Von back, but I couldn't let them know which buttons to press to make me jump.

When Geon was conversing with Luna, I made eye contact with Lang. He lifted his chin and made a gesture with his hand at his side for me to calm down and wait it out. He inched closer to the bars, and I saw in his hand a bit of the *baga* root I knew I wouldn't be able to breathe without in a few hours. I snatched it and shoved it in my mouth, chewing and swallowing before Geon turned around. My heart was racing, but I was breathing. Lang just bought me another day.

I didn't want to be in this cell another minute.

"Langgam, see to it the child gets a drink of water. It won't do to have her up and die in here. Imagine Ezra's protest then. I daresay he may even raise his voice." Geon and Luna laughed as they exited together, leaving Lang with me in the dark.

Lang's fingers lit up, sending flickers of candlelight over both our faces. He reached through the bars and held onto my hand. "So cold," he said of my fingers. His eyebrows pulled together in concern. "Stay strong. They won't hurt you more than a few punches. Sama wants you alive, and at this point, he's the only voice Father's listening to." His other hand reached through the bars so he could sweep his thumb over my cheekbone. "He got you good, didn't he."

I couldn't put words to the pain that still radiated across my face. "Lang, if the big bad baddy's army is on its way, I shouldn't be here!"

"You're in our prison, which is warded against any kind of porting. I would sneak you out, but the hallway is lined with guards. Be patient, *hani*. I promise I'll get you out before then."

"Von and Mason," I begged. "If you can't get me out, then at least get them Topside."

"The guards are working over Von and Mason for information right now. They've even fitted Mason with a collar to keep him from turning into a wolf, or from porting Topside."

I shuddered to think of the medieval torture I could only guess at the brutality of. If I thought I was panicked before, it was nothing to how I felt now. "You have to rescue them! You can't let them get hurt like this! Go!"

"Ruiz is trying to get himself assigned to Von's detail. Once he's in, he'll have a better way to sneak Von out."

"Where's Ezra?"

"Trying the diplomat route with Aranya, my brother. He's in a state down there. He's sent word to the other rulers, so hopefully they'll get here before Sama's army does. They can demand you better than just Ezra can. Ezra doesn't have an army. The kings in Terraway have threat of war they can hold over Father's head." He pulled my hand out through the bars and blew his warm breath on my icy knuckles. "If Sama's army gets here before the others, I'll find a way to sneak you out."

"Save Mason and Von first!" I begged again, growing frantic. "They don't deserve this! You have to find them. Please, Lang!"

Lang's face fell. "It's too late for Mason. They'd done their damage before I heard you'd been captured. Ruiz can help Von."

"Too late?" My mouth went dry and my palms started sweating. "You don't mean…"

"No, but I'm sure he'll wish for death soon enough."

"Please, Lang. You have to get them out! Your dad's cracked!"

"Why do you think I've been helping you in secret? I know, *hani*. Stay strong." He squeezed my fingers and pressed them to his lips before releasing me. He examined the fear in my face with sadness. "No wife of mine will be put to death in my father's dungeon. I'll find a way out soon."

"Hurry, Lang." I couldn't help the pathetic note that snuck through my resolve to stay strong. "I don't like it in here."

Lang drew my face to the bars so he could brush a kiss to my unmarked cheek. It was my blip of warmth in the cold, and I was grateful for the kindness. "Be patient, sweet girl."

Then he left me in the dark where there was nothing for me to do but count.

~

I KNEW THERE WERE FIFTY-SEVEN BARS ON THE CELL THAT caged me in like a bird in her pajamas. Fifty-seven was an odd number. I didn't much care for those. The compulsion to touch the bars was strong, so I counted them, running my knuckle across each one in case my figure was wrong and it was actually the nice even number of fifty-eight. Or sixty. Sixty was divisible by ten – a nice, round number. I liked those.

Fifty-seven again, so I started over, touching more times than necessary just because I needed to. I needed to touch things. If I touched the bars, maybe Bev wouldn't be so unhappy. Maybe she'd look at me and smile, like Judge, Darius and Terence's mama, who before she passed, hugged her hoodlum boys like they weren't capable of committing a whole slew of crimes. She positively beamed when her boys came home. Maybe if I touched the bars and came up with sixty this time, Bev would look at me in the same way Mama McCray had lit up for her children.

If I touched the bars, Allie might come back to me. She would decide she'd had enough space from us. I'd wake up and she'd be there, making eggs and pancakes with too much maple syrup. When we'd moved out, one thing she insisted on was only ever buying real 100% maple syrup. She was amazing like that.

If I touched the bars, Von would be okay. He'd smile and finally show me some of his paintings I'd been too shy to ask about. Mason would be fine if only I touched the bars. He'd come bust me out and look at me as if *I* was the thing that was precious to him, not the ghost of someone else I'd never measure up to.

I clawed at my arms, desperate for some kind of relief from the darkness that gnawed at my insides. I don't know how long it was until I fell asleep, but my eyelids closed finally, and somehow the darkness I chose felt less oppressive than the one that had been chosen for me.

39

MY BEAUTIFUL DISTRACTION

My dream life took off like I was being sucked into a vortex, dropping me into my house, which had been freshly polished. I could smell the homemade cleaning solution I'd always been a little proud of. It left everything smelling like lemon, lavender and a touch of vinegar. There were no footprints marring the carpet, but perfect vacuum lines that felt like a red carpet rolled out for yours truly.

I inhaled deeply, collapsing on the couch and picking up a mug of tea that my dream self was nice enough to have ready for me. It was sweetened with honey and lemon, just the way I like it.

"I was hoping to run into you here," said a deeply masculine voice that warmed me.

I turned to see the white-blond hair and hard body of Philip suddenly sitting on the couch next to me. I was relieved to see the pretend perfect guy I'd conjured up in my dreams to makeout with and chat about stupid stuff. Philip was a great distraction, and boy, did I ever need that now. I smirked at him. "You should've said, 'Come here often?' That's a better obvious pickup line."

Philip chuckled, reaching out to pull me into his side so he could trace the curve of my hip. He gave me a delicious kiss that made us both inhale at the sweetness. I never got swept away by hallucinations in my dream kisses; I got to be me, even if it was with a fake person. "I was worried I wouldn't be able to find you. Where are you?"

"In the living room." I waved my hand at the television, the coffee table and lamp on the end table. "Nice, right?"

"Any place can be a palace if you're with the right person."

"I missed you," I confessed, gazing over at him contentedly. I needed something beautiful to distract from the pain. Philip was my beautiful distraction.

He examined my face, looking almost like he was moved on an emotional level to see me. "That look. I don't get much of that."

"What look?"

"Unfettered admiration."

It was like he was overloaded by the burdens of the world, and had been waiting his whole life for me to relax him. Like I was his Puller. I laughed through my nose, loving the way he smiled for me. "Oh, yeah. You're a real ugly duckling. I'm sure I'm the first girl to pay you any attention."

"I get more fearful deference followed by resentment. Not this. You're practically glowing just to see me. It's... It's heady and quite addictive."

I traced the outline of his grand pectoral muscle beneath his white tunic. His shoulders were slightly broader than Von's, but not as inhumanly thick as Mason's. "Now that was a good line. Got me right here." I tapped my heart with two fingers.

Philip's fingers replaced mine, flirting on the edge of danger that thrilled me enough to encourage him with a flirty sweep of my thumb across his abdomen under his shirt. "Tell me where you are really. Not in this place. In reality. Don't you want me to be with you for real?"

I snorted, which I'm guessing wasn't the sexiest thing I could've done, but whatever. Dream Philip wouldn't leave me. He was fake, so there was no chance of him up and sleeping with Jessica, or comparing me to his saint of a former wife. It was my little world, and stoic though I wanted to be about love, in my dreams, Philip was devoted to me. "I wish you were real."

"Tell me. Let me send someone to come get you."

"I wouldn't tell you even if you were real. I wouldn't want you to be where I'm at. It's unpleasant, and our time shouldn't be crappy here. I want unicorns and candy hearts." The fear I tried not to feel crept into my voice as memories of the cell plagued me. I pressed my forehead to his and whispered a desperate, "I'm in the dark, and I don't like it."

He kissed my lips, his eyes closing to savor the flavor of me. "Let me come rescue you. Tell me what darkness has you so scared."

I slowly turned my head from side to side, our foreheads still joined so I could feel his breath on my nose. He felt so real. I wanted Philip to be real. "It's getting harder to hold on. I feel like I'm losing myself. Some days I'm all I have, and I'm afraid this time it's not enough."

He traced the outer edge of my breast over my shirt, and I couldn't help the quickening of my breath or the slight lean in that made his goal closer to his firm but gentle grasp. "Tell me, lovely thing. Tell me where to find you."

I shook my head, not wanting to think about where I was or the state I was deteriorating to. "It's cold there."

"Show me," he insisted, his voice turning firm.

I sighed, pulling away and staring out into my living room. I waved my hand as if brushing dust off a chalkboard. In the next breath, Philip was in the cell with me, plunged into darkness that was palpable. "I'm in Geon's dungeon, locked in a cell in Sakuna. He's going to keep me until Sama's army gets here, and he can turn me over to him." I started scraping my nails down the sides of my arms. I hated when I hurt myself in my dreams. "I don't like it here."

Philip was angry, pushing against the bars and

mumbling things in a language I didn't understand. It was sweet he was trying to bust me out – my very own dragon-slaying prince. But it was futile. He was a dream, and even if he managed to slay all the dragons and bust down all the walls in my dream, when I awoke, the world would still be filled with monsters. As I suspected, I would die alone.

After much heated effort, Philip sank down next to me, leaning against the concrete wall the cell was bolted to. "I'm sorry. I've failed you completely. I want to get you out, but it appears I'm limited."

I nodded. "Hey, you're pretend. It's alright. If I die, I die. Is what it is."

Philip let out an angry hiss. "Don't say things like that."

"I can say whatever I want; it's my dream. I can only live so long without food and water, Philip." Sadness engulfed me, and I let out an unbidden sob as my emotions swung loose from my control. "I'll disappear forever, and Ollie won't know what happened. He already lost Allie, and now he'll lose me. I can't... I can't stand it when Ollie's in pain. I can't leave him alone. He needs me!"

Philip's arm found its way around my form, pulling me to his side. "I'll return you to Ollie. Don't lose hope on me now. I'll get you out of here, and punish the man who did this to you."

"I'm going to die alone," I confessed, my heart breaking at my worst fear coming to fruition.

"You're not alone," he assured me. "I'm here. I'll never leave you."

"Bev doesn't love me!" I wailed, not caring anymore how childish I sounded. "Allie doesn't want me anymore. She... Allie left me, and I don't understand why! What did I do?"

"Nothing, sweet girl. You did nothing to make Allie leave. Some things are beyond your control."

"I love Allie, and she left! I try to love Bev, but it makes no difference. I love Judge, but he's still horrible! My love is useless! What a total waste."

Philip held me while I cried, not judging me or trying to talk me out of my feelings. "I'm here, Gracie."

"Geon's hurting Von and Mason!" I couldn't stick on one thought for more than a few seconds; everything was crashing down on me. I tapped my chest. "They're scared, and I can feel it. Something's very wrong, and I can't get out of here to help them!" I gulped down a breath between sobs. "There are only fifty-seven bars in the cell! I need there to be sixty!"

"Sixty? I don't understand. Will that help you better escape?"

"No, I just need there to be sixty bars!"

Philip clutched me tight and waved his hand to the dungeon, morphing three additional bars to evenly disperse through the periphery of the cell. "There. Does that help?"

I heaved out a gust of relief that at least one problem was fixable. I collapsed in Philip's arms, exhaling a little of my internal madness that polluted my mind. "Thank you. I just... Sixty. That's much better." The relief over something that shouldn't have had that much a hold on me pushed down on my psyche with a crushing weight.

Philip was frozen for a few beats, but eventually started to rub my back to soothe us both. We said nothing of my obvious crazy. All I knew was that through my fog of psychosis, Philip didn't let go, and I didn't push him away.

40

FRIGGIN' READY

When my dream was cut short by the creak of the heavy door, I wished for Mason. I wished for Von. I wished for anybody at all except for the voice that greeted me. "Have you decided to tell me where you've hidden the sagrado stone yet, child?" Geon's voice was light on the surface, but there was a menace to it that scared me afresh.

I maintained my resolve for silence, especially since I couldn't tell him where the stone was if I wanted to, which I didn't.

"Very well. I know you're worried about the other kingdoms, so I brought in one of Sama's spies." Geon clicked his fingers, and I heard another set of footsteps. "Andy, tell Lady October that Lady Mariang is holding up her mantle just fine."

I covered my mouth in horror when Andy, one of the

men Ezra had sent to guard me, answered through the dark. I could almost picture his goatee while he talked. He'd been the one who tried to keep me in the mansion by sucking my will from me, pulling so hard that I blissed out. I didn't much like Andy.

"Lady October, the quota's being met. Lady Mariang's upset, but she knows what's expected of her. She's adding to the number of souls you stockpiled."

I said nothing. I knew the only things that would fling out of me would be a perpetual catapult of insults, most of which would be lost on him. He'd guarded me. He'd pulled stress from me, or tried to, anyway.

Geon's voice was calm with a hint of a tease to it. "Andy's here to get you to talk. You're familiar with excessive pulling? Makes a person so relaxed and suggestible, they'd do or say just about anything you ask. Even a spitfire like you might become downright pleasant with the right persuasion. We could torture you to find out what you know about the stone, but see, if we send you back to Ezra with marks on you, that could start a war. This is the more civilized way to get information, don't you think? Andy." Geon unlocked the cell door and directed the spy toward me. "Get her to tell us where the stone is."

I wanted to rage against the bars in the cell like a gorilla, but knew that wouldn't get me anywhere. Instead I drew back, readying myself to fend off Andy and his stupid chin beard.

"I thought you'd cooperate," Andy chided me. "I

thought you understood what was at stake here. I don't understand why you, of all people, would resist the help Sama's rations will bring. With them, you wouldn't have to work so hard. Mariang could live longer if she didn't have to reap so much."

"Bite me," I spat, inching away from him when I heard his footsteps in the dark. "You don't give a crap about Mariang. You're working her ragged by keeping me down here. Spare me your utopian worldview."

"Fine. Have it your way." His voice turned playful. "They always have so much fight in the beginning. It's almost sweet."

Geon clicked his fingers, giving light to the cell. I could only see by the faint glow coming from Geon's hand, but it was just enough. This wasn't the time for pulling punches or biding my time. It was strike to incapacitate.

I was starved.

I was scared.

I was friggin' ready.

He took the first step toward me, and I was already pouncing. My leg flung out as it had so many times in the self-defense training I'd had to go through for the prison job, landing square in Andy's gut. He doubled over as I predicted he would, and I took my opportunity to cup the back of his head, shoving his cranium hard into the metal bars. I knew every chance he had to touch me, I would lose myself more and more, so each punch was quick and delivered force I didn't bother tampering in warning.

I picked Andy up by his shirt's collar and his belt, using his head like a battering ram against the cage, growling with bloodlust I didn't want to examine too closely. The bars didn't shake – they were sturdy, providing me a great place to take out my anger on my lot in life.

"Is that what you wanted?" I shouted at Geon, whose mouth had fallen open. I dropped Andy and stomped my bare foot down hard on his nose when his head lolled to the side with a moan. "Is this what you were picturing? I did my job! I did everything you people demanded of me! Now you want to take me away from myself so you can get your hands on a lousy rock I was going to bring you a piece of anyway? How long do you guess you'll get me to cooperate? You think you can control me?" I picked Andy's heavy limp upper half up again and slammed it hard into the bars, knocking out two of his teeth when his head bent the wrong way. "That's what I thought!"

There was no use playing civilized now. Andy moaned incoherently at my feet but didn't move, which was best. I was in no mood. "You wanted me in a cage? You treat me like an animal? Just you wait till I sink my claws into you!"

Geon wasn't in a place to be messed with either. He opened up his mouth, but instead of words, a mess of angry bees came out, swarming around me with purposeful buzzing. I'd forgotten that Lang was Prince of the Bugs or whatever, and that his dad no doubt had that same kind of ability. "That wasn't very nice," he scolded me, as if I'd stepped on his freshly mown lawn.

"Let me tell you, George, if even one of those bees stings me, you can forget about me ever going back to work. You care about your people? Attacking me's just going to seal the deal that they're dying young. You don't have the stone, and if I'm sent home with even one little bee sting, then you won't have me to help you anymore. Mariang's on her last leg, so like it or not, you still need me."

"Sama's army is on its way with rations. We won't need you for anything soon enough."

I threw out my arms to the sides and popped my chin up in defiance. "Is that so? Then where is he? Shouldn't he have been here by now? How many days was he expecting you to go without *buhay*? Wake up, Geon! Sama played you like the dummy you are." I beat my fist down across Andy's slack face three more times. "You think you hold the cards because you've got a cage? I own you! You're in *my* cage!" I stared him down, daring his anger to be bigger than mine. I feared the words that birthed out of me, but my fury couldn't be held back anymore.

I could tell Geon was questioning his plan by the note of hesitance before his reply and the forced bravado in his voice when he finally answered. "You own nothing. You belong to me as long as I say. I'll find that stone, and then you'll serve no purpose."

"Good luck finding what I've never seen!"

"Such a brave little fighter. Let's see how you fare after a few more days of this."

"Even after you return me to Ezra, I'll stop reaping and make sure everyone in Terraway knows why, so they have you to thank." I knew his type. He only responded to strength, so I gave it to him in spades. While on the inside I was screaming in fear, on the outside I remained steadfast, my chin raised to dare him to make the next move. It was a dangerous game of chicken I was playing, but to be fair, he started it.

Geon stared me down, migrating from a game of logic to a battle of who needed to save face more. I could play that game all friggin' day.

His bees encircled me, buzzing with a thousand little wings that were mindlessly waiting to be told which way to go to attack. The moments of silence were tense as a fiddle's string and piled up until there was a whole minute filled with only the ominous buzzing.

"Yes, I think I'll keep you locked up a little while longer. See how mouthy you are after you've been starved, as my people are. When Sama's army gets here, they can decide what to do with your mouth." Geon snapped his fingers, and the tiny lights went out. The head of the bug family left me with his buzzing minions alone in the dark with Andy, who was slowly bleeding out on the floor from the injury I'd given him to his head.

I was cold, terrified and alone, and as I scraped at the skin on my already bleeding arms, I began making peace with the darkness that swallowed me whole.

41

TORTURE

Enjoy a free preview from *Torture*
book three in the *Terraway* series.

*T*he worst thing about being alone with your thoughts is ignoring the ones you have no control over. The fears about my possible death if King Geon of Sakuna continued starving me were one thing. I could deal with those with some amount of quiet dignity. No, it was the childhood bag of crapfest that unleashed itself on me in the unending dark. Visions of the flies trying to burrow under our bedroom door plagued me, especially when Andy's body began to rot after it became painfully obvious that I'd killed him.

Lang had been sneaking in to feed me bits of the *baga* root, a handful of berries or two and a canteen of water I didn't have it in me to resist anymore. I'd begged him to take away Andy's body, but he told me his father wanted me as uncomfortable as possible, so sleeping with a corpse became my norm.

I tried to reconcile my screaming guilt over my homicidal rage with the logic that I'd killed Andy in self-defense. I tried to assuage my horror at the lowlife I'd always known was lurking inside me by telling myself that it was either him or me. I knew I would skirt to safety in a court of law, but my own personal jury had me guilty as charged. I didn't even know Andy all that well, and now he was dead.

And rotting.

The maggots started in after who knows how long. Those gave birth to flies. These were fat, hairy flies that had a whole body to feast on, and they did so with gusto. I'd promised myself when Ollie and Allie finally busted me out of Bev's place that I would never let myself live like that again. I didn't so much mind anymore when adults broke their word to me, but breaking my own promise to myself felt like a new blow I wasn't sure I would recover from in a day.

Or two.

My days were broken up by sporadic visits from Geon, demanding to know where I'd hidden the sagrado stone.

He'd come in with a platter of meat, my stomach lurching until he informed me it was roasted sigbin. After he left when I remained unwilling to divulge my secrets, I cried with the hope that Geon hadn't cooked up Edward, the sigbin I loved.

I fell asleep, restless and freezing, choking out a cry of relief when Philip appeared in front of the fire pit I conjured to warm my dream self. I ran to Philip, stumbling with my stiff joints, desperate to find some comfort, some connection in the stifling darkness. "Philip? Help me!" I crashed into him, pretending the dream warmth was just as good as actual heat.

"What happened? Are you still in King Geon's prison?"

I blinked up at him as I buried my fingers under his shirt to warm them up. "Yes. And I don't think anyone's coming for me."

Philip held me, warming my body and rubbing my back and arms to soothe my panic. "Are you hurt?"

"I'm okay. The dark's getting to me, though. I'm trying with everything in me not to lose it. Geon's keeping me here to hold me for Sama's army. This Sama jackhole wants to keep me locked up so everyone goes to him for help, instead of being able to feed themselves. It's so stupid! The whole thing, I hate it!"

Philip was stiff. "I'm sure this Sama character doesn't know you're being held in such terrible conditions. Are you well fed?"

"No! Geon's starving me, and I'm sitting in a cell with a rotting body that's got bugs in it. Help me," I begged, wishing I was strong enough to break down the irons and save myself. "Come find me, Philip. Don't leave me here by myself. I'm so scared." My arms banded around my stomach as the confession rolled out of me. "I killed someone! I killed a guy I don't even really know! He was Duwende. Andy was going to take my will so I'd tell him where the sagrado stone is. I didn't have a choice!"

Philip gripped my arms. "You know where the sagrado stone is?"

"Of course I do. Or, I did anyways. Hopefully Edward hid it somewhere safe."

"Who's Edward?"

"My puppy."

"You're not making any sense. Where's the stone?"

There was too much edge to his voice. It was like he cared about the stone more than he cared about me. "I don't want to talk about a stupid rock that's done nothing but ruin my life! You're supposed to be the perfect guy!" I started beating on his chest. "You're supposed to love me so much better than real people. I can't even imagine up a fake guy who cares that I'm starving and lying in a cold jail with a dead body? You suck, Philip! You suck!" I pounded on him over and over, taking out my frustration on the hard body he hadn't even had to work at to earn.

Philip softened, letting me beat on him with angry fists.

"I *am* the perfect guy. I'm the one you can tell all your secrets to." He held me and slowly sunk to the grass, keeping me close as I broke down into shameful tears that fell into his shirt. "Talk to me. Geon's got you in a dark cell. He's starving you. What else?"

"I want to go home. He's got Von and Mason somewhere, and I know he's hurting them! I can feel it. I can feel something's very, very wrong."

"Mason can handle it. I'm sure Von can, too. Matruculans can endure a great deal. And if your half-vampire's resisted the transition this long, I'm sure he has strength enough for a little torture."

"I don't care about strength! I hate Terraway! It's ugly and mean here. All they do is use me. I was doing just fine until they came along." I gripped Philip's shirt, desperate for a connection, however fabricated. "I need my medication. I'm going crazy, and I worked so hard not to be crazy! I'm losing my mind! I need it, or I'll get lost again. I don't remember what happened when I went off it a couple years ago. It was a week before Ollie found me. A week! He was gone and I was alone. When he found me, I was a basket case. Like, I could barely talk without counting. I was bashing my head against the wall and hadn't eaten or showered in days. I can't go back to that! I can't go under again! You have to help me. I work so hard not to be crazy. I'm not crazy! I'm not crazy!"

Philip's hands scrambled to hold me together as I

openly sobbed in his arms. "Quiet now, little one. We can't have you losing your mind. I'll come find you. My people are on their way. They'll get you out of there and take you to my place. We'll get you some food. My own special recipe. I don't want you crazy or dead. I want you with me, by my side." He clutched me, and I make-believed that he cared deeply about who I was, not what I could do for the kingdom. "I'll see to it Geon's punished."

I snorted my disbelief. "You're not real, though. I need actual help. I need my brother. I need Ollie." I let out a loud wail. "Allie! Allie left us, and she's not coming back!"

He kissed my cheek tenderly. "Tell me about Allison."

"My sister never would've let me live like this. She did everything to make sure I never had to live with bugs and rotting things. Now she's gone. She stopped loving me, but I never stopped needing her! If she was back, she would make me that chicken soup with the noodles Ollie loves and hold me so I didn't hurt myself. She would sing to me and wrap me in heavy blankets until I felt warm and calmed down."

"She loved you."

"She was perfect, and she left us. She knows I'm too much. She knows I can't be fixed. I can't be fixed! I can't be fixed," I moaned in Philip's arms.

He held my head to his shoulder, clutching me to him and providing the deep pressure that always calmed me down when I floated away from myself. "I can put you back together," he promised, and with everything in me, I wished my perfect guy was real.

But he wasn't.

Read *Torture* and continue with
the next book in the *Terraway* series.

ABOUT THE AUTHOR

USA Today bestselling author Mary E. Twomey lives in Michigan with her three adorable children. She enjoys reading, writing, vegetarian cooking, and telling her children fantastic stories about wombats.

While she loves writing fantasy, dystopian, and paranormal tales for her readers, Mary also writes romance under the name Tuesday Embers, and cozy mysteries under the name Molly Maple.

Visit her online at www.maryetwomey.com, and sign up for her newsletter, so you never miss a new release.

www.ingramcontent.com/pod-product-compliance
Lightning Source LLC
Chambersburg PA
CBHW011053130726
47906CB00010B/1013